Loving This Man

Other books by the author

Ladies of the Night and Other Stories
How the Star-Fish Got To the Sea
How the East-Pond Got Its Flowers
Being Black

Loving This Man

Althea Prince

INSOMNIAC PRESS

Edited by Richard Almonte
Copy edited by Lorissa L. Sengara
Designed by Mike O'Connor

National Library of Canada Cataloguing in Publication Data

Prince, Althea, 1945-
    Loving this man : a novel

ISBN 1-894663-06-3

    I. Title.

PS8581.R549L68 2001   C813'.54   C2001-902150-X
PR9199.3.P746L68 2001

The publisher and the author gratefully acknowledge the support of the Canada
Council, the Ontario Arts Council and Department of Canadian Heritage through
the Book Publishing Industry Development Program.

Printed and bound in Canada

Insomniac Press, 192 Spadina Avenue, Suite 403,
Toronto, Ontario, Canada, M5T 2C2
www.insomniacpress.com

The Canada Council | Le Conseil des Arts
FOR THE ARTS | DU CANADA
SINCE 1957 | DEPUIS 1957

ONTARIO ARTS COUNCIL
CONSEIL DES ARTS DE L'ONTARIO

Susan —

friends of struggle and friends for life,

In loving memory of my father and mother:
Gerald Simon Prince and Dorothy Maturin Sebastian Prince

Love,

Althea,

Acknowledgements
My thanks to my sister Jennette Prince
for mothering me through the storm of life;
and my brothers Arnold Prince and John Prince
for fathering me in good time.

I thank Mike O'Connor and Richard Almonte of Insomniac Press
for taking such good care of the manuscript.

I also thank my daughter Mansa Trotman,
my niece Janis Prince
and my friend Gabriele Hardt
for reading a first draft and giving excellent feedback.

This book was written with assistance from
the Canada Council for the Arts and the Ontario Arts Council.

All events and characters in this book are fictitious.

Book One
Reevah's Song

Chapter One

Sayshelle's Mama Reevah told her that she was born in a small-small house on Number One New Street. She said that the street was named that way, even though it was not new at all when she and her husband went to live on it. They never even questioned the name of the street. She was pregnant with Sayshelle, and they were grateful for the comfort of the house and the welcome they received from the whole neighbourhood.

The people who lived on the street never talked about its odd name. Some of the Old Ones who could remember knew that it was because it was a newer street than some of the others in the area. However, they did not really care about that any more. They had told their story many times to careless listeners; and now, not even a direct question brought an answer from them.

It was an odd name, "Number One New Street," but it kept company with another oddity in the neighbourhood called "Number Two New Street." It was odd too that although the street was no longer new, no one had thought to ask the people who lived on it if they wanted to name it something else.

The street held the people's homes, provided them with a place to be friends or enemies, to quarrel and to make peace; and it kept their children safe. It was in-between Number Two New Street and Drake Street on one side, and South and Tanner Streets on the other. A large gutter flowing out of West Pond divided Tanner Street in two, and served as a kind of central meeting place for the whole neighbourhood.

There was a high fence around West Pond to prevent anyone from venturing near to the water, whereas East Pond, on the other side, was a much shallower pond, running in a natural way to meet the ground.

Everybody knew all of the boundaries of the community and felt safe within them. If the children disappeared from the street, older brothers and sisters were sent to make sure that none of them had fallen into East Pond.

The bank of the pond merged with the path that the children used when they took the long route home from Girl School, Boy School, and Miss Davis School. They dug up pond-flower seeds from the soft mud at the edges where the water met the ground.

They would abandon their shoes and socks, and walk in the mud with their bare feet. It gave them a feeling of wild freedom, as they stretched dangerously over the water's edge to pick dried pond-flowers.

The pond-flower seeds were a source of delight to the children. Cracking the nut open with their teeth was such a laborious task that time would slip away from them unnoticed. Then they ran all the way home, fearful of punishment for being late.

The biggest hurdle of all was cleaning their feet and hiding the mud on their clothes. For they would adamantly deny that they had waded in the pond.

When rain fell heavy-heavy for days on end, West Pond, also known as Big Pond (the people used both names), became hazardous, overflowing and swelling up the gutter, running all the way down to the bay. In the rainy season, the children were allowed to wade in the water that overflowed from the gutter onto Tanner Street. At that time, even East Pond (or Little Pond, as the people sometimes called it) could drown a body easy-easy.

Everything looked clean after the heavy rains, because any rubbish lying in the half-dry gutter was pushed away out of sight in the greyish gushing water. It was as if God washed the place clean-clean. Even the trees glistened from all the rain that pelted them: the banana, the coconut, the *ginnep*, the raspberry, the cherry, and the breadfruit trees. The less hardy plants, like the rose-bushes, lost all of their flowers' petals and stood lonely and forlorn, praying for the sun to help them create new growth.

Everybody knew everybody else who lived on the street; and everyone knew everyone else's business. Sometimes that knowing would slide into malice and then harsh voices spilled out onto the street. There was love too, with neighbours helping neighbours; the elderly cared for, and the young nourished and loved. It was a comfortable, not idyllic, life, but it was the *doing of life* as the people knew it.

Although nobody thought about it, everyone knew that they had the right to be consulted about the renaming of their street. They just never thought much about those things and accepted that their street would keep its strange name forever. Then suddenly one day, the government changed the name from Number One New Street to Prince Klass Street.

"The change happened," Reevah told Sayshelle, "because the government accepted some white woman's name for the Antiguan hero who planned a revolt during slavery-days. The story goes that he planned to get rid of slavery by killing all of the white people in Antigua. They say that he and his comrades were going to carry out the revolt while the white people were attending the Governor's Ball."

He did not succeed, because somebody betrayed him; but Reevah said she thought it was a brilliant plan and it made her heart feel good to hear about him.

"The white woman wrote her book long-long ago; since in the nineteenth century they say. And our great men in government never think to check to see if the man's name was even correct." She shook her head slowly from side to side; it still made her sad to see the way in which things were done in Antigua.

"The story goes," Reevah said, "somebody give the government the book that the white woman write, and they just take it as Bible. It is also rumoured that is a member of the opposition party who give the government the book." She could not hold back a chuckle at the irony of it. Whether that last part of the story was true or not, it was a good joke.

Then Reevah stifled her mirth and continued. "Well, before anybody could say anything, they rename our street Prince Klass Street. And afterwards, people were heard to have observed that nobody think of giving *them* the white woman's book to read. Then we could at least know something about the man whose greatness cause our street to have his name. His story and countless other stories about slavery-days are things that none of us ever hear about in our history lessons."

Reevah made a "tut-tut" sound and shook her head. "Maybe if they did ask us something, somebody could have looked more deeply into the matter. Then the street might be called King Court Street. For I hear that the man's rightful name is King Court. But no. One day they just change the name to Prince Klass Street. One time! Just so! Bam!"

She paused, her eyes distant, as if she was awaiting the forming of a picture. It seemed to Sayshelle that her whole face was going through a change, and her body seemed to be feeling it as well. She held her arms around her bosom, as if she was comforting herself.

Sayshelle could see that her Mama Reevah was having a hard time speaking some small horror that her eyes already accepted. There was also a quiet about her. When she finally found her voice, there was no mistaking its mournful tone. Each word spilled out on top of the other. Sometimes she paused and caught her breath; and then she rushed on again.

"And is just so one day they wall up East Pond, so all like your age don't even know it had a pond named East Pond. They make it into a parking lot, and they put offices all 'round it...and just so...East Pond disappear from our lives. It is like slavery; is as if it never happen...as if it never had a time here on top of the ground."

Reevah shook herself. Speaking the words moved something from her body. For these things still rested in her: the image and the sense of loss. She shook them from her shoulders.

Sayshelle involuntarily shook herself as well. For she was journeying with her mother; she felt as though she was releasing the same feelings. The emotion of losing a whole pond from your life was a great thing to think about. A whole body of water...repressed...gone underground...to run on the land no more.

Not a word or a whisper passed from Reevah's lips as she prepared to comb Sayshelle's hair. She did not even speak the customary invitation to her daughter to come close. She simply cleaned the comb, picked up the low, wooden stool on which Sayshelle usually sat, and settled it in front of her rocking-chair. Then she fetched a cushion for her back and another so that her daughter could rest her head on her lap.

Sayshelle did not immediately move into the space that her mother made for her. She sat looking at the whole scene, drinking in the ritual...digesting it with her whole self. There was nothing new about it; but she always took pleasure in the sight of her mother making a space for her at her feet. There were few things that came close to this experience of her Mama Reevah combing her hair.

Now that she had finished high school, it was no longer a thing that they did every evening. They had long ago settled into a pattern of being together like this only on occasion. There were times now too when Sayshelle combed her mother's hair.

They had come to allow their hair-combing evenings to happen when they both needed the closeness. Sometimes they did not even need to speak; and Sayshelle would drift off into a light sleep. Then Reevah would work silently, moving her daughter's hair into smooth, tight rows of "Congo."

And then a tug of her hair with the comb would pull Sayshelle awake. It was a little agony that she had to bear as her mother smoothed out all of the knots in her hair with the teeth of the comb.

She remembered how when she was little, she would day-dream while her Mama Reevah tugged and combed and smoothed her hair into place. She would amuse herself by imagining the Carib part of her Papa Emmanuel's hair being forced out of place by her Mama Reevah's African hair. She would equate each tug of the comb as her Mama Reevah's African hair saying, "Go away!"

And then the softer, less powerful Carib hair would attack again; because her history books said that the Caribs were warlike people. The thought of both of the people whose blood ran in her veins fighting a war over the ownership of her head would make the tugging and the pulling more tolerable.

In the end, her Papa Emmanuel's Carib blood had managed to soften her hair only a little. As her Mama Reevah finished combing her hair, Sayshelle would mutter to herself: "The battle will continue; all is not lost."

When her Mama Reevah straightened her hair for her confirmation in the Anglican church, Sayshelle counted it as a victory for the Carib part of her Papa Emmanuel's hair. That thought kept her amused for most of the confirmation service—a boring, droning affair that left her entirely uninspired.

The most insulting thing for her was having to kiss the bishop's ring. She looked into his pale blue eyes, sitting in his pale-pale white face, and felt sure that he did not see her. It was not just her that he ignored; it was her whole confirmation class. They did not seem to really matter to him.

Mama Reevah's voice broke into her reverie: "Come!" It was a soft command, lovingly spoken; an invitation, moving warmly from the mother to embrace her daughter. Sayshelle willingly accepted the invitation and settled herself onto the stool at her Mama Reevah's feet.

They both knew that Sayshelle would loosen the plaits the next day. For they gave her a headache; but she loved having them done, for the closeness with her Mama Reevah. Tonight, she knew that she would not sleep; her Mama Reevah was in the mood to talk. And she would listen to everything that was said; she would take in every nuance.

As she plaited her daughter's hair, Reevah said, in a voice singing with gladness, "On the day I born you, right here in this house on Number One New Street, renamed Prince Klass Street, it rain and rain and wouldn't stop. It was the same kind of rain that fell on the day your father died."

Sayshelle *did* remember how it had rained on the day that her Papa Emmanuel died. It seemed to soak everything; and it washed the trees clean-clean. The rain never stopped until they lowered the coffin into the ground, said the first prayer, sang the first hymn, and threw the first sod.

"It was a funny kinda rain," Reevah said, "a kind of all-day, stop-and-start-again, heavy-and-light rain. And when it finally leave, everybody step outside, or look out of their windows, anxious to feel the air on their skin. We would feel a different air after the rain; as if all the flies and germs and punishment that the sun bring, gone somewhere else for the day."

Listening to her Mama Reevah, Sayshelle could almost feel that air on her face. She remembered the newness of everything after the funeral. There was a softness and a sweet-smelling moist feeling that was different from the usual dryness that the sun brought.

"On the day you were born," Reevah continued, "that stop-and-start-again, heavy-and-light rain never stop altogether until after a whole day, and a night, and a morning." She said that the rain left when the midwife delivered Sayshelle and she cried out from the slap on her first-time-into-the-world bottom.

Reevah's voice was now hushed with the awe of it. "And if anybody was paying attention, they would notice that the rain stop on the beat of your first pause for breath, after the pain from the midwife's slap."

Sayshelle had memory *stronger than who*; she even remembered being hit that first time. She had stopped saying it to anyone, though, as they said that it was impossible to recall the moment of your birth. But she remembered it through and through, clear-clear. She could recall before the birth too.

She had strong-strong memory of how her Mama Reevah sang to her while she lay inside her belly with her thumb in her mouth and her eyes closed. She remembered too that her Mama Reevah read to her, and told her stories.

And she remembered being wet—soaked through her skin; and her heart; and her soul. The rain reached inside her Mama Reevah's belly to embrace her, making her even more wet. It was a welcome into the world, a kind of baptism, as she moved from the womb to her Mama Reevah's arms.

Reevah said that Emmanuel smiled in a different way starting the day his daughter was born. She told Sayshelle: "Your father never stopped smiling that way, up to fifteen years later when he went to meet his Maker. Even though he was not so happy then, and was in plenty pain, yet, when he smiled, it was that same smile that his face learned to make from the day you were born."

She stopped plaiting Sayshelle's hair for a moment and, turning her daughter's face up to her, said, "You were the sun in his eyes." Sayshelle smiled at her Mama Reevah; she could see that in *her* eyes, *he* was the sun. Her Papa Emmanuel was the sun in her Mama Reevah's eyes, in her heart, in her whole life. Even though he had been dead all this time.

Some two years ago, Sayshelle asked Reevah why they had had only one child. Reevah explained to her daughter that she and Emmanuel knew that he was going to die for many long years. That is why they decided not to have any more children.

Silently now, Reevah recalled that the knowing still did not prepare her for burying Emmanuel. The rain falling all the time helped to wash the wound of the pain clean; but for a long-long time, she carried Emmanuel in her heart, wrapped in a wreath of sadness.

While her fingers continued to make deft lines in her daughter's hair, the sadness bubbled up in her throat. It made her voice come from her like a lament. "When your Papa Emmanuel died, it was as if one of those ugly nylon wreaths that people put at gravesites these days move itself inside my heart. It hold that sadness in there with all that purple mourning-colour." Then she fell silent, lost in her thoughts.

Sayshelle's hair was now neatly plaited in four large "Congos." Reevah smoothed her hands over her daughter's head. She kissed her on the cheek and handed her the comb with the little tufts of hair which had fallen victim to the pulling and the plaiting.

Then, as if she only just remembered that she was in the middle of a conversation, she said, almost absentmindedly, "I *too* hate them ugly nylon wreaths. Although of a truth, they do stay on the gravesite and help people to mark the place where they bury their loved ones. The thing to do is to plant a *snow-on-the-mountain* tree at the gravesite. And me *too* hate them purple flowers; make sure you don't put them on my grave when you bury me."

Sayshelle smiled and said nothing. Ever since her Papa Emmanuel died, her Mama Reevah spoke often of dying. Sayshelle knew that if the talk persisted, she would become upset and end up crying. She could not bear the thought of losing her mother as well as her father.

She noticed that her Mama Reevah used the phrase the minister said at funerals: "loved ones." Sayshelle thought it was funny how people who were terrible while they were alive became "loved ones" as soon as they died; not that her Papa Emmanuel was terrible; he really was a "loved one."

She was sure that she would never forget her Papa Emmanuel. People told her about him all the time, and that kept his memory even more alive than just her own knowledge of him. They were quick to say to her (when they met her in the street, or came to the house to pay their respects) that they had known her Papa; and sometimes they even described his decline from the cancer.

They never seemed to think of how she felt to be going over his death all the time. It was as if they wanted something from her, pouring their hearts out about her Papa. But she could never give what they wanted: some benediction, some blessing, some kind word, so that they could feel connected to her Papa through her and be comforted by him, even though he was dead.

Sometimes, Sayshelle sought in her heart for the words, for the gestures, but she never found them. She did not know how to continue her Papa's relationship with all of the people he knew. She felt that to make those connections would be to acknowledge that her Papa Emmanuel was never coming back. It was like stepping into his shoes while they were still warm, and that was uncomfortable to her. Sometimes, she felt her Papa Emmanuel's shoes big-big, swallowing her up in his personality and in his essence.

She loved her Papa Emmanuel and she emulated him; but she was *not* him, and she did not want his role in life. She was not sure what her own role was as yet, but she knew that it was different from his.

Her Papa Emmanuel seemed to have friends all over Antigua...and even the world. When he died, words of sympathy poured in from as far away as New Zealand. He had a friend who moved there after he met a woman from New Zealand in England and married her. Her Papa Emmanuel carried on a correspondence with his friend for years. He enjoyed the letters he received telling him of things going on in New Zealand, Australia, and England.

Her Mama Reevah said it made him bigger than the other people around him, because he stretched his mind to such great heights. He spent hours and hours writing letters, peering over his glasses at her with his eyes vacant as he concentrated on some sentence that he was constructing. He composed impeccable sentences and paragraphs. His penmanship was clear and finely sloping, and his words slipped easily off the tip of his pen.

Sayshelle knew that it made her Papa Emmanuel sad to know of all of the other countries in the world where things were happening—unlike Antigua—where, he said, "Nothing of any great consequence happened."

He would lament often: "No big political discussions among equals take place; no talk between the government and the people on topics of benefit to the country.

No reforms to things in the country that involve the people, so they could learn real skills and not just how to serve tourists. No development of ideas taking place; although they announce things on the radio as projects belonging to different ministers of government. But nothing t'all ever come of them, beyond the announcements."

He would look so sad when he spoke of the land, Sayshelle thought. He missed the countryside a lot and he was distressed to see how the whole island was being destroyed.

"Look at the land, for instance," he would say. "The government announce how much attention it is paying to environmental issues. Yet it allow hotel-owners to dig up sand; and it sell land so dirt cheap that people say they giving away the land to foreigners and government ministers. And they cutting down trees, and digging up harbours; and the list goes on and on and on."

Reevah said Emmanuel used to feel a sense of helplessness at all of the bad things that were happening in his island and the good things that were not happening. He grieved that he could do nothing about it. She said that try as she might, she could never get him to focus on the good things that were always taking place. "These are things that happen despite the government: the things that ordinary people do in life every day; year after year; whole generations of people."

She pushed her rocking-chair gently. "When he was a younger man, your father was active in politics. He go to all of the public meetings and listen to what the leading party and the opposition parties have to say. He go to all three meetings, every time they have them. He hear so much speech, he could predict how each speaker in all three parties would tackle a particular topic."

She threw her head back and laughed; Emmanuel's great intelligence was still something in which she took pride. Sayshelle laughed too, remembering how her Papa Emmanuel could recite whole passages of poems he had learned as a small boy. He also liked memorizing the speeches of famous men.

Reevah did not tell Sayshelle that at this moment she could feel her father's spirit close. She thought that it might make her uncomfortable. It felt as if he was showing his approval of her talking this talk with their daughter at this time. She smiled at Sayshelle and touched her face lightly.

"After several years and several elections, he lose hope that there would ever be a change in government. The last election before he died was too disappointing for him. Things looked very promising for the opposition party: the ruling party was brought up to public ridicule; the schools were in shambles; the streets were full of potholes.

A big scandal erupt over funds that was to renovate and update the airport runway going instead to the pocket of a senior government minister. And you know the people don't play with things like that; they give him the nickname 'Runway' as his middle name!"

Sayshelle laughed at this and Reevah said, "You don't hear anything yet. Another minister was disgraced by begging back for his job after he resign; so then the people put 'Beg-back' in front of *his* name!"

Reevah laughed so hard at that that her eyes were moist. Between her laughter she said, "Wait! There is more!" Sayshelle was still laughing when she asked, "What? There are more nicknames?"

Reevah said seriously, "No...more bad dealings. On top of all of that, the prime minister's brother was arrested for smuggling cocaine into the island. Then the newspapers and the people said that the prime minister send one of his ministers to pay his brother's fine. All he got for his crime was a little fine of some few thousands of dollars. His partner in crime, a man from Guyana, was sent to jail to await trial. Can you imagine that, child? Can you believe what I am telling you going on in this country?"

Sayshelle nodded. She knew of the case and she remembered her parents talking about it for days and days, running into weeks. It was the only thing that everyone spoke about at the time; even her friends brought up the topic. Nothing like this had ever happened in Antigua before. They could not believe that their little island was some big cocaine port, with the prime minister's brother involved to boot.

"It is like living in a horror movie," she said, and was gratified with her Mama Reevah's laughter, rippling up in waves through her body. Reevah threw her head back and let the laughter take her over. Finally she said, "You're so right; our own private horror movie. If only it would stop, then we could build our country in some small and some large ways; but these people make new horrors every day."

Reevah said there was nothing worse than the fact that there were so-called intelligent, educated people in the country and yet things continued in this way. She told Sayshelle that she would say to Emmanuel that if the well-educated people wanted the government out, they would get them out.

"As I tell your father, child: poor people could only get them out by going up to the Parliament buildings one day and whipping them on their behinds. Only then would they pick up their feet and run home."

They laughed at the image of the members of the government running home. Then Reevah continued in a firm voice. "I tell your father that elections were a waste of time, because everybody wouldn't go to vote; and so it was only the government supporters who vote in any large numbers. And as you know, people say the government pay them in one way or another for their support."

She paused and breathed deeply, letting her breath out slowly, releasing the things she was speaking with her breathing. Sayshelle looked at her mother with a new respect. She never used to listen carefully to the conversations between her parents. She appreciated her mother's clear perspective on Antiguan politics. Somewhere in the dim recesses of her memory, they were familiar to her. There was an echo...a faint-faint echo of all that had been said in her presence. It helped her to take it all in now.

She was more than ready to hear it all. In fact, there was a hunger in her for the things her Mama Reevah was telling her. It was as if the space to receive them was now mature inside her heart and in her belly. She had recently had her eighteenth birthday, and *did* feel more mature and focused somehow.

"Eventually, Emmanuel agree with me," Reevah continued, "but people like us don't have that kind of power to make people see the truth. We just support the people whose voice sound strong and righteous, and hope for the best. It is all we can do in the situation." She laughed, saying, "Besides, your father grow his hair long as a protest and I like how it look on him. He was so handsome with it; it give him a new kind of character. It also make the Carib blood in him come out; you could see his cheekbones more sharply somehow."

Sayshelle remembered how her Papa Emmanuel had made a decision to let his hair stay on his head until there was a change in government. It grew quickly, because he had Carib blood in him; and those kinds of mixtures produce people with long hair. Soon, with his thick curls falling to his shoulders, Sayshelle thought that he resembled Beethoven, the composer, and Shakespeare, the writer.

The way her Papa Emmanuel told it, he could trace his generation all the way back to the Caribs and to the last set of Africans brought to Antigua. His mother was from English Harbour, where most of the Caribs used to live. He said that he knew that his whole generation did not have any white blood in it.

"Only pure Carib and pure African blood run in his veins," Reevah said, her voice full of pride. She said that it was the two of them combined, the Carib part and the African part, that made Emmanuel such a nice-looking man.

Reevah felt that little thrill of satisfaction that always came when she thought of life with Emmanuel. She was grateful that she found Emmanuel just when she did; just when she was all wound up tight-tight in her head, wanting to love somebody bad-bad. She was only seventeen when she met Emmanuel, and she stuck to him like a bee to a honeycomb. He let her stick to him, never chasing her away from him, although she was sure that she was not the prettiest fly in his parlour.

Before she met Emmanuel, Reevah had a strong feeling that if she did not love somebody soon, she would explode. But she did not want to love just anybody; she wanted to meet the right boy and give her gift of love to him alone.

Emmanuel was a man, not a boy, but that did not stop her from wanting to be with him. He really had a parlour that was like the one in the story. In the story, the spider said to the fly: "Come into my parlour." And that is how it was with Emmanuel, with the difference that he did not entice any girls into his house. They came voluntarily, and he invited them inside. He gave them lemonade, and he did not touch them. Some of them were bold enough to touch him, but he stopped them, because he was not that kind of man.

He was stationed at the Newgate Street police station, and because he did not have any family in town, he rented a little two-by-four house in the Brown's Avenue area. This was far enough from her own house for Reevah to feel safe that her parents would not find out that she visited Emmanuel. And they never did.

Reevah smiled at her daughter and decided to tell her about that time; about how from the first day that she met Emmanuel, she found her way back to that house at every single opportunity.

"I was the one person your father allowed to be in his house, whether he was there or not. He show me where he keep the key, behind the doghouse at the back of the little yard. So then I would fetch the key, let meself in, and sit, waiting for him. While I waited, I would absorb his essence through his smell, and from looking at all of his belongings, without touching them."

Reevah gave a little embarrassed laugh and Sayshelle delighted in it. She had never heard such intimate things about her parents before. She was not at all embarrassed; she wanted to hear more. It was the first time that her Mama Reevah had ever revealed so much of the romance between her and her Papa Emmanuel. She was usually much more reserved and shy to speak to her daughter about these things.

Talking to Sayshelle about Emmanuel made Reevah remember so many other moments that she could not share with her daughter yet; and maybe she never would. They were things she did not know of mothers sharing with daughters, or with anyone else for that matter. They were her jewels, stored up inside herself. She smiled at her daughter and closed her eyes, just letting the memories wash over her. She knew that Sayshelle would be quiet and wait for the words to flow again.

Reevah relaxed into the joy of remembering how she would sit in Emmanuel's house, listening for his step, her eyes fixed on the door. That way, she could read his feelings on his face as he opened it and saw her. Sitting now with her daughter, she hugged the memories close of how he used to be glad to see her...always! His eyes would light up, and he would come to her, and hug her up really tight, and kiss her.

When the sweetness between them came, she was ready for it. She held on to Emmanuel and buried her face in his brown-brown-colour-of-cinnamon neck that smelled of Old Spice cologne.

She was wearing the Chanel No. 5 perfume that her godmother had given her for her birthday. The letter "o" was written small-small on the label of the perfume bottle. She smiled now at the memory of how she used to gaze at it, loving the artistry of it. The white lettering on the black background was so clear, so strong an imposition, the one on the other. She thought that it was classy; and even today, she still used Chanel No. 5 whenever she was going somewhere special: to church, or a wedding, or to visit her godmother. She had put some behind her ears on the day of Emmanuel's funeral.

Emmanuel was so pretty, Reevah liked to just watch him. For a long time, that is all she did: just watched Emmanuel while he talked. And when she talked, he would watch her.

She liked how his chin was almost like a square knob, and how it just kind of stuck itself out from his face, making him look like he was holding his whole head out from his neck. His chin made him look like a handsome version of the Dick Tracy character in the comic books she used to read when she was a girl, way back when.

His thick neck flowed nicely into broad shoulders, which supported his long, muscular arms. And his face, sitting on top of his brown-brown-colour-of-cinnamon neck, was a thing of joy to Reevah. She loved his mouth best of all. He had beautiful lips that seemed made for her to kiss. Just looking at his big, round, full lips would make her feel hot, wanting their petal-softness next to hers. Then she would pull him close, suddenly, urgently; and Emmanuel would laugh, loving her passion. He never tried to restrain her youthful, abundant need for physical closeness. It stayed like that between them throughout their whole marriage.

They would sit in his house, with the dog grumbling at lizards in the backyard. The curtains would be drawn to close out the light, the radio playing softly, the kerosene lamp lit for softness. The electric light and the sunlight were too harsh for the colour of their love. Emmanuel would hold her then, gently, softly, as if she might break. He would pat her back as if she was a baby, so that she soon fell asleep.

He did not sleep because he insisted that she not stay at his house beyond dusk and risk her parents' wrath. After she took a catnap, he would wake her and walk with her to the top of her street. Then he would watch until she reached inside the gate of her house and waved to him. If she did not wave, he knew that either one or both of her parents were sitting on the gallery.

In the light just before the sun went to sleep, Reevah would turn her face to Emmanuel at the top of the street, straining to put all of her love for him into her eyes as she closed the gate behind her.

Reevah brought herself back from her thoughts. She spoke of how she used to lie in Emmanuel's arms and look at his high cheekbones. "His almond-shaped eyes and his high cheekbones are the parts of him that show his Carib blood," she said.

Sayshelle had only seen pictures in textbooks of the Caribs; there were very few people in Antigua who still looked as if they had Carib blood in them. Reevah said that some people were part Carib and didn't even know it.

"Things were quite mixed up because of slavery and the white people taking charge of people's lives. I sometimes wonder how everybody still managed to keep track of their *generation*. But nobody really talk about these things; it is as if everybody want to forget that slavery ever happen."

She went on: "When my mother was alive, I try to raise the talk of slavery-days with her; but she say that it is too painful to speak about. So I drop the subject."

Reevah grew silent again. Looking at Emmanuel had made her keep memory of the Caribs and slavery-days alive; he was so Carib-looking and so African-looking. It was as if he was a last reminder of those two sets of people in pure form, brought together in harmony.

Even his cheekbones were a source of delight for her fingers; and soon, she would replace them with her lips as she kissed all of the places that her fingers had first worshipped.

If she closed her eyes, Reevah could still feel the *niceness* of touching Emmanuel. She recalled how they lay, wrapped in each other's arms, reaching for the sweetness that happened between them. The sweetness stayed, even up to a few months before he died. When his illness became unbearably painful, it was enough for them both when she caressed his hair, now grown long on his head from waiting for a change in government.

Emmanuel would moan at first when she touched his head, as if there was longing still in his loins. His longing reached its fingers up to receive her touch, so far away. Soon, his sounds were like a cat's murmur, as Reevah touched her lips to the places her fingers indicated. It was the same ritual with which she had first lovingly touched Emmanuel in those early days in his house. Now, she touched only his head. And so she satisfied them both, holding him gently, softly, in her arms, the way he used to hold her. Memory of how he had loved her would come to her, helping her to feel the sweetness inside her, without his touch.

He would sense her need for his touch sometimes, and it made him weep, the tears rolling down his face to wet her lips as she caressed his neck and his chest. She would kiss them away, loving his joy into being, out of the sadness. It was enough.

"So much more *story* to tell you, Sayshelle-child." Reevah took a deep breath. "So much more went on that you did not see or, even if you saw it, you were too young to take note of it.

The election came and went before your Papa Emmanuel died. He was beside himself when they announce that the party leader and his henchmen were back in power. In his view, they had not a single redeeming feature among them. He felt as if he kept himself alive just to witness the collapse of his dream.

And when it was all over, he had a full head of hair to remind him of how foolish he was to have hope. He knew that he could have died long before the election; he would feel his life's breath leaving him and pull himself back, willing himself to stay alive.

During that time, child, you will recall that your father eat little more than spinach; pieces of soft-boiled eggs; water; the juice from *sibber-sweets*; and sometimes, a little brandy mixed with Coca-Cola to help his digestion." She stopped speaking abruptly then, as if the memory of how hard it had been to watch Emmanuel's decline was more than she could manage.

Indeed, it was a very hard time for Reevah and for Sayshelle. They would feel so helpless as they watched Emmanuel's skin falling slack on his bones. It had a diaphanous, almost translucent quality to it, and it was only in his eyes that you could still see the power of his Spirit. Some days, all that passed his lips were sips of bush tea that Reevah or Sayshelle fed him from a spoon.

Emmanuel said one day that he felt as if he was like Jesus, fasting for forty days and forty nights. When he reported visions of meeting his mother and holding her hand, Reevah realized that his Spirit was travelling. She had heard Old Ones say that was the way it happened to people before they died.

It was Emmanuel's last gasp, and he lived it in a sullen humour that was unusual for him; but it made him interesting to people. His long hair and his words about "the winds of change in Antigua" gave him a different look and a different personality from the gentle, quiet soul people knew.

"Your father was retired from the police force for some time," Reevah continued, "but people from the villages that he used to work in still came to see him. They would call him 'Corpie' the way they always used to do. He liked that so very much; I was grateful for those people."

Reevah's voice was smooth and peaceful as she deftly carried on two conversations: one inside her head and the other out loud with Sayshelle.

"People from the villages where he worked brought provisions from their harvests and offered them to me. They would say: 'This is to help your husband get well.' I accepted their gifts gratefully. I really appreciated the help, as Emmanuel's pension and my small salary could hardly keep us going.

You know, child, I often worried about money then; because Emmanuel's pension would not continue after his death. That is the way they handle policemen's pensions. There is no widow's pension; and so I knew that I would be our sole support after your father died. It was a good thing that I knew how to plant a good garden."

Sayshelle knew that her Mama Reevah could only find work as a domestic worker. Her Papa Emmanuel's political work and open criticism of the government made it hard for her to find a job. Besides, she was a known supporter of one of the opposition parties. She and her sister Sage attended their public meetings. They carried their stools and sat near the platform. They wore sweaters to keep themselves warm. Reevah tied her head with a cotton head-tie, intent on shutting out the night dew.

In order to make a little more money, Reevah boarded two policemen. She provided their meals and washed their clothes. They were from Dominica and rented a house on Number Two New Street. It helped, too, that she grew all of her own vegetables right there in her own backyard. She taught Sayshelle how to plant and tend to the garden, the way Emmanuel had taught her.

"Just before your Papa Emmanuel died," Reevah said, "I observe that the last pumpkin-vine he planted was entirely filled with blossoms. He get really excited when I tell him this; and then he insist that I take him out into the yard to see it. Then he point it out to each visitor that week, observing that it was an indicator of something."

She smiled at the memory of his almost childish delight in the blossoms on the pumpkin-vine. She remembered how his voice was resigned, at peace with his approaching death, as he spoke about the flowering of the plant. Yet Reevah thought that she also detected a note of triumph. It was as if he was pleased to bring to a close a life he no longer desired.

Each day she told her heart to be still; for it lurched with fear at the sight of the blossoms on the pumpkin-vine. She closed her eyes now, bringing back the memory of them.

"They were so beautiful too, those blossoms on the pumpkin-vine." She tried to paint a picture to help Sayshelle remember. "You recall them? They were a deep-deep golden-yellow, and they were hardy, strong blossoms. Emmanuel said that the vine would produce all the pumpkins at the same time, unlike the usual three or four at a time."

She opened her eyes and looked at Sayshelle, making sure that she was paying attention. She was surprised when Sayshelle said that she did not recall any talk of the flowering pumpkin-vine. Then Reevah remembered that she had made Emmanuel promise not to tell Sayshelle about the sign of the blossoms on the pumpkin-vine. She felt Emmanuel close as she spoke: "This way of a fruit tree, or a pumpkin-vine, blossoming all at once, is the strongest sign, the old people say, that someone in a household is going to join their Maker. Usually, it is an old person; but sometimes, it is a sick person whose death could be forecast in that way."

Her voice dropped almost to a whisper. "It was the strongest sign I had that Emmanuel was going to die. I prepare myself and you then to face saying good-bye to him." She wiped her eyes and blew her nose in a tissue. She smiled bravely. Sayshelle recognized it as the smile her Mama Reevah had learned to bring to her face when she spoke of her Papa Emmanuel's illness and his passing.

"And you know, child, the rain that fall after your father died, that all-day-start-and-stop-again rain, it knock all of the blossoms off of the pumpkin-vine. The rain leave it clean-clean. Every single blossom went with your father. If I did not witness it myself, I woulda never believe it."

Chapter Two

By now, all thought of sleep left Reevah and Sayshelle. They lit coils and citronella candles to discourage mosquitoes from buzzing around. Sayshelle plugged in the kettle and filled a teapot with bush to make bush-tea. She picked pure *noo-noo* balsam from the yard. It was her favourite tea, and she knew that Reevah said that it always made her feel refreshed.

The smell from their cups of *noo-noo* balsam bush-tea was very sweet in the room. Sayshelle smiled to see her mother inhaling the deep aroma of the *noo-noo* balsam, as if it was having a healing effect on her.

As Reevah settled into her rocking-chair, Sayshelle propped herself up on the ottoman. She wanted to hear more; it was helping her to feel her Papa Emmanuel as a whole person in a way that she had not truly known him.

Once she was settled in her rocking-chair, Reevah picked up the thread as if she had never dropped it. "So, after the election, Emmanuel grew his cancer bigger and bigger, or deeper and deeper...I always think of it both ways." She remembered how agonizing it was to watch her man's handsome body lose its appeal for her, as well as for him. For the pain became too much for them to touch too closely.

She had seen other changes in Emmanuel as well. Before the election, his hair used to be the topic of conversations with friends and visitors. Sometimes they would ask him, "So you going to cut your hair as soon as the election over?" And he, loving the attention, would reply with humour. Towards the end, though, when he was asked if he was going to cut his long hair, he could barely answer "Yes" or "No." The sullen humour that replaced his hope after the re-election of the ruling party now sat on him like a scab. It was thick enough and big enough to cover the cancerous hurt he carried deep inside himself.

Reevah rocked her chair gently for a while, liking the rhythm its squeaking hinges made. She stopped moving the chair to ask Sayshelle: "Eh-eh...you're sleeping...?" It was not really a question, but Sayshelle opened her eyes and answered: "You stopped talking. Please tell me more. You know I love it when you talk about Papa Emmanuel."

Her Mama Reevah's laughter was deep-deep at hearing her say that. She needed no further prompting. She told Sayshelle that her Papa

Emmanuel was a beautiful man inside and out, even up until the day he died. She spoke of how on the night he died, he smiled at his daughter for the last time. Then he put his hand in a blessing on her head as she sat at his bedside.

When Reevah looked at Emmanuel that last night, she felt that she was truly blessed among women: she was fortunate enough to find and marry the man she loved and who loved her. She told Sayshelle that he looked very handsome in his funeral suit. That is why she got her uncle to take a picture of him, laid out in his coffin. After the funeral, she made copies of the photograph for all of the relatives.

Sayshelle kept her copy at the back of her photo album. She did not like looking at a picture of her Papa Emmanuel laid out in his dead-suit. By putting it at the back of the photo album, she could make sure that there was no other photograph on the page facing it. Then she would just never turn that last page.

By tucking his photograph away in the back of her photo album, Sayshelle felt as if she buried her Papa Emmanuel again. She knew that one day, she would find some more suitable place for the photograph of her Papa Emmanuel in his dead-suit. She had lots of photographs that showed him alive, smiling, looking happy, in the rest of her photo album.

She discovered that her Mama Reevah kept her framed copy of the photograph in the bottom of the drawer with her panties. It was an oddity, so Sayshelle asked her why she chose that particular drawer. Reevah said that it was because she could not stand to look at Emmanuel in that state every day.

Reevah never really thought about why she chose the drawer with her panties; and now that Sayshelle pressed the question on her, she felt her face get hot with embarrassment. She averted her eyes before saying: "I just opened the first drawer to hand." She was relieved when Sayshelle accepted her answer and became quiet.

When she tried to reason it out, Reevah thought that she must have buried her yearning for sex with the picture of Emmanuel. She realized that she chose that drawer with her panties for some specific reason. She knew that from the day she married Emmanuel, she never looked at another man; and he was enough for her, even in death.

Even when his sullen self formed a crust over his usually gently smiling features, Emmanuel could not stop himself from being a nice person. Nor did he ever stop being her loving husband. In the last part of his life, they did not touch each other deeply, creating the kind of sweetness that had produced Sayshelle. Still she liked to just hold him. She rubbed his feet and she touched his face, his hands and his head.

Sometimes she loved him with her lips on his hair and on his closed eyes, while he purred and drifted off to sleep. It was enough.

Reevah dressed Emmanuel in his dark-blue serge suit for the burial. She thought he would like that: going out in style. Some women of the party he supported gave yards and yards of cloth for the coffin. She used some of it to cover Emmanuel's own pants and shirts that were also used to *chak* his body in the coffin. The undertakers wanted to make sure that his frail body would not roll around when they moved it.

It was then that she noticed for the first time just how emaciated Emmanuel's body had become. In all that time that she bathed him, massaged him, dressed him, and loved him, she did not notice that he was merely skin and bones. Her eyes held on to the image of the man she had loved for all of those years.

Reevah also used some of the cloth from the party comrades to provide a kind of shroud around Emmanuel. So he went to meet his Maker framed in the colour blue. Reevah knew that he would be happy about this. For Emmanuel liked the idea of wearing that colour to show solidarity with the party. He had several select blue shirts which he always wore to political meetings. He even wore them to the ruling party's public meetings, goading their supporters into acknowledging his opposition to the government.

Reevah did not adhere to such behaviour, and wore any colour she felt like wearing, including red, the colour of the ruling party. She had no intention of having petty political issues stop her from wearing red. It happened to be her favourite colour and sat very nicely on her dark-black skin. Besides, when she first met Emmanuel, she was wearing red and it did not stop him from liking her.

"After all," she often told him, "it is just a colour." However, Emmanuel took the colour thing seriously. So soon after she married him, although she did not give up her red clothes, Reevah stopped wearing them to any important event. She certainly never wore red to any party gathering or public meeting.

She liked to tie her head with a red cotton cloth every night before she went to sleep, but Emmanuel really couldn't take that. He said that it made him feel like he was sleeping with the enemy. Reevah thought it amusing and laughed outright when he said it; but she indulged him and never slept in the red head-tie again.

It was long after his death that she pulled out her old red head-tie and began to wrap her head with it every night. She noticed that when she began sleeping in her red head-tie, she started dreaming of Emmanuel every night. Before that, it was only now and again that she would wake knowing that she had met him in her dreams.

The first time in her life that she saw Emmanuel, Reevah was wearing her red cotton frock, which fitted her close at the waist and flared out into a wide skirt. She was feeling hot and tight as she had felt for weeks. She was too young to have a boyfriend, her Mama and her Papa said; but she just knew that she was ready to have a boyfriend.

She knew it in the way her nipples tingled when they rubbed against the fabric of the cotton brassiere that her Mama made to support her thrusting, budding breasts. She knew it in the way she felt every time she saw boys whom she thought were good-looking. But she was not going to throw herself at any boy; she knew that she would recognize the right boy when she met him.

Her body was feeling those feelings when she turned a corner in the Recreation Grounds and saw Emmanuel for the first time. There he was, standing with his back against a stall, watching people walk past. He was in his policeman's uniform and Reevah caught her breath at how splendid he looked. He did not see her at first, because he was turned sideways, talking to another policeman. She worked her way around to where he was standing, because she wanted him to notice her.

It was her red dress that Emmanuel noticed, first and foremost. For the colour made him think that she was a supporter of the ruling party. He watched her closely, but not for the reasons Reevah wanted. When she said "Good afternoon" to him, he answered politely, hoping she would leave the area; he did not want to get to know any government supporter.

"Why you slighting me?" There was real hurt in Reevah's voice and Emmanuel took a closer look at her.

"No reason," he said. "I didn't mean to slight you at all!" Reevah seemed less hurt now and he noticed the nice way her mouth curved into a sulky little smile as she said, "Well, I speak nicely to you, but you ignoring me." He took in her eyes, the way they looked brazen and seemed to hold a promise of something that he felt sure he wanted.

"What's your name?" She asked the question of the other policeman and he answered, then told her Emmanuel's name. She said, "Pleased to meet you; and pleased to meet you too, Emmanuel."

He smiled at her and was glad when she smiled back. The other policeman turned away, and Reevah seized the moment of privacy to ask Emmanuel: "So where you live Emmanuel? Ah going to come and visit you."

"You sure your parents would allow that?" Emmanuel asked, not wanting to find himself in any trouble. Reevah laughed and said: "No, they would not allow that; but I am not going to ask them!"

He told her where he lived and added, "Please bring a friend with you; I don't want people to talk about you visiting a single man's house." She nodded, liking that he was concerned about her reputation.

The next day, Reevah went to Emmanuel's house at the time they had agreed upon. She went alone and continued to visit him alone until she left high school and they got married.

Sayshelle looked at her Mama Reevah. She was thrilled to hear of her parents' romantic meeting. She was also still digesting her Mama Reevah's response to the question about the photograph of her Papa Emmanuel in his dead-suit. She felt sure that there was something more to it than her Mama Reevah said; but she knew better than to be impolite and ask any more questions about it.

Besides, there was something she wanted to know about her Papa Emmanuel. It seemed to her that she always carried the question in her mind. It would come to her from time to time and she never got around to asking him about it. And now he was gone.

She propped herself upright on the ottoman; then swung her feet to the floor and turned to Reevah: "Why Papa Emmanuel was so concerned to see the overthrow of the government? Why it mattered so much to him? Why it seemed so personal?"

Reevah was startled. While Sayshelle's questions seemed to come out of the blue, they went right to the heart of some things that she wanted to tell her. She liked that their minds were together in this journeying, this reclaiming, and this releasing. The closeness between them pleased her. She laughed into her daughter's eyes, exclaiming, "So we knock one head! 'Cause you ask about the very things I want you to hear."

She leaned back in her chair and cleared her throat. Sayshelle thought that she had an air about her of someone who was opening a bundle of papers that were tied up in ribbon and put away for years. She could see them emerging from the bottom of a box, or from a bath-pan under a bed.

Her Mama Reevah took her time to dust off the memories. She resettled the cushions in her rocking-chair, then leaned back and said nothing.

Sayshelle let herself become still...a complete quiet settling over each muscle and each cell of her body. She could hear herself breathing; and she could hear her Mama Reevah's breath rising and falling, purposefully. Suddenly a thought rippled through Sayshelle: "I feel my Papa Emmanuel present."

And at last, Reevah spoke, her voice rising gently from the silence. "Your Papa was a good man. He was a good policeman too; the people liked him. They liked him because he was never hard on them. He always listen to what they have to say to him when he was breaking up a fight, or settling any dispute." She relaxed into the talking, as if now that she had untied the package of memories, the words just spilled out of her.

"Before you were born, he was put on duty during the time that the labourers in all of these islands went on strike and the English people say that they were rioting. The superior officers give all the policemen guns and tell them to shoot into the crowd. Your father say he not shooting at the people; and for that, his superior officer never forgive him.

They give the policemen the guns anyway, and all of them follow your father's example and they fire the shots up in the air, so that the people just scatter. They say one man get killed in St. Kitts; but because of your father, nobody in Antigua was shot."

Reevah hardly paused, but Sayshelle noticed that there was a newness to her voice. She spoke in a rush, as if the memory was too painful to air it for too long. "After that incident, the superintendent of police was out to get your father. He transfer him from village to village, away from St. John's, where he know that he live with his wife. So I was always alone."

Her voice rose to an almost shrill note as she relived the experience. "Then how was your father to get his meals? Imagine a young married man, stationed in Bethesda, Freetown, Willikies, Bolans, Old Road; everywhere but town. So we had to find people to board him in every village, then when he get his leave he would come home."

She looked out of the window into the twilight, thinking of this time. Her eyes misted over with memory and she seemed to almost forget that Sayshelle was in the room.

"During that time, I was very lonely, and several men buzzed around, trying to entice me to their bed. But my resolve was firm; I loved Emmanuel and he was the only man for me.

One night, he come home on leave from the country and he meet a man talking to me at the window. Well, it cause quite a to-do and even though he know I was blameless, he was vexed that I even entertained the man. But to me, it was only talking; so I didn't see what the problem was. Well, Emmanuel and the man had one big quarrel and the next day, the man went to the station on Newgate Street and take out a warrant on your father. He say that your father hit him. The next thing we know, we in the middle of a big-big court case."

She wrung her hands gently, rubbing her knuckles with her palms. It was hard to speak, but she had an air of determination about her as she continued. "That terrible man, the superintendent of police...he tried to get your father fired over it; but we get a good lawyer and your father win the case. For the man had no evidence.

Well child, something went bad for Emmanuel after that case. The superintendent of police was determined to get him in one way or another. He really hated your father. He had his favourites among the police officers. He does give those men the best duty: close to their homes, and where they wouldn't have to pedal a bicycle to get to work.

Your father and others like him who fell out of favour had to pedal a bicycle to any village they assign them...all the way from town. They supply him with a bicycle, as if that is any comfort! And he had to see to the maintenance of the bicycle at that!"

She shook her head slowly from side to side and made a sound deep in her throat. Her voice, when it came, contained disgust mixed with disdain: "Anyway, as I say, things progress from bad to worse. Then one day, the superintendent send your father to go and watch his house on the outskirts of town. He send him to watch it late of an evening, saying that he feel sure that his wife was keeping a man. His instruction was to go and see if any man come and visit his wife.

Well, your father study on it, and he decide say that kinda duty is not the kinda duty that a superintendent of police should send a police officer to do. And besides, why would he send a police officer that he did not like or trust to do such a sacred duty?

So he study on it some more and decide that it was a trap. He make a decision to go to do the duty one hour earlier than the treacherous superintendent of police tell him to go; and he also decide to stay some distance from the house. He hide himself in the bushes, so that he could see all angles and observe everything that take place.

Well, a few minutes after the appointed time, he see two big men arrive with cutlass in they hand. They walk right up to the location near the house where the superintendent did tell your father to go and hide. Emmanuel watch them for quite a while. They look, and they look, and they look for him. And then when they couldn't find him, they leave."

Sayshelle was quite shaken by the story. Although she always knew that there was great enmity between her father and the head of the police force, she never knew what was the cause of it. Throughout her childhood, she heard her father say, "Mm, Mm, Mm!" three times, just like that, every time he spoke about the superintendent of police.

Reevah liked nothing better than talking to her daughter about her father. There were things they were not able to tell her at the time that they happened, as she was very young. In fact, not until long after he retired did Emmanuel breathe a word of this particular story to anyone besides Reevah.

It was a dangerous tale to tell, for it meant that the superintendent of police would finally find "cause" to get at Emmanuel. No doubt he would take Emmanuel to court for suggesting that he tried to have him killed.

Now that she was telling the tale to Sayshelle, all of Reevah's old anger and old pain came back to haunt her. She remembered how she and Emmanuel suffered. She had a frown on her forehead as she continued speaking; she felt as if she was reliving the horror of it all.

"So, your Papa Emmanuel wait there in the bushes until the two men went about their business. Then he make his way back to the station on his bicycle and report to the superintendent of police. When he see your father, he almost faint dead away; but he catch himself and ask him if he carried out the mission he send him to fulfil.

Your father tell him that he go to the appointed place as he instruct him, but he see no one besides two big men with cutlass in they hand."

Reevah laughed, raising her head triumphantly, her face turned upward in rejoicing. Her pride in Emmanuel rang in her voice. "He describe to the superintendent of police how the two men search and search, seeming to be looking for somebody. The superintendent of police look your father right in the eye and realize that he find him out.

Well girl! From that day onwards, your father's life was hell in the police force. That is why he never get a promotion beyond the rank of corporal. That superintendent of police was so wicked; he was vindictive to the very end!"

The old fire and anger returned to her voice as she spoke of Emmanuel's persecution. She seemed to have become strengthened, sitting upright in her chair, her body held taut. Then Sayshelle heard an edge creep into her voice.

"Emmanuel was not a saint, but to my eyes, everything he do, I support him, though sometimes I didn't really agree inside. He was a good man and he always act from his heart; but he had this way about him that sometimes does make me wonder how to try to change him. It was a good way for some people, but for me, his wife, it leave me with hardship in life.

He feel strongly about the government and I agree with him, but he say too much to too many people and it get back to those in power. Soon, it come to the place where, between his police superintendent who didn't like him and the government persecution, they force him out of his job.

The way they do it was abominable! They wait until he was home, sick as a dog, and they send another policeman to spy on him. He was sent to see if he really getting bedrest, as the doctor say he was supposed to get."

She stopped speaking abruptly and looked down at her hands. Sayshelle leaned close and held her mother's hands as they lay clasped loosely in her lap. They were usually such peaceful hands. Now she saw them unfurling, letting go, releasing the holding and protecting of so much life.

It was as if the fingers could no longer curl too tightly over the memories; and yet, fear of reliving some of those bits and pieces of her life seemed to make her reluctant to open her hands too widely. It was enough that the bits and pieces were in her memory, but to think and speak them breathed new life in all of the corners that she had folded securely out of sight.

Her resolve was firm. She made a decision to tell Sayshelle and let go the horror that she stored with this story. For now, it could no longer hurt her, nor her daughter, nor Emmanuel.

Her voice was full of emotion, as if she was choking the words out of her body. "Well, the policeman come and find you father bending down, weeding in the yard. And he watch him for a good long time every day; and he see your father *heft* the big rubbish-drum out to the street. He didn't exactly *heft* it outside; inasmuch as he was really in pain, he just push it along. He kinda roll it on the side 'til it reach in place.

Girl, that policeman...he watch your father all day...day after day, he watch him. And we, not knowing, went about things as usual."

She took a deep breath, a sorrow seeming to descend on her. The anger did not leave her; it receded in the face of the sadness of speaking of Emmanuel's loss of his life's work. Grief forced her voice to an almost-whisper as she brought back that time in words.

"Your father's cancer did begin to grow then, and sometimes he had pain in the night. And of a truth, the doctor did tell him to stay in bed all day; but he wasn't able to stand that. So in the daytime, he do all the things he was used to doing around the house. He didn't go walking out anywhere, not even to the fish market; which as you know, he used to enjoy.

He missed English Harbour and the fishing boats; so he liked to go to the fish market in town and chat to the fishermen. Well, in this sick period, he didn't do none of that. He just do the things around the yard.

By that time, we did finish putting the addition on the house and it was now to-size. So now the yard-space was not big at all. Is not as if Emmanuel was doing any set of yard-work; just tidying up and putting out the rubbish. He loved that work; it make him feel that he doing something useful; and he get to put his hands in the soil, pulling weeds and moulding up the plants. In fact, it help him to feel better."

She paused and drew in a breath. There was a long silence, and when she spoke again, it was as if a fire had burned her throat. For now her voice was little more than a hoarse whisper, and her words fell harshly into the silence. "Well that policeman they send to watch Emmanuel was wicked. He make friends with the Montserrat woman who live down at the East corner; you know her, the woman name Harty-Di who live near to Cross Street."

Sayshelle nodded, "Yes, I know her; she's a nice lady."

Reevah agreed. "Thank God for that, or else we woulda never know the truth of the matter. Child, that policeman stay in Harty-Di house, quiet-quiet, watching your father day after day. We never see him enter and we never see him depart.

All we know is your father get a letter stating that he was observed doing strenuous activity for a certain number of days. It also summon him to a hearing before his superiors."

She shook her head sadly. "Afterwards, when it was all over, is the woman, the neighbour Harty-Di, who tell your father that she see the policeman watching him through her window, day after day. He never tell her what he was doing; and because she didn't see your father doing anything untoward, she had not thought to mention it to us.

Later, when she hear all about the sick-time and the 'hearing,' she put two and two together and realize that the policeman use her house to spy on your father."

Reevah pulled her hands over her hair, sweeping her plaits together, pushing their unwilling thickness into submission under her red head-tie. As night had fallen, the darkness brought the dew that came as soon as the twilight left. She liked to cover her head once the night-dew came.

Sayshelle inhaled her mother's clear beauty, shining from her face, damp with the night-dew. It was now no longer obscured by the thick plaits that she allowed to fall across her forehead after her evening bath. Her skin was almost as black as the *doving* pot that they used to cook meat. Her eyes were large and dark brown; her lips followed the curves of the soft frill of a hibiscus flower.

Sayshelle had long ago decided that her Mama Reevah's head was carved just for the purpose of fitting nicely onto her neck. So perfect was the symmetry of the construction of her head, neck, and shoulders that she sometimes caught her breath when she looked at her.

She watched her now, and was saddened to see Reevah's eyes clouding over as she prepared to speak. Her body was soft again, relaxed all the way down to her feet. She stretched them out in front of her, curling and uncurling her toes like a cat moving from a deep slumber. Her hands sat loosely in her lap now; the fingers of one hand gently caressing the palm of the other.

"Well, make a long story short," Reevah said, "that is how your father lose his job as a policeman. You were still just a young girl, so we never tell you about it. All of that is what make him resolve to stop them, come what may; these wicked people.

He lump everything that happen to him into one; because the superintendent of police was a high-ranking government supporter. He know that it was because he speak out against the government that he suffer in his job."

Sayshelle could see her Mama Reevah's feelings still making the journey out of the long-long tomb of their confinement. They were scraping a raw passage, using a new space that was tender from holding them in safe-keeping for so long. The words tumbled out, and in their wake, they left ease.

Reevah stopped speaking as abruptly as she had started; she now sat, her eyes distant, her face untroubled. She was visiting a memory of Emmanuel, at peace at last, when the superintendent insisted on his early retirement.

For his retirement gift he was given a stone bust of the English prime minister, who was still alive then. His name was Sir Winston Churchill. The bust had a metal cigarette in its mouth; and it was long after they had brought it home from the retirement ceremony that they realized it was a cigarette lighter and not just a statue.

Such a thoughtless gift, Reevah thought then and still; for no one in their family smoked any more. It was years of smoking that caused Emmanuel's cancer. The strange thing is that he decided one day to stop smoking, and gave up his Camel non-filtered cigarettes immediately. It was not until several years later that he was diagnosed with lung cancer.

Everyone knew about it, so how could they go out and buy him a life-size cigarette lighter? And not only that, given how strong a man Emmanuel was against those colonial white people in England, how could they think he would want to look at a bust of some old English prime minister?

Years later, when the bust of Sir Winston Churchill up and mysteriously disappeared from their house, Reevah suspected a thieving relative to be the culprit. She said nothing of her suspicions to Emmanuel, for she was relieved to be rid of the offending symbol of his bad treatment at the hands of the superintendent of police and the government. She would say nothing of it now to her daughter.

The secret memory brought a smile to her lips. She decided that it was best to leave it buried with the passing of time. For the superintendent of police was now dead, and the then prime minister grew into a senile old man who fell asleep in Parliament. He too was now dead and all and sundry had attended a big state funeral. The thieving relative was still alive and well; but she figured God would bring retribution on his head for his actions.

She would tell Sayshelle about all of that on another occasion. She said to herself: "For now...tonight...I want to be more direct with my child about her father's goodness; his virtue and the odds that he fight against for his whole life. That way, she could celebrate him."

Now they were becoming tired. Reevah felt light and dreamy; ready for a good night's sleep. As she said "Good night" to her daughter, she felt a deep sense of peace. She kissed Sayshelle on the cheek, saying "Sleep well." She was rewarded with the radiant smile that her daughter turned on her. "I will," she said. "Better than ever before."

As she lay in bed, Sayshelle thought about all that her Mama Reevah had told her. She had a much fuller picture of her Papa Emmanuel, her Mama Reevah, and even Antigua. There were other things that stood out for her...things that her Mama Reevah did not say, but which she could read. These important to her; for they told her how her parents were with each other. They told her much more than words.

She noticed how her Mama Reevah's face changed every time she talked about her father. It was not a big change, but it was sufficient to make the colour of her eyes deepen to a luminous darkness at the memory of him. Her lips softened, and her hands reached up to touch her cheek. Sayshelle thought that she was reliving the memory of Emmanuel's fingers on her face.

Ever since she was a little girl, Sayshelle watched her father caress her mother's face. He always seemed to get such pleasure from stroking her forehead and tracing a line down her nose, to touch her lips with his fingers; then his own lips would brush hers.

Emmanuel and Reevah were always reserved in front of her; but often, she heard them talking softly into the night. Then she would wonder if her Papa Emmanuel was touching her Mama Reevah's face again. She would smile happily into her pillow at the thought of the soft love she always saw between them.

It was so different from what she saw and heard about in the relationship between her Aunt Sage and the man she lived with, named Rommel. Although she never asked about it, Sayshelle knew that her Aunt Sage's life worried her Mama Reevah and caused her pain. It was as if they were from two different families, the way in which they lived their lives.

She wondered what caused them to have such different lives, her Mama Reevah and her sister Sage. She heard her Mama Reevah ponder this very question many times, saying that Sage just seemed to be born weaker and a prey to all of the things that could destroy her. "She is nothing like me and Juniper Berry," she would say, referring to her younger sister who had only recently returned from living in Trinidad.

Chapter Three

They sat on the gallery of his house every night. It was always after supper and before the evening news. Rommel knew when the evening news began, because while he sat out on the gallery, he turned the volume up really high on the radio and on the television set. Although both were tuned to the government stations, he liked to have them playing at the same time.

Sage thought that he gave himself the challenge of trying to listen to the two of them together. She heard him say often to his friends, the pride showing in his voice, "I heard it on the radio and on the television at the same time. I like hearing what they both have to say."

Sage did not have the courage to tell Rommel something he refused to acknowledge: that the news on the television and on the radio were one and the same government propaganda. The way Rommel saw it, the news was real: it had something to do with movement and change in the country. The government was getting things done. He never thought to ask himself what became of the projects they announced on the radio and on the television. Sage thought that they were like banners, waving in the wind, going nowhere.

Rommel would not accept that his party ("My boys," as he called them), were wastrels, numskulls, who were not getting anything done. In the early days of their living together, Sage reminded Rommel that the opposition party said that his "boys" lined their pockets and their families' pockets with the people's money.

She knew that he had heard the rumours about bribes. Anyone with enough money could get a piece of the island. It even came to pass that the government leased land to an Asian businessman to set up an "Asian Village" on a little island off Antigua. As usual, nothing came of it, even though it was announced over and over on the radio, and on television. Many jobs were promised to Antiguans; but they were all still waiting.

Then there was the hospital, and the airport, and the vendors' stalls, the library; the selling off of land to all and sundry. The list just went on so long that Sage wearied of even thinking about all of these non-existent, failed projects.

She reminded Rommel that one of his numskull "boys" (or was it his son? She couldn't remember for sure) was caught with a briefcase of money chained to his wrist in some airport in Europe. She pointed out to him that that kind of event was not reported on the news. The news did not tell people like Rommel about things like that. It was at the opposition parties' public meetings that people heard the *real* news. But Rommel didn't go to the opposition parties' public meetings. The fact that Sage went to them was, to his mind, a kind of treason.

He judged and sentenced her for being so ungrateful to the government that she and her sister Reevah would go to the opposition parties' meetings. As Sage dressed to leave the house, Rommel would say, "Both of you going to listen to the stupidness that those guttersnipes and numskulls have to say." He went so far as to admonish her, calling her "an ungrateful dog" that "bites the hand that feeds you." Sage knew better than to respond when he became abusive in his language. She knew that he could easily work himself into a frenzy of abuse that might last for days, eventually turning into slaps to her face.

In the days following any talk of the opposition parties' stupidness, of guttersnipes and numskulls, they would sit on the gallery in the evenings. As usual, the radio and the television set would be blaring inside the house, in anticipation of the news. Suddenly, Rommel would turn to an unsuspecting Sage and slap her. And so it would begin.

Every now and then he would hit her one hard slap, for no reason that she or anyone else knew or could figure out. But *he* seemed to know why he hit her. There were intervals as long as two hours between the slaps, but she was never sure how long they would last. She just had to sit next to him on the gallery, waiting for the next slap.

Meantime, in between the slaps, he picked his teeth as if nothing unusual was taking place. If she attempted to leave the gallery, he slapped her hard again, saying, "Where you going? Sit down!"

Sometimes the force of the blow, when it did come, was so strong that it knocked Sage off her seat on the bench. She would pick herself up from the floor of the gallery while he nonchalantly went back to picking his teeth.

Once Rommel went to Canada to visit his sister in Ontario. When he came back, he showed Sage a bull-pestle that he had bought on his travels. She was shocked to hear him say to her, "If you bother me, Ah going beat you senseless with this!"

It was only then that she started to plan her escape. It was as if the bull-pestle sank her to some animal place that made her wake up. She could take the slaps when they came, twice or so a month; but she could not take even one beating with a weapon.

She could not believe that he went to another country, walked into a leather-goods store, and bought the bull-pestle with his hard-earned money. That was too much somehow; too much purpose to his hitting her. Sage could not quite stomach that.

She tried to find out from Rommel how much he paid in Canadian dollars for the bull-pestle, but he would not tell her. She really wanted to know. Somehow it seemed important to her to figure out how many pounds of flour, sugar, or cornmeal from Rommel's shop went into the cost of the bull-pestle. She wanted to see just who Rommel really was, by knowing the amount of money that he had spent on an item with which he intended to inflict pain on her.

All those times when he hit her, she took the slaps that came to her at long intervals, in between picking his teeth. They came with no words and they came for no reason, but Sage knew that rum did not need a reason. It was only when he had had a certain amount of rum-soaking that Rommel hit her. Then if he did not have a reason lying in wait to account for the slaps, the rum would help him to make one up.

He did not bother trying to justify the slaps, the way he used to in the beginning. He could never really justify them, but because they were new with each other, he used to try. He would make excuses to her afterwards, saying that he didn't know why, but ever since he was a little boy he liked to hit people, and also lizards, and cats, and ants, and dogs.

He told her that he used to tie the feet of cats in four paper bags and then laugh and laugh as they tried to walk. He said that he used to make little fires to kill ants, and would sometimes drown them, just to watch them struggle to stay alive.

When he described how he used to throw stones at lizards, his face came alive with enjoyment at the memory of the sound of the thud on the lizards' thick skin. He laughed as he described how he would aim at them as if he were playing *cushew* with his friends. Then his laughter turned to annoyance, as he spoke of the day that a lizard turned to attack him. He was shocked that a little creature like a lizard thought that it could have a fight with him; all the same it startled him into leaving lizards alone. "Unlike lizards, dogs know who is master," he told Sage, launching into a description of a dog he used to have, but which had died suddenly one day.

He said that it was agreed between him and the dog that he would hit the dog every morning, every afternoon, and every evening. Sage shrank from the cruelty on his face and in his eyes as he said, "That dog used to come and stand up at the appointed hour, just as if it could tell the time, ready to take its blows, morning, noon, and evening."

Sage felt a rage rise up deep inside her. She told it to be quiet. It was the bull-pestle that woke up that rage, and gave it permission to be with her daily, strumming the music behind her whole life.

Sage never had a conversation with herself about leaving Rommel. She never discussed with herself whether it was a good idea or not. She just knew that she was leaving him. It was just a matter of time. "Reason I stay so long is because it was convenient for the moment," she told herself. He paid the rent and he bought the food.

It was not that Sage didn't want to work, but her right hip was hurting her again. In fact, it had been hurting her for the last two years. It put a stop to anything called work, even looking after children. She couldn't move up and down to find food, let alone cook and wash for the set of children that she had. Along with that, she had had a journey into rum living with Rommel. She was only recently able to give up both of them. That is why she farmed out her children to different people…for a combination of reasons; but mostly, it was about the rum and about Rommel.

She thought of leaving them with her sister Reevah; but at the time, Emmanuel was sick with cancer, so it made no kind of sense.

Now she was just waiting out the pain so she could leave Rommel and go and get her children. She knew the pain would go away; it always did. Last time it came for only a month or two; the time before that, it came for a year. She knew this pain well; it had been with her since she was fifteen years old.

The first time it came, she was walking home from school with her two sisters. She stooped to pick a yellow rose and a piece of fern from Mrs. Weisinger's garden and she felt her hip lock itself into a knot that she could not untie.

Days later, she still could not loosen it. She said nothing about the pain, because she did not want to have to explain that she had been stealing Mrs. Weisinger's rose and fern. Whenever she was in an adult's presence, she pretended to walk straight, gritting her teeth as the pain racked her body.

By her sixteenth birthday, she accepted the pain whenever it arrived, stoically kneeling in church, or during sports activities at school, or sitting in class, or even just walking. Her sisters and her friends soon thought of her as having a bad hip, because she did not hide it from them. They learned to slow down for her when she was having her sessions of pain.

It was not until she was walking down the aisle on her father's arm to get married to Junior Tobias, the young man she married soon after high school, that he said to her, "Why you limping? Your shoes too small?" Sage shook her head, tears burning behind her eyes from the pain. She was angry that the pain had chosen to come now, on her wedding day.

She never told her father the truth about her pain then, nor later at the reception when he asked her if she was all right. She nodded, not trusting herself to speak about the pain. Here it was, going into her marriage with her, and she wondered if it would never go away.

She never did get around to telling her husband the truth about her pain, because he did not stay with her for longer than it took for them to make one baby. They were like two children fighting over the smallest things, and eventually he ran away to St. Thomas to seek work.

Within a few short months, Sage received divorce papers in the mail and an agreement to support his child. She signed the papers and sent them back in the mail, but she never heard from him again. Some time later on, she heard that he had gone to live in New York.

It seemed to Sage that the church bells rang louder than usual tonight. They merged with the barking dogs, the swoosh-swoosh of the cars, to create a din that at once embraced her and seemed to be shouting at her. She suddenly thought of her children; it was as if the noise was trying to reach inside her head to make her focus on them.

It was in her thoughts all the time that her four children had four different fathers. Her marriage to Junior had been so brief that she had trouble remembering being with him, even though he had fathered her first child, named Joyling. Junior stayed permanently in her mind as "the man I married."

The second father she remembered well, because she hated him with such a passion, she could never forget him. She never agreed to be with him; he merely took his pleasure with her, against her will.

The other two fathers were the beginning of the blur in her mind, because she had started drinking by then. They were two men, that is all; two men with whom she hardly noticed that time passed. They ignored her and their children with her, beyond the handouts they reluctantly surrendered. She would accost them in the street with her swollen belly and shame them into giving her money.

When her two youngest daughters Ruth and Naomi were born, she made sure that she showed them to their fathers. She wanted them to see their offspring staring them in the face. These bold steps yielded few results. She soon tired of the humiliation of going like a beggar to these men. Eventually, she gave up and set about being the sole support of her children.

Sage was proud of the second child, because her father was a light-skinned man from a good family. Not that she profited from any of that, because he completely ignored her and his child. But Sage made sure that she told everybody his identity. She thought that he had some nerve denying that he was the child's father, after she allowed him to rape her, night after night.

He used to do his deed in the quiet light of the street-lamp while her first child slept right there on the same bed with her. He would get hot from drinking rum at the rum-shop at the corner. Then he would stumble into her little two-by-four house and climb on top of her.

He did not care whether he woke her child or not with the clumsiness of his alcohol-soaked body. How she loathed him then! How she hated the stench of his breath as he poured himself into her, night after night.

She endured it all, because his father employed her to clear *cassie* from his yard for a measly sixty dollars a month. So she said not a word, because that was her largest source of income.

Anyway, when all was said and done, she had a pretty child to show for it; and besides, he never came near her from the time she told him she was pregnant. One day, his father called her aside and told her that she ought not to be such a loose young woman. He told her that she had no business getting herself pregnant. Then he fired her, saying that she was "too big with child to do the yard-work."

She was so humiliated that she could not find her voice to tell old Mr. Dimitrius that she had little to do with getting herself pregnant. She wanted to scream at him that it was his son who did all that there was to be done to make her pregnant.

As she stumbled home, tired, hungry, and feeling the child heavy in her, she thought of all that she wanted to say to old Mr. Dimitrius. She told herself: "Now it is too late. And anyway, what would be the purpose of it?" She sighed. Then she focused on how she was going to find work to feed herself and Joyling and Rogain Dimitrius's child.

Once or twice a month while she was carrying his child, Sage ran into Rogain Dimitrius on the street. With elaborate flourish he would stop her and hand her some money. She knew that he did it to pretend to people that he was being kind and considerate. No one knew that she was carrying his child. People would likely think that he was just helping out one of his father's employees; a fired employee, to boot. She smiled now at the irony of the whole thing.

The child was born with a pretty bronze colour, like a shiny, new copper penny. Her hair was a darker shade of gold, mixed with the same bronze colour as her skin. It made people always ask: "Who is this one's father?" And Sage would smile proudly and say, "Rogain Dimitrius, from the Dimitrius family in town."

She knew that Rogain Dimitrius's mother and father had come to Antigua from Dominica in the early years. At that time, all of a sudden, Dominicans started to come and live in Antigua. Many of them had the same light skin as the Dimitrius family. For although not all Dominicans were that colour, the high-class ones were red like that.

Rogain-Dimitrius-Child was the lightest-skinned of her children; and she had good hair. The fathers of the other three children were black-skinned men with coarse hair. Ruth and Naomi were darker-skinned even than Sage, and neither they nor Joyling had hair that slipped through her fingers when she was plaiting it. Their hair did not move sweetly into place, like the hair on the head of Rogain-Dimitrius-Child. It was as if the seeds of the four men pushed themselves right through her daughters' hair.

Sage thought that her daughters all looked a little like her; and they all had her same kind of body. When they were babies, she washed their feet and marvelled at how much their toes looked like her own toes. They had her broad shoulders; and their hands were shaped like hers, with smooth knuckles and long, tapering fingers. They were all tall like her too; although life had caused her to hunch her shoulders, so that she could not even be sure just how tall she really was.

Sage used to day-dream that she would one day send her daughters to Miss Simon for piano lessons. And that they would have the kind of running shoes that cost four hundred dollars a pair. For Sunday school, she would buy them each a pair of black patent-leather shoes; they would wear them with dainty white nylon socks.

In the day-dream she would meet a man who would marry her, even though she had four children. He would be father to them so lovingly that she would relax for the first time in her life and just live life. They would live in the same way as the high class people: casually.

She would take her children for walks, instead of sending them to look for water, noisily clanking through the streets in the early hours of the morning. It would hurt her heart every morning to hear them going down the street. They sounded like an iron-band at Christmastime as they pulled their metal buckets on the noisy, hand-hewn cart.

She would have a maid to comb their hair, and to wash and iron their clothes, using running water from inside the yard. It would make Sage smile to think how she would have the maid cut the crust off the bread to make delicate sandwiches. She would have her fill of sandwiches with ham and mayonnaise and lettuce and cucumber; and some would be made with cheese of different colours.

Maybe she would even send her daughters to a hairdresser to straighten their hair. Even Rogain-Dimitrius-Child, although her hair hardly needed any straightening. Still, she would do it just for the specialness of it.

Then she met Rommel and all of those dreams faded into a fog of cotton-wool. She let go of the flights of fancy that used to keep her going. Now they made her head hurt. It was too hard to recall how it was to be so free as to dream.

At first, she did not take any notice of Rommel. He bothered her every day when she went to buy food in Mrs. Martin's shop. He worked in the shop, weighing out flour and chopping up *ling* fish and mackerel for the customers.

She asked him for a pound of *ling* fish, and noticed that he put a whole extra big piece on top of the pound before wrapping it for her. Her eyes met his; guilt seeped through her stomach and her heart at his invitation to be complicit in the theft from which she would benefit.

Sage did not like what he had done. She appreciated the extra *ling* fish, but she was not a thief. Besides, she did not want to be beholden to this man with the hard line in his jaw, a wicked mouth, and brazen eyes.

Not wanting to make a scene in the shop, she said nothing and took the *ling* fish. Each time she cooked a piece of it, the memory of that man in the shop with the wicked mouth came back to haunt her. It made her feel very uneasy, and it spoiled her taste for *ling* fish.

In the end, she made fish-cakes with the rest of it; they were easier to get down without the image of that man's wicked mouth coming back to haunt her.

The next time she went to the shop, she wanted a pickled mackerel, but when she saw Rommel at the pickle-barrel, she changed her mind and asked for a tin of corned beef instead. She felt really angry that she changed her meal because of him. She did not know his name then and thought of him as "the man with the wicked mouth."

After a while, Sage stopped going to the shop altogether and sent her two older daughters with a list. One day, they came home and said that the man in the shop whose name was Rommel said to tell her "hello."

This made Sage feel angry, because she knew that he had probably been sending her stolen pieces of *ling* fish, or mackerel or pig-tail. She realised that there was nothing for it but to confront him and make him stop.

Armed with this determination, she set out for the shop one Saturday. As soon as she entered the doorway, she saw Rommel and he saw her. She walked right over to the pickle-barrel and said, "I want one mackerel please; and don't cut it up." Then she asked for a pound of *ling* fish, adding: "And make it only one pound please; no more, no less!"

Next she said, "And give me one pig-tail in one piece; just mark it with the knife in four places for me please." Rommel looked at her with an amused smile on his face; then he spoke to her for the first time, dropping his voice to a barely audible whisper. "And how you going to feed those four daughters you have with no one helping you?"

Sage felt humiliated and angry and yet kind of pleased, at the same time. She thought that he was forward to be minding her business, but she was flattered that he took the time to find out about her. She also liked it that he wanted to help her. She did not answer him; she just took her purchases and swept to the cashier, her head held high. She didn't want him thinking that he could buy her favours.

All in all, she did not like being beholden to any man; but he offered to help her, openly and honestly. That felt different, although she still didn't feel good about him stealing, even if it was from his family.

After that, she let him give her the extra goods, telling herself that he wasn't stealing, as he was the shopkeeper's nephew. She justified it all by saying to herself that it belonged to him anyway. Deep down, she knew that he was stealing. In a way, she was relieved when it came to a halt. It had to stop some time, she always knew, but the turn of events surprised her. One day, Mrs. Martin the shopkeeper died, and left the shop and her house to Rommel, as he was her only living relative.

Before long, Rommel started to deliver all of Sage's groceries to her every Saturday, and he would take no money for them. Soon he began staying on her step, talking to her, after he delivered the groceries. Sage knew that he would try to get close to her. She felt as if he was trying to buy her and she resented it. She wanted him to help her because he was good. Then she would likely approach him, and it would be out of love, or at least desire, and not out of obligation. She would have loved him completely if he had not shown that mercenary side so quickly.

That hard line she saw in Rommel's jaw when she first met him was now full on his face. It seemed to spread across his eyes and all, especially when he slapped her. Then the line jumped in rhythm with a muscle in his jaw; and his eyes would be cold-cold, jumping in that same rhythm. At those times, Sage felt raw, naked fear rising in her belly. She would think: "It as if say he don't even know me."

She left Rommel and set out to look for her children. The bull-pestle motivated her; but it was the well-being of her children that catapulted her into action, not fear of the bull-pestle.

It started with her wondering if somewhere one of her daughters was being degraded as she was; sunk so low that a man could leave a poor country like Antigua and go all the way to Ontario, Canada and come back with one thing for her: a weapon to beat her. It made her mind snap back into place so sharply, so suddenly, that she was sure she heard a "crack-crack" sound.

Sage never answered Rommel that day when he showed her the bull-pestle. She just made sure that she knew where it was at all times. She knew that if he hit her with it, she would kill him for sure. She laughed crazily inside when she thought of how much power she had over Rommel's life. She cooked his food, washed his clothes, and stayed wide awake while he lay snoring next to her.

She thought of how she could pour quicksilver in his ear, easy-easy. She murmured fiercely under her breath: "Rommel feel he own me, but me-Sage...I am my own owner." She didn't even feel that she owned her children, having given them away...farmed them out like orphans to work in people's kitchens.

She shook her head, muttering to herself, "The way I see it, no matter how those three decent women say that they going look after my girl-children like if they was their own, they are my children and nobody care for your children as well as you. Some little something will always be missing. Oh yes, without a doubt, some little something will always be missing."

Just thinking about her children made her heart hurt. She remembered how when she gave them away, her heart was full of Rommel and the yearning for alcohol. She needed alcohol drunk with Rommel; dancing to calypso with Rommel; singing calypso with him; making love with him.

The time when he was helpful just as a benefactor was long past; it was overshadowed by her desire for him. She found herself longing to feel his chest pressed against her breasts as his body rose to hover above her. He would move way up, deep and so sweet inside her; and Sage would wait in ecstasy for the passion to explode between them. She would feel his tenderness toward her then; and she grew devoted to him completely, but not wisely.

She could not recall just when it was that the tenderness stopped. It just kind of crept into their conversation, their interaction, their love-making. The love-making was the last place that Rommel inflicted pain on her; long after he began to call her names and to assault her body with his fists.

It was soon after those early days of sweetness between them that she cried one night, feeling him hurting her inside. It was as strong a fire as the pain in her hip. After a time, her body seemed to betray her, getting excited by his touch even when she started to hate him deeply.

After the slaps, after the pain, would come the make-up. Sage knew the rhythm well now, and she hated him for so successfully engaging her in this violent, sick way of doing life. She became resigned to it; but there was a part of her that did not want this to be the way she lived forever.

And so she waited and watched, knowing that the time for her escape would present itself. She did nothing without this stealth; even her breathing was regulated by her surroundings. When Rommel slept, she breathed deeply, feeling safe to let her energy recharge itself freely, without interference from him. When he was awake, she breathed in a shallow place at the top of her chest, hoarding her pure air in her diaphragm. She became so good at holding her breath that it hardly made her feel faint any more.

Sage remembered that a woman with whom she had left one of her daughters asked to keep the child. It was Rogain-Dimitrius-Child, the one in whom she took the most pride. She remembered shaking her head "No," not wanting to speak the anger in her chest. She could taste on her tongue how much she needed a drink. At that time, she was hiding the drinking from herself, let alone anyone else. She thought now of how shameful it was that the woman was trying to buy her daughter from her; her prettiest daughter to boot!

It was rage that made her raise her head so that her eyes were level with the woman's chin. It was a strong chin, she remembered. She wanted the money the woman offered her; but she had her pride; and she wanted her child back when she was ready.

She wanted to make things secure with Rommel. She just could not manage children and Rommel and the drinking. It was too much; but she wasn't giving away or selling her children. She was going to come back for them. Later, much later, after she went deep into the places that drinking rum with Rommel could take her.

After the announcement of the bull-pestle, Sage saw her life straight in front of her. As soon as the pain left, she would leave. She would go and see if her daughters were sinking as low as she had sunk; and she would make sure that they did not sink any lower.

She left the rum altogether; just like that, she stopped drinking. She always knew that she could stop drinking whenever she wanted to; but it seemed like she never had a reason that was strong enough to win over her blood's need for the alcohol. Now, her children were the reason; the bull-pestle reminded her of what she had never really forgotten.

Some days her hip hurt her so much that she thought she wanted to cry out; but she would grit her teeth and bear it. She had to wait and watch for her chance to leave. She had to be prepared; there was no use in letting the pain stop her.

Her mind was full of the steps after the leaving: the children, how to get them back from the three women. It was not so easy. She would have to go to three houses scattered all over the island.

She had made sure not to ask any of the women in the area where she lived to look after her children. She did not want any of those people in her business. They had already cried shame on her for being with Rommel in the rum shop every night while her four children were at home sleeping.

They were very moralizing, and she always felt that they looked down on her. The nearest woman was in Mongotung, and to Sage's mind, even that was too near to where she lived. It was just that Mrs. Morissey was such a nice lady that she knew it was the right place for the two youngest children.

People in her area had a lot to say about Sage farming out her children to three different homes. They had a lot to say too about how she lived with Rommel, drinking rum, and singing calypso, and taking slaps. They didn't count the alcohol as having any power over her; they simply declared her worthless to leave her children and go and live with a man and drink rum.

They had no way of knowing how drinking with Rommel took away the big knot in Sage's belly; just behind her navel. They had no way of knowing that if she did not go with Rommel, she would disappear. She would become smaller and smaller, and just slip entirely into nothingness. And that would have been worse, worse even than dying; at least dying would mean that there was a body the children could bury, and mourn, and grieve over.

She knew that she made a mistake by going with Rommel, but at the time, it felt right—correct—like some kind of equation in a schoolbook. She could see from early on in the course of things between them, however, that he and her children did not have a good spirit-taking.

The children's spirits just did not *take* Rommel...none of them. Although Rommel tried to be nice with them, he wasn't *really* nice with them. She knew from watching them interact, the first time they were all together, and so she kept them apart after that.

Soon, her craving for Rommel was as strong as the craving for the alcohol. She could not take one without the other, although she tolerated alcohol without Rommel better than she tolerated Rommel without alcohol. It was pure and simple to Sage: something inside of her just said that she was tired of minding the children and needed those two things more and more.

Everybody thought that she didn't love her children; but she knew that it was love for them that made her send them away from her in this different time. The pain was with her then too, she remembered. It was a terrible memory, the picture of her, a mother, limping away from her screaming, crying, and whimpering children.

Only Rogain-Dimitrius-Child didn't scream; she just watched Sage as if she was looking at a crazy woman. She watched her without blinking, until she limped around the corner. It was only then that Rogain-Dimitrius-Child turned to face her new keepers: an elderly woman with a daughter and the daughter's husband. The daughter had a young baby that she was to help look after.

The child had heard the older lady ask Sage to keep her for good and felt her mother's response in the way her hand tightened over hers. She peered at Sage's face and could tell from the way she hung her head and tightened her lips that she did not like the idea of the lady keeping her.

The thing was: Rogain-Dimitrius-Child liked the idea very much. Now, when Sage turned the corner, leaving her with these total strangers and a baby to mind, she decided that she was never going back to live with her mother. She did not hate her, she just pitied her. She wanted a better life for herself than the one her mother was creating.

She loved her mother, but she wanted to live better than worrying about her drinking all the time. She knew that Sage thought that she hid her drinking from her children; but they all knew about it, even the last child, who was only five years old.

She smiled at the lady whose hand held hers warmly and comfortingly. She knew that she had found the heaven her Sunday-school classes glowingly described. She decided then and there that she was never going to give it up for the hell of life with Sage.

The lady smiled back at her and asked, "So what is your name? Your mother only referred to you as Rogain-Dimitrius-Child. What is your real name?"

She made a decision then and there that that was to be her name. She answered: "Rogain-Dimitrius-Child."

She decided that if everybody was going to need to be told whose child she was, the way her mother was always being asked, then she might as well say it at the beginning. That way, people could say: "I could see it in her hair," or "Rogain Dimitrius can't say you give him a jacket!" or "Oh yes, I can tell from the hair and the red skin."

There was always some comment like that about her skin colour, or her hair, or her nose, or something that was like her father's family. She had twice seen some of her father's family in town and rather admired their looks. They had lighter skin than hers, but their hair was the same copper colour as the hair on her head.

Once she saw a boy in the family who looked so much like her that she was startled. When their eyes met, he looked at her with the same surprise she felt. Then he put a hand up to his face and she laughed and brought her hand up to *her* face. She laughed again as he checked to see if she were his mirror image. She shook her head in a circular motion, making her copper-coloured plaits swing wildly around her head. He laughed and swung his head in the same way. His hair was cut low and a riot of copper-coloured curls covered his head.

She noticed that his eyes were light brown and were framed by thick, curling lashes, like the ones she saw framing her own light-brown eyes when she looked in a mirror. His mouth, big and shaped just like hers, opened to reveal the same white-white big teeth that earned her the nickname "Box-a-Chiclets." At last she had seen someone who looked just like her. For the first time in her life, she felt affirmed in her existence in the world. Their identical large lips smiled at each other until the woman who was with him (probably a maid, she decided, given her dark skin colour) hurried him into a store. Seeing this boy changed how she saw herself forever. No longer did she feel like she did not belong anywhere. She knew that she belonged somewhere, with one person at least who looked just like her.

After that day, she dreamed of meeting him again, just to look at this replica of herself. She wished that she could touch his hair to see if it felt like hers. She remembered this now with a confused pull in her heart. She wanted so badly to feel that she belonged somewhere. It was so hard being the only one in her family who looked so different. The only one whose hair slipped through her mother's fingers, as she so often heard her say.

"Rogain-Dimitrius-Child is my name," she repeated proudly. The elderly woman tried not to laugh. "All of it?" she asked. As the child nodded, she queried: "Should I call you the whole thing?" She tried again to repress her laughter as the child nodded, saying, "Yes, that is my name: Rogain-Dimitrius-Child."

The woman was glad that she had a friend who would register Rogain-Dimitrius-Child at school without a birth certificate. She was given no documents by Sage and had not thought to ask for any until now that the child was declaring this impossible name. She wanted to spare this poor child any further trauma. She figured that being born to such a mother was enough of a cross to bear. She wished that she could keep the child, but she realized that Sage was determined to take her back.

She explained gently to the serious-faced little girl that she could call herself anything she wished to, but the school would only register her real name. She was surprised when the child looked crestfallen and hung her head; she seemed to be considering the situation for a moment. Her next words showed her decision to capitulate: "My name is Seleena Dimitrius," she said. Then she added: "Ma'am," in the way she had been taught to speak to her elders.

Rogain-Dimitrius-Child immediately caused a stir in the private high school for girls. Her place in society was established by the fact that she wore the light-blue school uniform, instead of the navy-blue tunic designed for the dark-skinned girls. The school had two colours and styles of uniforms. The white girls and the light-skinned girls wore the light-blue version and the Black girls wore the navy-blue version. This was not a choice they made. When parents registered their children, they were handed a sheet of paper that contained the version of uniform their daughters were expected to wear.

Rogain-Dimitrius-Child's status was also defined by the fact that she was driven to school and picked up from the school by her guardian. In addition, her guardian was a light-skinned, well respected, high-class lady.

Rogain-Dimitrius-Child's "class," as everyone called it, was also assumed by the way her hair was plaited in two, or in one. This was unlike the hairstyle of the darker-skinned girls, who had small plaits all over their heads, or rows of "Congo."

Lastly and quite importantly, her colour and the softness of her hair gained her entry to a rung on the social ladder that she never knew before. However, her colour and her hair did not count as much as they would normally have counted, because everyone knew that she was Rogain Dimitrius's *outside* child. Besides, his *real* children (the *inside* children whom he had sired with his wife) also went to the same school.

Word spread around the school that the Dimitrius girls had an illegitimate sister who wore the light-blue uniform usually reserved for white girls and high-class, light-skinned girls. Not the least astounding piece of news was that she called herself by a sentence: "Rogain-Dimitrius-Child," even though she was registered under the name Seleena Dimitrius.

The whole school heard the stories about how some girls took turns asking Seleena her name, just to hear her say "Rogain-Dimitrius-Child." Then everyone laughed.

The two Dimitrius girls were mortified to encounter in the flesh the result of one of their father's nightly escapades. After the first two weeks of the school term, they went home to their mother in tears; and finally, Mrs. Dimitrius confronted her husband about the child.

She was not jealous or angry, but simply wanted to know the truth about her. Given the fact that the child was a whole two years older than her first daughter, she knew that she was born before Rogain Dimitrius became her husband. Her oldest daughter came exactly ten months after her marriage.

She did not believe her husband for a moment when he said that he had been seduced by Seleena's mother. He first denied knowing of the child's existence, finally pronouncing her "the product of a fuck." He said that he had never even seen the child, not since she was a small toddler. "She was still a baby then, really," he said, "maybe all of three years old."

Mrs. Dimitrius never knew of her husband needing to be seduced. On the contrary, when he told her that the mother was an agricultural worker on his father's land, she suspected that he had either raped her or exerted pressure on her to have sex with him.

She knew that he and his brothers routinely raped their father's female agricultural workers, or at least pressed them into sexual unions. She therefore always insisted, despite his protest, that he use condoms whenever she allowed him to have sex with her; something she still suffered, but which she planned not to allow for too much longer. She felt sure that she took her life in her hands every time she allowed him to touch her, because she did not trust her husband to use caution in his liaisons with women. She was sure that he was full of life-threatening organisms.

He was a promiscuous man who was given to bouts of rum-drinking; in her view, this was a deadly combination. She sometimes felt as if she were caught in a vice that began the day she left Dominica and set foot in Antigua.

Only one member of her family met her husband-to-be before she married him; and that was her grandfather. He and old Mr. Dimitrius had been friends in Dominica. One year he came to Antigua to watch cricket and met Rogain Dimitrius. From the time he returned, her grandfather talked of nothing but the possibility of a marriage between the two families. She had not minded the idea. Dominica held no promise for her: neither in a career, nor in a mate. She had outgrown most of the young men of her childhood and the photograph they showed her of a handsome man with a devilish smile fed her romantic soul.

Her mother and father had advised her to accept Mr. Dimitrius's offer of his son Rogain's hand in marriage. They showed her photographs of a house with a lovely garden, two maids (one to wash and one to cook), a gardener, a car, and a driver. She would also have a fabric store and would get to keep the profits.

Seeing Rogain Dimitrius confirmed the image in the photograph. His handsome face was even more appealing in person. His rough way of speaking bothered her; but she thought that after they were married, she would help him to become more cultured. She planned imaginary trips to Dominica to stay with her family. That would let Rogain Dimitrius develop a close relationship with her brothers, who were refined gentlemen. She was sure that some of their good manners would rub off on this rough and tough husband of hers.

However, she bargained without the fiercely dominating will of Rogain Dimitrius. He had no intention of changing anything in his life; except perhaps the availability of her warm body in his bed whenever he wanted it there. This was novel to him, this feeding of his sexual appetite at will. It meant that he no longer needed to go through the effort of pretending to court some unwilling, nubile, middle-class young woman in town. That kind of courtship cost him a pretty penny, not to mention the fact that he had to pretend a civility and gentlemanly behaviour he did not feel.

It was only the workers on his father's estate whom he got to lay a hand on at will and without any finesse. Marriage simply meant for him that he had a woman at his beck and call.

Mrs. Dimitrius did not get the life she was promised. To begin with, the profits from the store were used to cover household expenses. Secondly, Rogain Dimitrius drank a lot of the money he earned from his father's business.

So soon after she arrived in Antigua, Mrs. Dimitrius started to pay their household expenses. This included the salaries of the two maids, the gardener, and the driver. Eventually, she gave up the driver and one of the maids and only used a gardener occasionally. She enjoyed working in the garden; she found it therapeutic as a way of coping with living with Rogain Dimitrius.

Mrs. Dimitrius felt compassion for this little girl, desperately reaching for an identification with a father who denied any knowledge of her. She went to see her guardian and asked to meet the child. She then discussed with her husband the possibility of asking the girl's mother for custody of his illegitimate daughter. He reluctantly agreed, and thus began a chain of events that altered the life of Rogain-Dimitrius-Child forever.

Chapter Four

Sage began her journey to take back her children with her oldest daughter, Joyling. She had left her with a family of shopkeepers in All Saints. She thought at the time that at least this child would have enough food to eat, seeing that they sold all kinds of food.

Nothing could have been further from the reality, and nothing could have prepared Sage for the change in Joyling. When she saw her child, she let out a sharp cry. In the three months that she had been away from her, Joyling had become nothing but skin and bones. Her eyes were sunken in her face and her cheekbones protruding below them, made her look even more like a skeleton.

The bones of her elbows stuck out sharply in her thin arms, which hung almost below her knees. "And her legs!" Sage's eyes caught sight of them, sticking out below her skirt. "Oh, her legs are so spindly!" She drew her breath in sharply at the sight of them. Her little girl resembled a poster child for starving children in other parts of the world...but not in Antigua!

As she looked at Joyling, Sage felt the tears rise in her throat; but she held them back. She did not speak to the people who almost starved her daughter to death. She took the child's battered suitcase, which they handed to her, and gripping Joyling's small hand in hers, she stumbled from the shop. She was startled at the thinness of her child's hand. The bones felt as if they were soft. She held it gently after that.

By the time she turned the corner, Sage found the tears hot on her face. She said nothing to Joyling, but she stopped walking and turned now to look at her. She tried to speak; she wanted to say something, anything. All she managed to say was: "I am sorry."

Joyling stood at her mother's side crying softly. Sage stood still in the street and put her arms around her child as together they cried. She knew that people stared at them, but she did not care. This was the first time she had felt her tears since she met Rommel and started drinking heavily.

She dried their eyes, and they walked to the corner to catch the bus back to town. Sage breathed deeply as they stood in the hot sun. She thought of how glad she was that she finally managed to leave Rommel to go and get her children. She smiled at Joyling and hugged her close.

Sage had woken up that afternoon with a fire behind her eyes. She always slept during the afternoon, waking in time to cook Rommel's dinner before he came home from the shop. The night before, she had kept watch as usual, unable to sleep while Rommel was in the house.

She got up carefully from the bed, anticipating the pain. Whenever it was with her for a long time, she would wake with the memory of it, making her move cautiously. But now, as she swung her feet over the edge of the bed and touched them gingerly to the ground, she discovered that the pain was gone.

The fire behind her eyes now made sense. This was the day! The pain was gone, and Rommel would not be home for four hours! She had four whole hours to get the hell away from him and go for her children.

She would move fast to make sure that she did everything right and still have time to do a check before she left the house. First, pack the bull-pestle. She had not included that in her careful planning, but it came to her now in a flash: "Take the bull-pestle with you and burn it!"

She obeyed the command her mind gave her and put the bull-pestle in the bottom of her suitcase. Next, she took the money she had been hoarding in a hiding place ever since Rommel came back from Ontario, Canada with the bull-pestle.

It took only a few minutes to pack her clothes; she did not have many. In fact, she had fewer clothes than when she first moved in with Rommel, because the generosity he showed when he courted her had soon given way to a meanness that left her impoverished. He supplied sufficient food for them to eat, and enough rum for them to drink; and that was all.

He gave her only a little money for those items that his shop could not provide: like cooking gas, and ground provisions, and vegetables. Everything else came from the shop. Sage scrimped and saved to be able to put away a little money each week without arousing Rommel's suspicions.

She thanked her dead mother in her heart for teaching her as a child how to make nutritious, inexpensive meals. She also had a lot of help from Reevah, who supplied her with vegetables that she and Emmanuel grew. She wore many of her sister's skirts and blouses, knowing that Reevah pretended that they were cast-offs. She knew that Sage was reluctant to accept charity, so she pretended that they were too small for her and that she would have to throw them away if her sister did not take them.

As Sage walked away from the house, she did not look back. She did not want to carry any last memory with her of the gallery on which she sat to receive Rommel's slaps. She did not look around the street either, as she wanted no keepsake of the place of her captivity.

It was not that Rommel had held her captive, but she had felt like a captive. Her prisoners were alcohol and the earlier excitement of being with him; dancing to calypso and drinking rum with him; loving with him and living with him. The excitement and enjoyment of love-making was the first to go; and then the bull-pestle woke her from her alcoholic stupor.

Soon, she could derive little pleasure from the sound of calypso, let alone dancing to it. As she came to reject the hold that Rommel and alcohol had over her, all of the areas in which she had taken pleasure became repulsive to her. She would receive his body on hers when he inflicted it, grateful that he was too drunk to notice that her responses lacked the fervour of her earlier passion.

It was bush-tea and fish-broth that helped her get rid of her need for alcohol. There were days when Rommel drank, and the smell drove her crazy; but all she had to do to hold on to her resolve was to go and look at the bull-pestle.

The hardest time for her was during the day when she was alone and the liquor was right there in the house. She would fight hard to overcome the way her dry mouth ached from the desperate longing for even a drop of rum on her tongue. Whenever she felt weak, it was the thought of her children that kept her going. She found that if she kept her mind focused on them, she would feel stronger. Even the pain in her hip would recede to a manageable place if she kept her mind on her children.

Ruth and Naomi were well looked after and they were happy to see Sage. She decided that she would leave her three children with Reevah and Sayshelle, and go alone to get Rogain-Dimitrius-Child. Reevah had agreed that they could all stay with her until she found a job and could afford to rent a house.

She was confident that the woman with whom she had left Rogain-Dimitrius-Child had taken good care of her. Sage knew her to be a good person and she remembered that the woman had even wanted to keep the child permanently.

There was a surprise in store for her when she arrived at Reevah's house. A letter had been hand-delivered from a lawyer's office. Reevah was waiting anxiously for her to return home and read it.

Sage's hands shook with fear as she opened the letter and read it out loud. It told her that her daughter, Seleena, had been removed to the house of her father Rogain Dimitrius. It also stated that Rogain Dimitrius had made a petition to the courts to receive permanent custody of the child.

Sage sat in the nearest chair. She felt dazed, numb almost. It did her heart good to look at her three daughters. She was grateful that she had not had to fight to get them back. The two younger ones, too young to understand what they had heard, talked to her constantly; it was as if they had never been separated from her. Joyling, however, remained quiet. Like Sage and Reevah, she seemed dazed and unbelieving.

Sage wept inside her heart as she looked at Joyling. The way she looked made her even more determined to have all of her children together with her again. This time, she would be their mother in the right way. She had gone deep to the bottom of the world and she had come back up. She knew that she had no job; but that was nothing compared to how strong her mind was and how free she felt. She was not only free from alcohol, she was free from ever allowing any man to take advantage of her. She knew that she would find the right work situation so that she could feed, clothe, and house her children. All of her children. She was not giving up Seleena.

It was as if some big tent of peace had come and set itself up over her life and nothing would ever be the same. She would never look back; she would remember what was behind her without turning to see what it looked like.

That same kind of determination propelled her forward; it helped her not to look back at the house where she had suffered and the neighbourhood in which she had done penance. She felt like Lot's wife in the Bible, needing to keep her eyes fixed on the future. She felt that if she looked back, her heart would turn to stone.

Chapter Five

Joyling could not speak very much. She only had feelings and she had no words to speak them with; no voice to say them with; no way to shape them and give them form. She had given up hope of ever seeing her mother again. In fact, to her mind, hunger for her mother and her sisters was a bigger hunger than her yearning for food.

As she sipped juice and water and nibbled at the meal her Aunt Reevah forced on her, she thought of how full of love she felt. The love of her mother and her sisters was filling her up in a way that her Aunt Reevah's food could not.

She was happy just to sit and listen to Ruth and Naomi talking. She missed Seleena most of all, because they were the closest in age. They were the only two children for their Mama for a long time, until the last two girls came. Her Mama took care of the younger girls, leaving her and Seleena to look after each other. Joyling loved Seleena as if she was her own baby.

She did not quite understand what had happened to Seleena. She wished they could all go with her Mama Sage to pick Seleena up, the way they had all stayed together until now. She didn't like the idea of her Mama leaving her again. She was afraid that she would not see her for another long-long time.

When she looked into Sage's eyes, Joyling could see that she understood her silence. Her Mama held her face in her hands and kissed her, saying, "Ah going to get your sister Seleena."

It was the first time that Joyling could remember hearing her Mama call Seleena anything other than "Rogain-Dimitrius-Child." She could tell that it meant something from the way her Mama said "your sister Seleena." Her voice sounded hard and strong, with a fire burning around the words. Her jaw was set and she had the air about her as if she was preparing for a battle.

A fear crept into Joyling's heart: a fear that Seleena might not come back to them. She started praying to herself from that moment, deciding that she would never stop praying to have Seleena back with them, living with them, completing their family. And she prayed that at least her Mama would come back.

Sage never made any plan about when she was going to burn the bull-pestle she took from Rommel's house. Half a mind told her to just keep it to remind her of what she had come through. She kept it in the bottom of her suitcase at her sister Reevah's house; and every time she felt weak, she only had to remember that she had it.

She was pleased with herself for taking the bull-pestle away from Rommel's house; that felt really good. She had a mind to take it and beat Rogain Dimitrius with it to get back her child. She laughed crazily at the fleeting thought; she knew that she could do no such thing, because that would give him more evidence that she was an unfit mother. And besides, she was half his size.

Imagine that: "unfit mother!" She never ever thought that she could be called such a thing in her life; and yet, deep down inside her, she knew that she deserved it. For now that the rum had left her system, she fully realized that it was a great wrong to leave her children. What mother in her right mind left her children for rum? What sane mother gave her children out in servitude to total strangers? She could see that in others' eyes, she looked like an "unfit mother."

She had not been in her right mind. That is how crazy and sick for rum and Rommel she was; so crazy and so sick that she could not keep her children with her. When she made that decision, her mixed-up sick heart held only concern and caring for them.

Now that she was at risk of losing one of her children, and seeing how Joyling had almost starved to death, Sage wondered for a moment if life with Rommel would have been worse for them than these things. It was hard to judge it; and besides, she reminded herself, "How could I have known beforehand how things would go?" She sighed, her heart and her head full-full of grief and worry.

She walked to Rogain Dimitrius's house with her knees shaking, a growling in her belly, and a hollow feeling inside that nothing eased. In the end, she kept on praying "Give me back my daughter, God."

It was not from hunger that her belly growled, her head reeled, and her eyes misted over. She was just so full up of emotions, all struggling with each other, that she felt off centre. She was full of anger and hatred; and her mouth salivated with the desire to hit Rogain Dimitrius with Rommel's bull-pestle.

At the same time, she was also full of love for her child Seleena whom she so longed to see. This was her favourite child; her golden princess child. This child was the hardest child that she had made. Her love for

Seleena was like a testament of her being so much more powerful and strong than Rogain Dimitrius and all like him. He degraded her to make this baby, holding money as the key to her prison.

And the baby came and saved her from him…a golden baby with pretty skin and pretty hair; much prettier, she was sure, than any of the other children in the whole Dimitrius family. Out of the dregs of her life came this golden child to put a stop to her torture. She felt that she had reason to love this child more than any other. For he stopped touching her after she became pregnant with Seleena.

Sage hugged herself tight; her arms ached now from wanting to feel her child in them. Her mind beat a rhythm: "Soon, soon, Seleena; soon, you will be in my arms, child."

The gate at the front of the house presented itself before she was really ready for it. She stood fixing her clothes, wiping her eyes and smoothing down her hair. She held on to the gate with one hand, leaning on it for support. The pain in her hip was coming back and she knew that she was racing against time to get her child before it hit her really hard. She knew the pain so well, she could tell how many days and sometimes even how many hours she had left before it would strike her again.

A voice called out to her from the yard: "Who's there? Do you want someone?" The owner of the voice revealed herself to Sage from behind a rose-bush: a tall, light-skinned woman with perfect features, dressed in perfect clothes. She wore an apron that was so white, Sage wondered if she wore it for decoration, as a part of her outfit. Her ears carried the gold of Dominica earrings, and she sported a thick gold chain around her neck. Gold bracelets adorned her wrists and when she moved her arms, they jangled loudly, making a sound that grated on Sage's nerves.

Sage raised her chin a little higher. She was not going to come with humility for what was rightfully hers. She held her body upright and said in as firm a voice as she could muster to the woman she assumed to be Mrs. Dimitrius: "Good afternoon. I am Sage, Seleena's mother."

It seemed to Sage that the woman's face became flushed under her freckles. Her light skin was full of freckles from being in too much sun. She put down her garden shears, took off her garden gloves, and opened the gate.

The woman was embarrassed and more than a little flustered. She held the gate open for Sage to enter the front garden and immediately, a large dog bounded from out of nowhere and knocked Sage off her feet. Its paws soiled the front of the white blouse and navy-blue skirt that she had borrowed from Reevah.

Mrs. Dimitrius was very upset at what the dog did and offered to lend Sage a house-coat while she took the stains out of her clothes. Sage felt completely derailed as she sat in her underwear and half-slip in the kitchen, wrapped in the expensive fabric of Mrs. Dimitrius's silk house-coat. The fabric felt foreign against her skin.

She hoped that she looked calm sipping lemonade while Mrs. Dimitrius worked on the stains in her clothes. She noticed that the robe carried the same strong scent of the perfume that she smelled hovering around Mrs. Dimitrius. As she moved her arms in the large sleeves of the robe, she got a whiff of a man's cologne. This added to her feeling of being an invader, intruding in this woman's home, her life, and even her house-coat.

She shivered. She tried to concentrate on what the other woman was saying. She was explaining that because they had not known that she was coming, Seleena and her two daughters were visiting their cousins, a few streets away.

Mrs. Dimitrius left the room to make a phone call to ask them to come home, and Sage took in the opulence of her surroundings. She could not help but compare the warm comfort of this large kitchen to the little two-by-four house she had lived in when Rogain Dimitrius used to rape her nightly.

She hoped that Seleena would not arrive before she was once again dressed in her clothes. She wanted to reclaim the look of respectability that she had accomplished when she first arrived. That was not to be; for it seemed like only seconds after the phone call when the three children came running into the house.

The two Dimitrius girls came to her and shook her hand politely when their mother introduced them. Seleena stood a few feet away from Sage, staring at her.

Sage said: "I come to get you Seleena." She held out her arms but Seleena did not walk into them. Sage was shocked; for she realized then that she expected Seleena to *run* into her arms! Finally, with coaxing from Mrs. Dimitrius ("Go and say hello to your mother Seleena!"), she walked slowly into Sage's arms. Sage felt her heart sink at the coolness of her daughter's reception. She was also grieved to notice that even though she held Seleena close and kissed her, the child held her body stiff and unresponsive, unyielding to her embrace.

She wept inside, feeling that she had already lost her daughter and the court battle had not even started. She expected resistance, but not from Seleena. She asked Mrs. Dimitrius for her clothes, feeling that she at least wanted to look respectable in her daughter's eyes.

As she got dressed in the bathroom, she thought of the fact that the lawyer had advised her that she was only allowed to visit her daughter with another adult whom either Rogain Dimitrius or his wife chose. She planned to ask them to just let her have her daughter back. She returned to the living room and said as much to Mrs. Dimitrius, feeling her eyes filling up with tears.

After she spoke, she could see on Mrs. Dimitrius's face that if it were up to her, it would happen that way; but it was Seleena who objected. She said, "No! I don't want to live with you again. I want to live here with my sisters and my father and my stepmother."

Sage was so shocked that for a few minutes she could not speak. Then she tried to embrace her daughter, but again Seleena resisted her, holding her body stiff in her mother's arms. Still, Sage held her and kissed her, because she could see in her child's eyes the hurt that she had caused her and the need she had of her.

This child was not starving for food the way Joyling was; she was starving for love; not just any love, but her mother's love, Sage's own love. The starvation gave her eyes a hungry look, different from the kind of hunger that she saw in Joyling's eyes. Joyling had managed to survive that hunger for Sage's love, but Seleena had not.

Sage was frightened for Seleena. Before she came to the Dimitrius house, she was frightened for herself, afraid that she would not get her daughter back. But now, she was frightened for her daughter; because if what she said with her lips helped her father to keep her, she would starve to death for lack of her love.

She could see it in her eyes, sure as sure could be. She tried to think, to figure out what to do to help Seleena make the right decision for her life. She asked her to come with her again, telling her about how much her sisters missed her and wanted them all back together. Then she said it: "I am not drinking rum any more, child. I move out of Rommel house; I stop all of that kind of life now. I am looking for a job to support our family."

Sage saw Seleena waver in the face of her humility and then at that very moment Rogain Dimitrius burst into the room. His rage showed that he knew that Sage was there and she realized that his wife had quietly left the room. Obviously Mrs. Dimitrius had heard Rogain Dimitrius arrive and went to apprise him of the situation. She likely hoped to avert his rage, but that was not to be.

Sage was too focused on Seleena to notice that it was only the two Dimitrius girls who were left sitting in the room. Just as their father entered, Sage looked at them for the first time, noticing, even in the midst of her anxiety, how much they resembled Seleena.

Rogain Dimitrius was a tall-tall man with red-red skin and a bellowing voice. His face, permanently mottled from alcohol, grew beet-red as he shouted at Sage to get out of his house, calling her a drunken slut and a whore. She was sorry afterwards that she said it in front of her daughter, but she reminded him that she never whored with anyone, not even him, seeing that he never paid her when he raped her, night after night.

At that, Mrs. Dimitrius, who was quiet during her husband's tirade, drew in her breath and said, "I thought you said that she seduced you?" Sage laughed, saying in a voice that sounded shrill, even to her ears: "Seduce him? Why me would seduce him? Me find him disgusting, always drunk, pushing aside my other child I had at the time, to climb into my bed and rape me. I keep quiet about it, because I didn't want to lose the little job I had with his father."

Mrs. Dimitrius turned then to Seleena and asked, "What do you want to do, child?" Seleena did not hesitate. "I want to stay here," she answered.

Sage did not know what happened inside her in that exact moment—that precise second—but she gave Seleena away suddenly, in her heart. She lost the strength of her resolve at the flatness in her daughter's voice and the coolness she saw her bring into her eyes. She felt that she had already lost her and the court case would be a complete waste of time. Right at that moment of discovery, the pain came back fully in her hip.

She turned on her heel and walked out of the house, unashamed of limping for the first time in her life. She walked out of the yard, out of the gate, and onto the street.

As she walked down the street with her hip-and-drop limp, Sage ripped up the court papers that she had carried in her bag. She would not go to court and sign away her daughter. She would just let them have Seleena until she didn't want to be with them any more. For she was quite sure that day would come. And when that day came, she knew that she would receive Seleena again in her arms.

She heard it all in her daughter's voice, saw it in her eyes. She felt that she knew her babies very well; she had raised them close-close to her in Spirit.

Chapter Six

"Living with strangers is not so bad after all," Rogain-Dimitrius-Child thought. It had been a long time before she had become accustomed to the order in the two households she had lived in since her Mama Sage left her. The sense of security in both of them made her feel safe and well looked after, although she didn't really feel loved. And she missed that, because her Mama Sage was loving to her and to all of her children. That is why she could not believe it when she left her that first time.

Sometimes, when she thought about it, she missed her Mama Sage's love so bad, her heart hurt her. Even though she loved being clean and safe and no longer hungry all the time...still, she missed her Mama Sage's love. She was not sure that she could live without that touch, that soft-soft touch that her Mama Sage gave her, beginning at the top of her head. She could still call it back to her heart, that gentle, sweet touch on her cheek, on her arms, on her hands, on her forehead.

Her Mama Sage really knew how to make her children feel like they were somebody; and especially Seleena, because out of all of her children, her Mama Sage really loved her best. That was a thing she just knew. Seleena remembered how her Mama Sage's hands used to linger on the top of her head, as if she received some kind of good feeling from keeping it there.

Although she missed all of that loving, she did not want to go back to living the way her Mama Sage was living. She liked the way she didn't have to worry every day about whether she was going to eat well or not. She liked too that she went to the private high school for girls, instead of the government school that she and her sisters used to attend. They never used to have desks and her Mama Sage could not afford to get a desk made for them.

She only had to close her eyes to remember how she could see hatred and meanness in the eyes of Rommel, the man her Mama Sage allowed in their lives. She was not sure that she could trust her Mama Sage to be able to stay away from him, and also from the rum. And then what if one day she came to her and Joyling and their little sisters and told them again that she was going to leave them with people "for a time"?

Just like that, they would go through another big upheaval and she just could not stand that kind of life again. It made her head hurt her all the time; and then the music she heard inside would fade into the background.

She always knew that she and her Mama Sage were close. For one thing, they both had a pain that would come and stay and then go away, as suddenly as it arrived. Her Mama Sage's pain prevented her from walking, but Seleena's pain prevented her from talking. When it came, she would go silent, sometimes for days at a time; because the vibration of her voice made her head sting even more sharply.

When she lived with her Mama, she got that pain when she was hungry; but now, it came all the time. Every time her father talked to her, she got the pain; and it stayed until he left the house. She wished she knew what it was, this pain.

Every doctor tried to find out the cause of it and gave up. This was the first time that Seleena ever went to a doctor and she never imagined that there were so many doctors on the island; and that was just in town. She felt sure that somewhere in the world, there was a doctor who would know what was wrong with her.

She wished that she could find her voice to say this to her father, because she did not want him thinking that she was too sick to live with them any longer. She wanted to stay here and live with his family in this big house with the big yard, where everything always stayed the same.

She liked too, that she had other people in her family who looked like her. For besides her two half-sisters, there were her cousins, including the boy she saw in town that day. She liked going to their homes as well, because playing with a whole group of children that looked just like her felt good.

Living with her Mama Sage, nothing ever stayed the same for too long, including how they ate, where they slept, and what her Mama Sage did to get money to feed them. When her Mama Sage came for her, Seleena thought that her heart would break in two from yearning and longing for a hug-up from her.

Then when her Mama Sage put her arms around her, she found instead that she wanted to scream in pain and hurt and anger: "Don't touch me! How you could just leave me? Where you was when I did need you, every day, every morning, every night? Get away from me!"

Instead, she said nothing; but her screams were in her body. She kept herself stiff when her Mama Sage held her, for fear that she would shout out all of the hateful things she wanted to say to her. Her skin burned where her Mama Sage touched her. It was as if there was such a fire in her

Mama Sage's hands that not even holding herself stiff could cool those places where they touched her.

And yet she could not leave with her Mama Sage. She could not let go and allow herself to love her enough to live with her again. She was terrified that she would do the same thing to her another day.

She could not touch her Mama Sage. She could not hold her; and she could not walk with her, nor sleep in the same house with her. She did not trust her any more. She felt sure that her Mama Sage was capable of murdering her. For did she not already almost kill her by leaving her with strangers who passed her on to another set of strangers? It was that last thought that had given her the strength to tell her Mama Sage that she wanted to stay with the Dimitrius family; and it had felt easier, somehow, to speak to her using her school-voice and her school-language.

Rogain Dimitrius was the most alien of them all in this new world that Seleena inhabited. And yet she shared that most binding thing with him: blood. Proof of that blood was obvious to her every time she saw him. She looked so much like him that it hurt her, because she despised him with every fibre of her being. Even at twelve years old, she knew the true meaning of the word "hate." Every time she looked into the face that most resembled hers in the whole island—in her whole world—all she felt was hate.

Soon after joining his household, Seleena stopped telling anyone that her name was "Rogain-Dimitrius-Child." She no longer wished to be so closely associated with this man whom not even his mother could love. For old Mrs. Dimitrius would come to her son's house only when she was sure that he was not at home.

She made no bones about what she thought of her son. The first time she met Seleena she told her: "Is I bear him into this world, child, but Lord forgive me, I have regretted it ever since. He was a bad baby, a bad child, a bad young man; and now he is a big man, he is still bad." She laughed and said, "In fact, I think he is even worse now as a big man." Then she shook her head, making a clucking sound in her throat.

She took Seleena's hands in her kindly old hands and, rubbing them gently, told her, "Child, I welcome you into my family...you did not ask to be born into it. Remember that in me you have a place of refuge whenever you want it." Seleena felt tears come to her eyes at the kindness in the words. She blinked them away, and in a gesture of appreciation, kissed the old lady on the cheek. She wanted to kiss her hands, but held herself back, not knowing if it would be accepted. Her Mama Sage used to kiss her children's hands all the time.

She liked the way that old Mrs. Dimitrius's kind heart seemed to reach all the way through to the warmth in her hands. Her fingers looked as if they had so much love in them that they could soothe away any pain; maybe even the pain in her head.

She was glad that she got a chance to meet her grandmother, for it showed her that she was not from some bad seed. She decided that her father just chose to be a bad person, all by himself. It was not in his blood...it was his special curse.

In no time at all, Seleena realized that her father was indeed a terrible man. She heard him doing "it" with his wife one night, after he told her at the dinner table: "You not going to get away from me tonight!" When Seleena asked her half-sisters about the violent noises she heard during the night, they explained that those were the sounds of their father making their mother do "it" with him. They knew that their mother refused to do "it" with their father and that he sometimes made her do "it" against her will.

They were so used to their father doing that all the time that they did not even hear it as strange any more. It was a part of the rhythm of their lives; that was just the way life was in their home. Then they would wait for the tension to pass, until the next time.

After that, Seleena felt even more terrified of the man whom she was so anxious to claim as her father. She wondered about the relationship between him and her mother. She thought that maybe he made her with her mother by making her do "it" with him. She thought how horrible it would be if that is how she came into the world. She realized too that it was probably the way her two half-sisters came into the world as well.

"All of us are just accidents," she thought, "accidents that just happened from the behaviour of a cruel, cruel, cruel man." She shuddered at the thought of being just another accident. Her Mama Sage never acted as if she was an accident.

Ever since she heard her Mama Sage speak of how she was conceived, Seleena thought of Rogain Dimitrius as the man who forced her mother to bring her into this world. He was not worthy of being called "father." She made the decision that her voice would never utter those words to him or about him.

When Rogain Dimitrius treated his wife harshly, things became bad for Seleena, because Mrs. Dimitrius would change towards her. She did not ill-treat her, but she hardly paid her any attention. Seleena knew that her stepmother was the one who made Rogain Dimitrius take her into their home. Now, whenever he made her do "it" with him, she would be upset and unhappy. She even neglected her own children. They were not physically neglected, but she just did not seem to remember to notice that they were there.

The housekeeper did all of the work of supervising the children's dressing, eating, bathing and sleeping. She was always the one who combed their hair, and she made their meals and cleaned the house. But Mrs. Dimitrius's added touch was missing altogether in these times when she suffered at the hands of her husband.

Seleena would feel as if she did not exist to anyone but herself. Her half-sisters still found her an embarrassment and merely tolerated her. And now Rogain Dimitrius drank more than ever before. Seleena made sure that she kept out of his way, not seeing him sometimes for days on end.

For days running into weeks, Seleena was haunted by the memory of her Mama Sage's face closing down in front of her. She could not forget it. It was like a curtain coming down at the end of their school play. It happened very suddenly and quite completely; and then the play was over.

That is how it was with her Mama Sage's face that day. And she ached for her Mama Sage; but she hardened her heart against the ache, telling herself that she would learn not to need her love any more. She would make sure that she had everything she wanted, so that she did not have to live anywhere or be anywhere unless she wanted to be there. She vowed that when she grew up, she would make sure that she did not need anyone's money or love.

The night she refused to leave with her Mama Sage, Seleena put on her nightgown and knelt beside her bed to say her prayers; and it was then that the big-big thing that she had done hit her. She had chosen not to live with her Mama Sage ever again. She knew that that was what was in her heart and in her eyes that shook her Mama Sage so much that she turned and left. And now here she was, living forever with Rogain Dimitrius and his family.

She was not able to say her prayers because she did not know what she should ask God to do. She had a wish, deep down inside her, that her Mama Sage would turn around and come back and make her leave with her. She wanted her Mama Sage's love; but she also had a real wanting inside her to stay in this nice-nice house and live this nice-nice, safe life.

She tired herself out with all of this thinking as she knelt at the side of her bed. The pain lurked nearby, threatening to come and visit her if she did not stop thinking so much. She climbed into bed and pulled the sheet up under her chin. Closing her eyes, she made a wish for everything to be perfect when she woke up the next day.

She willed the music to come into her head and make the pain go away; and it did. Finally, sleep came to her and took away all of the thinking and the wishing.

Chapter Seven

Sayshelle's youngest aunt called herself "Juniper Berry." She used the two words together each and every time she said her name.

Juniper Berry returned to Antigua after she had lived in Trinidad and married a man named Ferdinand Berry. They got divorced just one year after the marriage, and now she was back in Antigua.

Whenever anyone commented on the combination of her first and last name, her aunt asked them if they knew what a juniper berry was. The response was usually: "No." Then she told them proudly of the real name, the botanical name: *Juniperus communis*. She also explained that it was used to flavour gin and as a scent in pot-pourri.

She never failed to add that she did not drink gin, for she knew it to be a harsh drink. She also did not mention that it was used as a seasoning for stews. That seemed too ordinary an attachment to make with her name, but flavouring gin and pot-pourri, now that was interesting!

Sayshelle always wondered if her aunt sought out a man named "Berry" on purpose. She did not put it past her to engineer the exotic lilt of her name. Of course he would also have to be a man of some means, because her aunt detested poverty. She thought that her Aunt Juniper Berry had a lot of style and was a directed, driven kind of person. It seemed to Sayshelle that she got exactly what she wanted out of life. Of the three sisters, she was the most independent and the most free.

Sayshelle wished that she could live life the way her Aunt Juniper Berry did: joyfully, while being steadily focused on her own goals. Soon after returning to live in Antigua, Juniper Berry set up her own business, importing small packaged goods from North American companies. She imported and distributed everything from yoghurt to paper clips. She was very successful at it and was already exploring buying her own home.

Juniper Berry told her sister Reevah that she was not searching for a man to look after her; but she also did not want a man who expected to be looked after. "After all," she said, "why would I want to buy any man? Who could be worth buying? I want a man who is respectable and who has self-respect. I also would not mind if he was good-looking; but most of all, I need to be able to talk with him about things that matter."

Reevah took that to mean that she wanted someone intelligent who had his own source of a good income. She told Sayshelle that she felt sure that her Aunt Juniper Berry decided that Clifford fit the bill very nicely. He was a man of means, he was intelligent, he was ambitious, he was handsome, and he was respectable. *And*...he was newly widowed!

Clifford knew that the only thing his wife Mabelay contributed to their making love was the passive acceptance of his body on hers. He could tell that she barely tolerated him pressing himself on her flesh. She lay under him, silently letting him have his way with her. She was being careful not to show her deep-to-the-soul rejection of his intrusion of her person. He could feel that way up inside her where he could not reach her soul, she rejected him. Her rejection of him was so deep that he felt that it hovered close to the bone.

He would always try to approximate that ball of fire that used to be ignited between them. He knew that she had the power to let her fire be lit by him; for they had both gloried in that all-consuming combustion throughout their courtship and marriage. Even though he realized that she withheld that part of herself from him, Clifford kept on trying to light her up, all by himself. It became a personal challenge for him, and he approached it with the tenacity, endurance, and determination of a long-distance runner, or a mountain climber.

Mabelay knew that Clifford sought to light that fire inside her. She therefore took her passion purposely, wilfully, and knowingly deeper and deeper up inside her, where he could not reach it, could not touch it, could not ignite it. She held her feelings right up inside her soul, carefully shielding them from the flame of his passion. She held all of herself away from him in that way; so that after a while, her feelings grew into one big sore spot. It was a hardness that could only be softened by love of life. Instead, she condemned all that was not a part of her religious focus.

When it grew too big to keep it in her soul, she had to release it. And it spread, all over her womanly areas, even up to her breasts; but that was after it had filled up her uterus and her ovaries. It was a wild kind of fire, and it turned cancerous when it could not find release into the playing field of love of life for which it was designed. It spread as rapidly as fire in a dry cassie bush, creating burnt, petrified coal, standing grotesque against the blue sky.

That is how Mabelay's cancer ravaged her, until even her lips were blue-black; and the wisps of hair left on her head turned brittle from the sickness and from the drugs. For her doctor tried to keep holding her in this life, against her will.

At the funeral, Clifford felt a deep anger as he put the wreath on the stand that held Mabelay's coffin. He whispered fiercely under his breath, "You didn't have to die to get away from me, Mabelay! You could have just told me you wanted to leave me!" He felt the tears slide down his face, but he did not wipe them. They felt good and cooling on his hot face.

He never understood the way Mabelay had changed. He tried everything in his power to win back her love. She could not forgive him for not joining her religion. Her religion dictated that making love was wrong unless they were making a baby. They decided not to have any children for another two years; so Clifford saw himself facing a sexless union for that long-long time. He soon tired of persuading her to grant him a small favour now and then. He felt like a beggar for love in his own home.

Outside of the issue of baby-making, Mabelay definitely thought that his intimate touching and fondling of her was an abomination. That was what she said after she joined her religion. She would say, her voice sharp and high-pitched, filled to the brim with annoyance, "I told you, I am not doing all of that any more! Not until we ready to have children."

Before she was converted, Mabelay would "do all of that" all the time, making love freely whatever way he wanted and whatever way she desired. She would respond to his fingers strumming her body, moving in rhythm with him, not just lying there, passively receiving him. She used to love holding him in her arms; and she used to tell him how much she loved him. And she would kiss him all over his body, as if his flesh was her flesh.

It was not just the sex that grew sour between them; everything grew hard and cold in their relationship. When she pursed her lips and looked down her fine, aquiline nose, Clifford would feel himself shudder. He knew what was coming next: a lecture on one of two or three things: she reminded him to say his prayers when he came to bed; or she pressed him to say prayers with her.

Or worse yet, she gave him a lecture about needing to change his life in a more righteous way. It was pure and simple: "It is time for you to consider receiving the teachings of my religion in your heart."

Mabelay's nose still looked fine and aquiline, even in death. Clifford was sure that her spirit still hovered, looking down that nose at the people at her funeral. He almost laughed out loud at the image that formed in his mind.

He was sitting on the chair that the funeral director insisted on providing for him. He suggested to Clifford that he should stay at the side of the coffin with Mabelay's body lying in it. That was the place designated for the "grieving husband" to sit for a time next to his dear, departed wife.

Soon, a stream of people walked by and shook Clifford's listless hand or patted his shoulder. He was well aware that he hardly acknowledged the condolences that were offered by friends and family. They all mistakenly blamed grief for his limp handshake and for a cheek barely proffered to receive kisses that were themselves barely formed.

It was not grief that perplexed Clifford; it was frustration and anger and hurt, for he never stopped loving Mabelay; not even for one day. Long before Mabelay died, he gave up trying to make love to her. Her clenched insides, strangely accompanied by her loose, relaxed body, eventually got the better of him. She was receiving him and yet rejecting him; so that he could not say that she was not doing her duty as a wife.

He did not remember when it was exactly that he stopped touching Mabelay. He thought maybe it was when he turned thirty-eight or thirty-nine. One night in bed, he turned to her hopefully; but the sight of her closed face cooled his desire completely. He could see no trace left of the woman he fell in love with and married three years earlier. It was as if he beheld a spectre in their bed as her face came to resemble the punishing doctrine of her religion.

The religious fervour that first took hold of her grew into a cold, menacing dogma that threatened his very existence. He saw it all on her face and he recoiled. Not only did he lose all desire for her, but he was repulsed by her. That night, he lay carefully on his side of the bed. It was not until the edges of the fore-day-morning that he finally drifted into a light, tortured sleep.

The next day, he created a bedroom for himself in the little half-room that Mabelay used as a sewing room. He said not a word to her about it. Late that night, long after she had gone to bed, he tiptoed into the sewing room and changed into his pyjamas. He breathed deeply, feeling sure that Mabelay was dreaming by now and would not notice his absence until morning.

He was just drifting off to sleep when the lights snapped on in his new bedroom. Mabelay stood framed in the doorway. "Is what you doing?" Her voice was indignant, maybe even belligerent, and yet Clifford thought he heard fear in it too; a note that he secretly relished. He thought that at least he had got her attention.

He did not expect his move out of their bedroom to bring any change in Mabelay. That was not his motive. He was entirely motivated by the repulsion he now felt in her presence. It was as if her coldness made her give off a bad feeling; just by lying close to her, it seemed to penetrate his pores.

His revulsion was so strong that although Mabelay had no bad smell,

Clifford could almost make himself believe that she did. He concluded that the hardness of her soul had an offensive odour. It made good sense to him.

He tried to shake the sleep from his eyes so that he could focus on her. She continued to stand menacingly in the entrance to his makeshift bedroom, waiting for him to answer her question. Try as he might, Clifford found that he could not come awake sufficiently to focus on her question, let alone answer it. He wished he could remember it, so that he could answer and then he would ask her to turn off the light and bid her "Good night."

Finally, she asked it again: "Is what you doing?" Clifford went for an innocent rejoinder. "Trying to sleep," he said and closed his eyes. By now, he was sufficiently awake to enjoy the moment. "Pay back," he thought, "pay back time." Even though his intent was not vindictive, he felt that Mabelay deserved to be paid back in her own coin and he was enjoying it. "Actually, I *was* sleeping," he added, almost laughing at his bravado.

Mabelay could not believe that this was happening. She sounded genuinely puzzled as she asked: "How come you sleeping in here?" Clifford never did answer her. He felt himself drifting back into a warmly satisfying sleep. Mabelay left as abruptly as she had entered the room. Her words hung in the air still, like a lullaby to the now sleeping Clifford. Those were the last words that she ever addressed to him directly...up to and including the day she died.

It was five years before Mabelay developed the cancer that took two years to kill her, but she never spoke to Clifford again. Not even on her deathbed, when he held her cold, dry hand and begged for her forgiveness, did she speak to him.

She still had enough control of the muscles of her face to bring to it that look that Clifford hated. It was the look she always wore when prodding him to join her religion. The look made her seem not so sick, not really dying. Clifford almost allowed himself to feel relief; for how could she be so mean-spirited and be on her last legs?

She never answered him when he begged for her forgiveness; she just gave him that look. There was also no mistaking the dismissive fluttering of her fingers when she struggled to raise them from the bed-sheets. Then she turned her head away from him. Clifford released her hand, feeling a little pang of hurt creep into his heart. She died then, making a great heaving sigh that sounded to him like it was full of relief.

It was during the funeral service for Mabelay that Clifford saw Juniper Berry for the first time. She took his breath away and he wondered: "Who is that beautiful woman with the brazen eyes?" She was sitting between two older women and the contrast between their mature faces and her youthful vigour was striking. He noticed her smooth skin first; even the skin of her hands was smooth, as smooth as that of her face.

She wore white and it contrasted sharply with the matronly navy-blue and black clothes of the rest of the congregation. Her painted lips were a sensuous gash of dark wine-red in her jet-black face. Whenever she opened her mouth to join in the hymn-singing, Clifford let out his breath at the whiteness of her teeth.

He noticed that she was tall and towered over the other two women in her company. She was directly in his range of vision, and so he did not have to turn his head to look at her. Once she caught his eye and smiled. He smiled back, feeling his face get hot and knowing that his light skin would betray him. It was not the first time that he cursed his light skin. When he was growing up, it made him an oddity in his neighbourhood, in his community, in his family. He was always cursing the American sailor who dropped his seed in Antigua and went on his merry way on his big ship. As far as Clifford knew, he was still unaware that his son even existed.

His mother told him that she was a young girl who ran home (as did all decent girls and women in Antigua) when an American ship full of sailors entered the harbour. The sailors chased girls and women through the streets, and it was assumed that anyone who was caught would be raped.

Although no one had ever heard a first-hand account of a woman or girl being raped by the sailors, the story was that it had been known to happen. Someone would raise the alarm: "Sailor-ship in town!" and all of the decent girls and women would hurry to their homes.

His mother did not tell him that there were some women who did not run away. He heard it in his community, as he grew up. In fact, those women who did not run away got dressed in alluring clothes, put on lipstick, and went to greet the sailors when the ship docked. They were considered prostitutes by decent people, although no one could attest to all of these girls and women committing any acts of prostitution.

And later, when some of these women gave birth to light-skinned babies, everyone cried shame on them behind their backs for having prostituted themselves with the sailors. People referred to their offspring as "sailor-pickney." Their light skin brought their children shame, instead of elevating them to a higher status in the society, as light skin usually does.

Yet within their small communities, they had a special position; not as someone of a higher status or caste, but it was a difference. It gave them mention, made them stand out; and so in the end, they were still given some sort of *place* that was special. They were singled out for attention based on their colour, although it was not always favourable.

Some of these offspring of sailors and Black Antiguan women were dubbed with the nickname "Backra," which was usually reserved for white people. There was the undercurrent of an insult in the nickname; for it was hooked to their first names without their permission. It was the same way with a young man whose father was a known and convicted thief. His father had been nicknamed "Thiefing-Judas" and the young man found himself answering to "Thiefing-Judas-Son."

Clifford felt lucky that he had only been called "Backra-Clifford" by one boy, way back when he was so little, not old enough to understand what it meant. He was not as fortunate about escaping the label "sailor-pickney" as he was in escaping being called "Backra-Clifford." His skin colour, his age, and his position in life identified him as a "sailor-pickney." For he was among the small number of light-skinned people of that age who lived in a poor community and whose parentage could not be traced to some middle-class, light-skinned father.

At that time, all of the light-skinned people in Antigua lived together in the heart of town. Certainly none of them lived in poor communities full of black-skinned people.

Clifford once asked his mother to tell him the identity of his real father, because he called her father "Papa" and knew no father of his own. She simply said of his father: "He was a white man from America or England. I did not realize I would be pregnant, or I woulda find out more about him."

When he asked her if she knew his name, she looked upset and embarrassed and told him that she promised not to give anyone that information. By the time he became an adult, Clifford had come to understand the stories surrounding the circumstances of the creation of all like him. He decided not to embarrass his poor mother with any more questions.

He saw the beautiful woman with the brazen eyes laughing at his reddened face. She put her hand over her mouth and as he saw her long, red nails, he experienced a little thrill of pleasure. He thought of how it would be if he could feel them on his back. Then he felt ashamed of himself for thinking such thoughts while they were singing burial hymns for his dead wife...for Mabelay. He made himself keep his eyes away from the beautiful woman with the brazen eyes. It was only when they were at the reception that he saw her again.

She walked right up and spoke to him. Her voice fell in his ears like gentle music: "My deepest sympathy."

He answered: "Thank you." He spoke almost in a whisper, because his throat was dry at being so close to her. He knew that she would take it for sadness, and was glad of that; he still felt ashamed of himself for blushing earlier.

"I hope you're not too sad..." He thought he could hear amusement in the way she asked the question. She trailed her voice off slowly.

He looked closely at her; it was clear to see that she was laughing at him. She seemed to be telling him that she knew that he was not as sad as he was pretending to be and that there was no need to feel ashamed of his feelings.

Of course, Clifford knew that she was correct. Still, he did not like her knowing so much about him, reading him so well, seeing through his act. He was not completely overcome by grief.

To his shock, he heard himself saying, "My wife and I were not happy together." And now his voice did contain grief: a kind of wrenching sadness seemed to have settled over each word.

Juniper Berry's whole attitude changed. She smiled sweetly up at him and put her hand on his arm. "I am so sorry." Her voice was warm and gentle. "Please accept my deep, deep sympathy." Then she paused and said in a firm voice, "I am very sorry."

He was quite sure that that last apology was for laughing at him. As she turned to go, walking some few feet behind the two older women, he touched her shoulder and asked, "How could I see you again?"

The smile she turned on him was dazzling, "I am listed. My name is Juniper Berry," she said. And with a swirl of long, white skirts, she was gone.

Whenever Clifford thought of Juniper Berry, he remembered the way she left the funeral reception. Her skirts sort of swirled around her body and around her ankles. He guessed at the curves of her body, because they were well-hidden under the loose, flowing lines of the fabric of her clothes. Her dress seemed to have been created to hide and yet entice.

He had felt dizzy with desire for her that day at Mabelay's funeral. Her perfume lingered around him long after she had gone. Later that night, after he said a final good-bye to Mabelay, he realized that Juniper Berry's scent was in his coat, where she had touched his arm. He sniffed the coat sleeve several times the next day, desperately trying to recall the image of her more strongly. He wished he knew the name of the perfume she wore. Then he could have bought a bottle and been able to have her scent around him whenever he wanted it. He realized that he was smitten.

He found her telephone number and dialled it every day for a week, but hung up every time she answered. He felt scared. He feared that she might reject him once she knew his age. He was not worried that she might just be after his money. Everyone knew that he had inherited Mabelay's share of her father's large estate, including property and half of a hardware business. He would not receive the cash for two years, when her sister could buy him out, but it was worth at least half a million dollars.

Yet he knew that Juniper Berry was no more interested in the money than he was. She seemed like the kind of woman who would always have her own money and would never be beholden to any man. He could tell that about her just from looking at her: the way she carried herself, the way she seemed so confident and secure.

Other women had made overtures to him and he easily identified the fortune hunters. Even at the funeral there were two women who seemed bent on inflicting themselves on him. He felt it like an intrusion, because at no time did he indicate that he welcomed their attention. Yet they kept on trying to stay at his elbow. Whenever he turned around, he bumped into one or the other of them. Eventually he excused himself and retreated to the safety of his mother and Mabelay's aunt. He sat on the couch between them and allowed their conversation to wash over him. Meantime, his mind was full of the image of the calves and ankles of a woman named Juniper Berry. They were only sometimes visible as she moved in a swirl of flowing white skirts, but they occupied a firm space in Clifford's memory.

Her lips, parting around her teeth, also swam before his eyes. He made himself concentrate on the tut-tutting and cluck-clucking sounds of the two elderly women. They spoke with grief of "Mabelay's untimely death," and Clifford found his eyes filling up with tears. He truly loved Mabelay; he was just not prepared to be who she wanted him to be. He allowed his tears to spill out of him, at last. He released all thoughts of Juniper Berry and said a final good-bye to Mabelay. The two women held him and let him cry. One of them brought him a cup of bush-tea, saying: "To make you sleep well tonight, boy...drink all of it."

The tea relaxed him and he drifted off to sleep with Juniper Berry's scent still hovering around him. For the first time since Mabelay's death, his dreams were peaceful and loving. He woke up determined to speak with Juniper Berry on the telephone.

Finally, on the first day of the second week, Clifford did not hang up the phone when she answered. He held his breath and kept the receiver at his ear. "Hello?" he heard. Then after a pause, she asked, "Is anyone there?" Clifford tried to breathe without sounding like a harassing caller. He could not speak.

Softly, Juniper Berry said, "Is that you Clifford?" He knew that she heard his very audible intake of breath, but still he did not speak. Now he felt like a real fool. She tried again: "Clifford? Speak to me, please." Her voice was cajoling, not angry. He even thought he heard laughter in it.

Clifford found his courage and his voice. "Hello," he said feebly, feeling quite ashamed of himself, like a little boy who was caught doing something bad.

"Hello Clifford," she laughed, but he did not feel that she laughed at him. He thought he heard relief in her laughter.

"I'm sorry. I hope I didn't scare you." He heard himself working at sounding overly contrite.

Juniper Berry laughingly asked, "Have you been calling me every day?" He knew that she knew the answer to her question, but he replied, "Yes." Then he apologized again. Juniper Berry stopped his apology, saying, "It's all right. You were shy. I'm shy too. I wanted to phone you, but didn't have the nerve. At least you got as far as dialling my number."

"You didn't have my number either," he said. Her pretty laughter was her first response; then she explained: "I got it from my sister Reevah." She laughed again, saying, "At least you dialled my number; I couldn't dial yours." She made an embarrassed little chuckle. "I tried, but I always stopped before the last number. I know your number by heart now."

Clifford felt pleased that she wanted to speak to him. He also liked her honesty. He confessed his own inhibitions and then, that over, he got right to the point. "When can I see you?"

She shot back at him: "Right now!"

He was taken aback, but rose to the moment. "Okay. In a half-hour? I'll pick you up; where do you live?"

"Slow down," she chided him. "I'll pick you up in one hour. How's that?"

He liked her take-charge attitude and her complete comfort in driving him. He gave her directions to his house, without asking why she wanted to pick him up and why she needed a whole hour just to drive the ten minutes across town. It never occurred to him that she would need to bathe and change her clothes before coming to pick him up. His mind was in a fog and his heart was beating like a thumping drum in his chest.

Juniper Berry's red dress took Clifford's breath away. It was as skimpy as her funeral clothes had been voluminous. The skirt stopped mid-thigh and the top held her slim body in such a way that it shamelessly outlined her breasts. He was sure that she had caught him salivating over her hardened bra-less nipples pushing themselves against the snug bodice of the dress.

It was cut in such a way that you could see where her bare arms joined the smooth slope of her shoulders. Their slide into her long, even smoother black neck was accentuated by a high neckline that ended in a bow tied at her throat. Clifford thought that looking at her was like looking at an ebony swan swathed in a small piece of red fabric.

As his eyes made their way over her body, he avoided looking directly into her eyes, for he was afraid she would see the raw desire he felt rising in him. She laughed, saying with a coquettish tilt of her head, "Look into my eyes. I want to see the feelings that gave you that erection." And at his shocked look, she said, "You can't hide it; it's leaping out at me." And she put her hand on his bulging crotch and squeezed.

Clifford felt it, even in his toes. He groaned. Juniper Berry unzipped his fly and held him tightly. At that precise moment, she stabbed her tongue between his lips and worked it in and out of his mouth, playing with the inside corners and rubbing his teeth. In an odd sort of way he felt as if she was soothing him with her kiss, even though it was a far from soothing kiss.

Clifford was gasping for breath now. He reeled from the sensation of her tongue and her fingers, and even the smell of her. He held her tightly while returning her kiss. She was now moving her hips against his muscular legs. He nibbled at her through the fabric of her dress, then pulled down the top of her dress and took her left breast into his mouth. He sucked it as if he were a newborn baby, moaning with fulfilment at being fed.

Juniper Berry cradled Clifford's head at her breast. They were still standing, now partially clothed, in the middle of his living room. "Come! Show me to your guest room," she commanded him, and, holding his hand, let him lead the way. He was glad that he did indeed have the extra bedroom, because he could not have managed to be in Mabelay's bed with Juniper Berry.

Juniper Berry made love to him with what she thought of as unbridled passion. He responded by seeking to know what pleased her; he wanted to give her as much pleasure as she was giving him. She took charge sometimes, and at other times succumbed to his touch. She was unselfish and caring, touching and soothing him, when all at once he became so excited that he twitched uncontrollably at the moment of ecstasy.

He kissed her lips endlessly, worshipping them with his own, taking them into his mouth as if he needed to drink from them to quench a great thirst. When he freed her lips, Juniper Berry put them to his ear and whispered, "Now make love to me the way you always wanted to make love to your wife." Clifford was startled, but grateful for the invitation to be free, free from the imprisonment of Mabelay's passive love-making.

He devoured Juniper Berry's whole body then, taking little pieces of her skin into his mouth and kissing and licking her. He felt all of his senses tingling and his mouth salivating, as if he were eating the fruit and drinking the nectar of some precious, rare fruit. Finally, Juniper Berry screamed and pushed her face into his neck, gasping her passion against its soft inside curves. But Clifford had not finished giving Juniper Berry pleasure. He put on a condom and slowly entered her. He did not move inside her, but kissed her gently, helping her to calm down and letting her rest. He kissed her closed, dry lips and licked them to make them moist. He kissed her eyes, ran his tongue over her eyebrows and then kissed her cheeks, her nose, her chin.

When Juniper Berry's breathing calmed right down, Clifford's kisses became more insistent, more purposeful. He concentrated on a spot on her neck that made her moan and showered it with kisses and soft bites. And finally, he sucked the spot, rhythmically, first hard, then soft, almost like a loose, wet kiss. The contrast drove Juniper Berry wild. She did not move her lower body, but she squeezed him deep inside her until they both exploded together, gasping for breath and kissing each other passionately.

Their love-making grew better and better, day by day. It was as if they were one body that had somehow become divided by an accident of birth. And now, at last, each had found its missing half. They thought the same thoughts, dreamed the same dreams about life. They talked about all of the ways in which they fit and wondered how they managed to be so fortunate as to have found each other. It was not just in their love-making that they fit: their personalities were also a harmonious blend.

Soon, they spent all of their non-working hours together. After a while, they rarely slept apart from each other. Most of the time they stayed at Clifford's home, as Juniper Berry lived in a small bachelor apartment, while Clifford had a three-bedroom house. Finally Juniper Berry sold her apartment, Clifford sold his house, and they bought a house together.

The closeness between them was so natural that there were times when Clifford's heart sang as he awoke in the morning and saw Juniper Berry's head cradled in his arms. They slept as if they were peas in a pod, reluctant to let any space between them. They found ways of positioning their heads so that they could breathe clearly while wrapped in each other's arms.

Sometimes, as they slept during the night, peacefully dreaming, their bodies would separate. Then they would find each other again and embrace closely as they again fell into a deep sleep.

Clifford felt sure that in dreaming, he would meet Juniper Berry, yet on waking, he could not remember the details of the dreams. She had no recollection of meeting him in her dreams and would laugh when he suggested it. "You just don't want to let me go, not even when we're sleeping," she said and she laughed, hugging him tightly to her. "I'm never leaving you, my darling, never, never, never; not even in sleep."

"You got that right!" Clifford said; and he laughed. However, he secretly determined to meet her in his dreams and to remember the dream afterwards so that he could tell her about it. It never happened; but something much more profound occurred that affirmed his belief that he and Juniper Berry were divinely connected.

One day, as Juniper Berry turned to walk into the living room from the veranda of their new house, Clifford saw a vision of her dressed in old-fashioned clothes. At the same time, he saw a quite different house, one that resembled the nineteenth-century architecture of New England. He looked down at his own clothes, not surprised to see that he too, like Juniper Berry, was dressed in old-fashioned clothes.

He noted with surprise that he felt quite calm, despite the strangeness of the experience. He looked at Juniper Berry again, but the moment had gone, and all was back to normal. He thought about calling out to tell her about the vision, but something stopped him. A strong, clear voice inside his head, resonating in his heart, making him shiver, said "Not now!"

It was said very sharply, as if he were being given a really strong directive. He sat silently, reliving the experience and wondering what it meant. By the time Juniper Berry returned from the house, he had digested the experience but had no idea what it meant, how it happened, or why it happened. He was thoroughly puzzled, for he had never experienced anything like that before.

Clifford realized that he and Juniper Berry had a few dreams that were very similar; but he had never thought of reincarnation. He looked up at Juniper Berry, considering how and when he would tell her about his bizarre vision. He knew she would not doubt him; but in a way, he was still wondering if he had imagined it. After a little while, he became more comfortable with the vision he had seen and just then, he heard that sonorous voice inside his head again.

He had heard it before today, and had come to equate it with his intuitive voice. Now the voice said to him that it was not his imagination. He supposed now was the right time to speak about it, because he did not feel any further need to process it himself.

He turned to Juniper Berry and said, "I have something to tell you." She looked expectantly at him. Clifford felt his courage fail him, but he persevered. He told her about the vision, noticing that as he spoke, Juniper Berry looked shocked. Finally, when he had finished speaking, she told him that she had experienced the same vision several times, complete with even more details. She saw the same house that he had, as well as two small children. They walked beside her, holding on to either side of her skirts. She had not wanted to speak about it before, because she wondered if he would believe her.

"And I knew that we were happy," she ended, "I could feel it. My eyes felt happy when I saw us in that period."

"So why are we back together?" Clifford asked playfully. "Didn't we do things well enough the last time?" He laughed, taking Juniper Berry's hands in his. "We're sure doing things beautifully between us this time."

He kissed her, holding her close against him. Suddenly he felt afraid, although he did not know what he was afraid of. He knew that it had something to do with the vision. He held Juniper Berry close to his heart, kissing her softly, sweetly. He felt so blessed. It was such a long time since he had felt the beauty of love in his life that he was frightened of losing it.

Juniper Berry looked deeply into his eyes. She seemed to sense his fear. "I feel sure inside that I needed to understand that it was possible to mother your children. I take it as a sign that it is right and fitting in this lifetime with you to have your children."

She was silent for a moment, thinking. Then she said: "I believe that there was another time when I did not do so well with mothering your children. It felt like a warning that I was to either get out of the relationship now or be prepared to be presented with the same challenge. Clifford, I had no intentions of having children; none whatsoever. This vision has made me rethink that."

Clifford held his breath as he looked at her. The fear was still hovering around him. "And do you want to have children?" As he asked her the question, he realized that he had never before contemplated being a father. His relationship with Mabelay was so bad that bringing children into it would have been a disaster. He had dreaded facing the issue; and then Mabelay became ill and the decision was taken out of his hands.

He had not thought of Juniper Berry as a mother of children. His image of her was all wrapped up in her wonderful mind, the things they talked about, her sensuousness and the way she loved him. He just enjoyed being with her and would have been happy to go on doing so forever; children were not in the equation at all.

Now he wondered if children would ruin their relationship. She still did not answer him, so he probed, "Do you? Have you thought of having children?"

Juniper Berry nodded. "Yes, I have thought of it now that I've had that vision. I have thought about it a lot; and I think that it would actually be a good thing for me...for us. I feel sure that it would enhance and not ruin our relationship. We have a great love and a great friendship; we would simply extend ourselves and give that same love and friendship to our children."

Clifford laughed. "You make it sound so simple; children are a big responsibility, you know."

"I know." Juniper Berry's voice was firm and clear. "I know," she repeated, "but I am prepared to give that kind of nurturing mothering love to another human being." Then she looked carefully at him. "And you, are you ready to be a father?"

Clifford surprised himself by saying, "Actually, I think I am. I had no father and I think that would make me want to be a devoted father. I don't know how fathers behave; not from my own experience; but I know what I would have wanted from a father."

He was quiet for a moment, then he said, "It certainly would be good to give a child the respectability of having a father, unlike my experience. I grew up with the stigma of 'sailor-pickney' hanging over me, no matter where I went...even if people didn't say it, I could see it in their eyes. I would feel good about fathering children and having them feel secure about having parents."

The die was cast in their minds...they were going to be mother and father to those two children whom they both saw in their visions. They felt sure that it was a sign, like a silent message that was revealed to them in order to complete their happiness.

Several months later, Clifford and Juniper Berry were walking down Market Street on their way to have lunch. Suddenly, Clifford experienced another version of what he now thought of as "the vision." He saw himself as the lover of Juniper Berry, whereas before he had assumed that they were a married couple; for they obviously shared a home. He did not know how he became aware of the nature of the relationship. He simply had a clear *knowing* that they were two people in love who were not married. It was not lost on him that this was just like their relationship in their present lives.

He turned again to look at Juniper Berry and she caught his glance and smiled at him. Immediately the vision faded and he felt himself relax. He did not tell her of the vision he just had. He supposed that he would have to learn to come to terms with these visions. He would then be able to casually turn to her and say, "I just had one of those visions of you and me in another time."

He felt obsessed with the vision, especially now that Juniper Berry told him that she experienced it as well. When she missed her menstrual period, they excitedly contemplated the possibility that the vision foretold the advent of twins.

Juniper Berry had just come from a visit to their doctor, so Clifford knew that she had some news for him. But she asked him to wait until they were seated in the restaurant before she would tell him the news.

As they sat down, the puzzle of the two children in the vision was solved. As soon as the waiter left their table, Juniper Berry turned to Clifford and told him her news. The doctor's examination had suggested the possibility of twins, although it was much too early to be certain.

Clifford's head reeled. Twins! "The boy and girl from your vision," he said to Juniper Berry, laughing nervously.

It was as if their lives were being blessed after all that he had suffered with Mabelay and Juniper Berry had endured in her marriage. He said as much to her and she agreed. She too felt that they were being shown the gift of new blessings in their lives, given the past pain in their marriages.

"There's a God after all, Clifford darling," she said and kissed the fingers of his hand, in which hers were tightly clasped.

Soon after they had had their meal, Clifford held out his hands to Juniper Berry with the palms upturned. She put both of her hands in his and smiled into his eyes. He felt the tears well up in his eyes as he said, "Will you marry me, mother of my children?"

Juniper Berry laughed out loud at the quaint nature of his proposal. "Yes, of course," she said, feeling as if she were shouting. Clifford pulled her close to him across the table and kissed her softly on the lips. He felt that at last, his hungry, weary soul had found its resting place. Juniper Berry said to him, "And maybe now those two children will stop haunting us. We have agreed to look after them." They both laughed.

"Let's toast our good news," Juniper Berry said. And as they turned to pick up their water glasses, they each saw a fading vision of the little boy and girl, walking away from them and then turning to wave. Clifford and Juniper Berry turned to look at each other, a look of wonderment on their faces. Then they turned back to the vision, but it was gone, faded from sight. Juniper Berry felt as if that chapter was closing, just as the new one inside her began. She knew that she would soon welcome those two children into the life that she and Clifford had agreed to provide for them.

She touched her glass to Clifford's and said: "To our family." He smiled, echoing her words: "To our family."

Chapter Eight

When Reevah became aware of the relationship between Juniper Berry and Clifford, she expressed concern to her sister. "Remember he just bury his wife. What people going to say?"

Juniper Berry answered, "That would assume that he was in a true marital relationship." Her sister knew that Clifford and Mabelay's marriage had soured years ago. She discussed this with Reevah, suggesting that Clifford had experienced loss of the marriage long before Mabelay's illness and subsequent death. She felt that his heart had a space that needed to be filled...had needed it long before his wife died. "Besides," she concluded, "we don't care about what people say."

Reevah was still concerned that her sister was being a little too daring. She had watched Juniper Berry make a subtle move on Clifford at the funeral; smiling deeply into his eyes, holding his hand just a little too long for a handshake.

She had not expected that a close relationship would develop between them in such a short time. She liked Clifford and she always thought that Mabelay had taken her religious fervour too far. In fact, over the last two years, she had not stayed too close to Mabelay. Although they had grown up together as friends, she came to want to put some distance between them. For every time she ran into Mabelay, she would subject her to long lectures on the benefits to be had from joining her religion. While she had no quarrel with Mabelay becoming a fanatically religious person, she used to wish that she would stop trying to make everybody else join her.

"Still," she thought, "I would prefer if Juniper Berry and Clifford waited for a while longer before starting such a serious relationship."

She thought that it was a little disrespectful for it to be happening so soon after Mabelay's death. It was one week after the funeral when she realized that they were always in each other's company. She sighed and made a decision to speak with Juniper Berry yet again, if the moment presented itself.

Juniper Berry felt ready to love another man. She had no way to explain why she stopped loving her husband. One day she looked at him and knew that it was not really worth the effort she was putting into the marriage. Besides, she wanted a career and he kept on talking about not wanting his wife to work. On top of all of that, her husband had the morals of an alley cat.

Soon after she came to the realization that she wanted to leave the marriage, she came home one day and found him humping their maid on the kitchen table. This was just weeks after she came upon a bottle of medicine for crab lice. He explained that he had had a one-night stand with a woman from whom he had contracted crab lice.

Juniper Berry declared to him then that he was never to touch her again. When she walked in on him and the maid, she just sucked her teeth, going *"choopse."* She packed her things and moved into a hotel. Then she immediately sued him for divorce, naming the maid as a co-respondent.

The only people she knew in Trinidad were all *his* friends; and she discovered that they were his support system and not hers. So she did not even bother to ask any of them for shelter.

It was a terrible scandal. She did not care; she simply withdrew all of her money from her bank accounts, cashed in the settlement she got from him for her half of their assets, and booked a one-way plane ticket to Antigua.

"No problem," she told herself, "I will get over this." In fact, she felt that Ferdinand Berry had done her a big favour, because she had already begun thinking of going back to Antigua. He made it easier for her by providing her with evidence of adultery.

All in all, she was thankful for the experience; especially as it provided her with a wonderful surname to go with her first name. It was after the divorce that she began to use her full name "Juniper Berry" as if it were her first name.

Juniper Berry loved Clifford. He made her world feel whole for the first time in her life. She looked at her older sister Reevah's marriage to Emmanuel and liked the closeness between them. She longed to ask Reevah how she had known that he was so right for her; but the sisters never talked that kind of talk between them. The closest they came to such a conversation was when Reevah cautioned or advised Juniper Berry about any man with whom she saw her.

Juniper Berry remembered watching the way Emmanuel's eyes lit up when Reevah came into the room. She also liked the way they raised Sayshelle. Watching them brought her an understanding of what real love should look like and feel like.

Whenever she had visited Reevah and Emmanuel, she felt their warm love embracing her. It was that kind of household that she wanted to create; full of love and ease, where no tension, lies, or betrayal were harboured. That was no environment in which to raise children.

When Emmanuel died, she saw how devastated Reevah was, and she thought: "That's how real lovers feel when one is gone from the other."

Her sister Sage was another whole kettle of fish. Her choice of men and the way she abandoned her children was a horror story that Juniper Berry just could not believe occurred in their family. When Sage farmed out her children and went to live with Rommel, Juniper Berry was in Trinidad, trying to make her life in a new country in a new marriage. She heard of what was happening through Reevah. She was glad that Sage had left Rommel and was staying with Reevah.

She also heard that Rogain Dimitrius and his wife had petitioned for custody of Sage's daughter, Seleena, whom he had fathered with her. She felt that the fact that she was already living with them was going to make things hard. For it would mean in the court's eyes that they had already taken over her guardianship.

Rum had made Sage careless, so that she had nothing in writing; and so in the eyes of the law, she simply abandoned her daughter on the woman's doorstep. Juniper Berry understood from Reevah that Sage had not even given the woman the child's birth certificate as proof that she was formally leaving her for a period of time. The woman went to the courthouse and obtained the birth certificate herself in order to register Seleena in school. It was all wrapped up very tightly as a case of abandonment.

Juniper Berry went to see Sage several times lately, but she never met her at home. Sage was working very hard in different cleaning jobs. She promised herself that she would help Sage to stay off alcohol. She would reach out a hand to help her, especially with the law case. She thought that it was important for a child not to be raised in the household of the man who fathered her through rape.

She was determined to help Sage get Seleena back from Rogain Dimitrius and his wife. But she was worried about the success of the undertaking, because Seleena wanted to stay with her father, and at her age, she would have a say in the court proceedings.

Just thinking of Sage's life and her four daughters by four different men made Juniper Berry sigh. She was so grateful that she did not have a child with her husband. Now she was pregnant for the right man; for she felt without a doubt that Clifford was her soul-mate.

When she saw the effect she had on him, she simply relaxed and made sure that they got plenty of opportunities to be together and to see each other alone. It was all they needed: time to be together, so that they could live out what was obviously a strong-strong, soul-to-soul connection.

As time passed, Clifford became accustomed to seeing the vision. It occurred more often now, and it was becoming less jolting. Now, when it happened, he eased into it, actually enjoying it, strange though it was. Before long, he came to look forward to the experience, welcoming the warmth that came with it. After he had experienced the vision, he would feel very much at peace. If he was with Juniper Berry at the time, it would be enough to just hold her and rub her growing belly.

Lately, he felt more and more concern about finding his father. Eventually he approached his mother. Tentatively and despite her discomfort (he could see it in the way she wrinkled her brow and shifted her eyes away from his), he persisted in asking for an answer to his questions about his father.

She said that she did not know anything about his father; did not even know his last name. She only knew the name he told her the night they met: Robert. After much prodding from Clifford, she admitted that she was one of those girls who did not run from the sailors, but rather dressed to go on board the ship to meet them.

Clifford was not shaken by this revelation. In fact he had suspected as much; and over the years, he came to terms with the possibility that he might have been conceived as the result of a monetary transaction. His only concern was that now that he was going to have children, he wanted to know the health history of his father's side of the family. Now that he knew that information was closed to him, the full import of being a fatherless child hit him.

He always loved hearing the song "Sometimes I Feel Like a Motherless Child," especially Paul Robeson's rendition of it. He had always known in his gut, even as a child, that that song had special meaning for him. He had a loving mother, but his father was not only absent, but lost to him forever.

He vowed to be present in his children's lives, especially in the life of his son. He would provide him with the role model that he had not had in his own life, except from his grandfather.

He remembered a joke one of his classmates told when he was in grammar school. He was not able to laugh at the time, even though later he chuckled in private. Apparently, it really happened in the market and concerned two women who were cursing each other about some age-old conflict between them.

That morning in the market tempers flared to a great height. One woman who was holding a baby on her hip thrust the child into the arms of a woman standing in the crowd and said: "Hold this product-of-a-fuck, let me beat this woman!"

As his classmates laughed heartily, Clifford smiled and held his head down on his chest, pretending to be shaking with laughter. But he was almost in tears, thinking that that might be all he was: "a product of a fuck"; nothing more, nothing less. It was much later, when he was alone, that the sick humour made him chuckle despite himself.

It was from the day he heard the "product-of-a-fuck" story that he vowed to become financially successful. He decided that he would make sure that his mother wanted for nothing ever again. She would never have to sell her body to anyone, let alone some sailor passing through Antigua.

He wondered if the man who deposited his seed in his mother would remember her first name, just as she remembered his. He wanted to spare her any more shame. He no longer considered the way he was conceived a shameful thing, having long overcome the taunts of "sailor pickney" that he received as a child.

The spectre of marauding sailors was no longer a part of people's lives, and as time passed, the stigma receded to a distant place in Antiguan life.

He was at his office at his accounting firm when the call came: Reevah told him that Juniper Berry was in labour. He left his office in the capable hands of his accounting clerk and drove to the clinic. He got there just in time to put on a surgical robe and hold Juniper Berry's hand while Reevah, the nurse, and a doctor helped her to deliver the twins.

By now, they knew for sure that she was expecting twins, but they arrived much earlier than anyone anticipated. They even surprised the doctor.

The babies were big and healthy, with eyes that opened wide as soon as they were bathed and cleaned. They also looked much older than newborns and seemed to be aware of everything that was going on around them. Everyone in the clinic talked about the two babies who were born with their eyes wide open.

Clifford and Juniper Berry smiled secretively at each other whenever people spoke about their babies' being born looking so old and wise and with their eyes wide open. They knew that their children were special and had been with them before.

Clifford insisted that Juniper Berry marry him before they christened the babies. He told her that he thought it would be improper for them to be offering the babies up to God when they themselves were "living in sin."

Juniper Berry did not have those kinds of feelings, but she went along with Clifford. She knew that she would be with him forever and did not feel obliged to go through the formality of a marriage. Besides, she was not Christian any more, but she went along with it to please him.

She also thought about the consequences of her children suffering from the status of "bastard"; it was a term that still resided in the law books. She was persuaded more than anything by his reminder that in one of the visions he had had, there was a strong impression that they were unmarried. Clifford thought that this was a message suggesting that one of the things they ought to do differently in this incarnation was to be properly married.

"Loving this man must not be a hard thing to do. Loving this man must be an easy thing to do; so easy, that you just love him and don't mind that it takes a lot of hard work for a woman to love a man."

Juniper Berry was speaking to Sayshelle. She paused for a long time, as if she was mulling things over...wanting to speak precisely and truthfully. "I didn't really need to be married, but Clifford needed to be married. It was in his vision that the issue of marriage appeared; not in mine. In my vision, the message was to be softer; to pay attention to my children, not have them pulling at my skirts as I walked around my property. When I saw that vision, I felt the woman's annoyance at the children and the man; all demanding love of her, needing her to touch them and hold them; making them demand it of her, rather than giving it freely. So I chose to be with a man and to have children. And how I love them...how we love each other is important for the greatest outcomes in all four of our lives." She laughed and Sayshelle laughed with her. It was well-known in the family that Juniper Berry had not planned to have children. Yet here she was, the proud mother of two babies. It was a big change.

Juniper Berry said, "I am perfecting love, loving this man in this way, including having his children. It is not such a big thing to do." Then she looked closely at Sayshelle and said, "I would not accept some other things that I see some women accepting. I set my standards in the relationship, just as he sets his. I won't cheat on him and he won't cheat on me. I will love him well; so long as he loves me well. The day he becomes one of those doggish husbands that I see flying around Antigua, our marriage will be over."

Sayshelle had watched her Aunt Juniper Berry go through a metamorphosis. It was not just the transformation of her body as her pregnancy had advanced through to motherhood that had changed her; she had changed spiritually as well. She seemed to have acquired some deeper understanding of life that she was using to create a happy life for herself, Clifford, and the children.

Sayshelle knew that the babies were a source of delight and pleasure for Juniper Berry. She told Sayshelle that she thought that they looked at her and at Clifford as if they knew them. "When Clifford holds them, they settle into his arms, as if they had always been there," she said, her eyes shining with delight.

The babies had smiled early. Juniper Berry also told Sayshelle that very-very early, they made sounds that seemed like language while looking at her, smiling at her, as if they had known her for a long time. She was quite convinced that she had mothered these two children before; although she did not think that they were twins in that lifetime. Their arrival helped her to complete one part of the change in herself that she wanted to make. She stopped running long enough to make a home. "I am nesting," she said to Sayshelle. "And ain't nothing wrong with that; when you feel to nest, then you should nest."

Now that she had her own children, Juniper Berry thought often of her sister Sage and her children. She wondered what it must be like to live without your children; worse yet, to just give them up to strangers. She realized that for Sage, it was a kind of numb period in her life. Juniper Berry thought that now that it looked as if she was going to lose Seleena, it must be worse. And now too, she was sober.

Juniper Berry often tried to persuade Sage to go to court to fight for Seleena; but her sister was determined that when Seleena was ready, she would ask to come back to her. She said that that was the only way that Seleena would be happy living with her.

Sage's voice was full of pain as she told Juniper Berry: "I see it in her eyes; I felt it in her heart when I put my arms around her. She is too angry with me; and she is angry because she missed me so much, it hurt her so much. I think she is the one that missed me the most. No, I can't fight for her in court; it would not matter. She have to want to come back."

By the time she had said all of this, Sage was drenched in tears. It was the only time she cried, when she cried over losing Seleena. She was upset about losing her daughter and she missed her too; but most of all, she was angry that that awful man Rogain Dimitrius was raising her without any love.

She felt comfortable about his wife, though; it was a comfort to know that she was such a nice person. Sage could tell that she treated Seleena properly, even though she might not be capable of giving her the warmth and affection that she needed.

She was sure that Mrs. Dimitrius did not give her own daughters too much warmth and affection either. She did not seem like an unkind woman; she was just a reserved, cool woman. She wondered why she had ever married a man like Rogain Dimitrius.

Juniper Berry accepted Sage's decision about waiting for Seleena to come to her senses. That is how she saw it, as "coming to her senses," although Sage's perspective on it was from a much different space—a spiritual space. Sage viewed it as a journey of spirit that Seleena was undertaking—if she were to interrupt it, their relationship would suffer.

Juniper Berry just hoped that it would be before adulthood that Seleena would have the epiphany that would send her back to her mother's arms. As she sat talking with Sayshelle and playing with her babies, Juniper Berry had a clear-clear image of Seleena peering at her, with her eyes full of sadness and longing. Just as soon as she had the image of her niece, it was gone; she was left with a sense of alarm surrounding Seleena. She made a mental note to continue to encourage Sage to try to get her daughter out of the Dimitrius household.

She looked at Sayshelle to see if she had seen anything, but she was busy patting the back of one of the babies. Juniper Berry decided to say nothing.

Chapter Nine

These days, gone was the name "Rogain-Dimitrius-Child" from Seleena's lips. She now knew that she was less that than she was anything else. She felt her Mama Sage's essence flowing in her veins more strongly than anything. It was her Mama Sage's love that she held fast to in her memory. It helped her to look after herself.

She lived life as a daily struggle, but she endured it all in order to receive the material well-being and stability she craved. She felt like an old woman inside, even though she knew that she still looked like a child. Not that much time had passed, but it felt to her that she had lived a whole lifetime already.

Mrs. Dimitrius was a cool-cool person and Seleena did not feel close to her. Rogain Dimitrius was like an alien being to her, and her two sisters treated her like what her Mama Sage would have described as "a poor relation." She always used to say to her daughters: "Never let anybody treat you like a poor relation." School was her great saviour, and her teachers acted like they were her parents. Two of her teachers in particular paid close attention to her, encouraging her musical ability and her writing of poems, which they said were really songs.

Under the generous tutelage of the music teacher, Seleena learned to play the piano. She hugged the gift of music close to her in those times when she felt bad, when her life felt like more than she could bear. Those times came often now; more and more, she felt the loneliness of living with people who did not love her.

One day she found herself in the neighbourhood where her Mama Sage, her sisters, her aunt, and her cousin lived. She did not make a decision to go there; it was more like her feet just took her to Prince Klass Street.

For the past few days, it had rained heavy-heavy without stopping, and Seleena could feel the moisture under her skin. She wanted to watch the children in her Aunt Reevah and her mother's neighbourhood. She knew that they would be wading in the water overflowing from the gutter dividing Tanner Street in two.

She would stay far away from them so that no one would see her and call out to her. She wanted to see her Aunt Reevah's house. Even if all she did was just catch a glimpse of it, that would be enough. "Maybe I will even get to see Mama Sage and my sisters; or even just Mama Sage and Joyling," she thought.

In the two years that she had lived in her father's house, her Mama Sage and her sisters had visited her four times. Each time she sat uncomfortable in their presence, feeling like a stranger to them, just as they were strangers to her.

Only Joyling had felt like someone with whom she could still remember closeness. Her mother's touch was now such a fading memory that she sometimes wondered if she had invented it in her imagination, or from a desire for close touch.

Her childish memories receded: they were like a bundle of old clothes, covered over with dust, and reeking of camphor balls. It felt too painful even to allow her eyes to rest on them.

She was now accustomed to feeling her old life in that way. She smiled inwardly at how she thought about it: "my old life." She was a cat with nine lives, in the middle of living life number two.

Obeying the impulse to see all those whom she loved and held dear, Seleena let her feet guide her to Number One New Street, now renamed Prince Klass Street. As she turned onto the street and saw her Aunt Reevah's house, she became agitated. Her heart began to beat thump-thump in her chest so loudly that the fabric of the blouse of her light-blue school uniform moved up and down in accompaniment.

She felt a movement and a laughter inside as her heart made music with her blouse. She always heard everything in music—every feeling was a rhythm, every pain was orchestrated in notes cascading around her.

She knew that she was a vessel for the music she heard inside her. She felt it growing and growing, going through certain changes, arriving in the form of the music she played on the piano.

This day, as her feet moved her past her Aunt Reevah's house, her step beat a rhythm that kept time with the movement of her heart. As she walked, she said in a little whisper, with lips that barely moved, "In that house is my whole family."

She passed the house, grateful that no one was on the gallery or at the windows. She was disappointed, though, that she did not catch even a glimpse of her Mama Sage and Joyling.

As she walked, a memory flashed before her of a dog that her Mama Sage used to keep around her just before she went to live with Rommel. One day the dog (which her Mama Sage named "Dog") disappeared; they searched high and low for him to no avail. Then several weeks later, they looked up and saw Dog walking casually down the street.

He behaved as if his leaving and his return were nothing unusual. He thirstily gobbled up the water that her Mama Sage offered him, rested his head on his paws, and went to sleep.

The next day, a neighbour told her Mama Sage that she used to see Dog all the way in Parham. They could not believe that Dog made his way back home. "Like a homing pigeon," her Mama Sage said, shaking her head and laughing.

"That is what I am," Seleena thought wryly, "a homing pigeon." She rather liked the idea, for it sounded so stable, and mature, and knowing. She did not feel stable, or mature, or knowing; but it was good to think of how it would be if she could return to her family, just like a homing pigeon, just like Dog. Her Mama Sage would feed her, the way she fed Dog. And best of all, she would hold her and pat her head, rub her shoulders, and sing to her. She missed that most of all.

She felt that she had no home really; no place that she belonged in. She lost her place with her Mama Sage, and she never really found her place in the Dimitrius home. She was a poor relation, begging for food, clothing, and good schooling from this family that was not really her own.

She was proud that she never begged the Dimitrius family for love. She kept to herself, listening to the music inside that kept her happy. She noticed that when she paid attention to the music, her headaches went away almost completely.

Now as she walked past the house where her whole family lived, she felt the familiar ache creeping along the back of her head, making its way to the centre of her forehead. She knew its journey well. She focused on what she saw around her, trying to make the headache go away.

She longed for the familiar: the old neighbourhood where she played with all of the other children walking home from Girl School, Boy School, and Miss Davis School. She longed to experience with them the feeling of freedom as they waded in the water overflowing from the gutter that divided Tanner Street.

Her hurrying feet took her quickly back to Tanner Street. She felt as if she were racing with the headache that was threatening to overtake her. Finally, she stood under a big *stinking-toe* tree at the top of Tanner Street. She hoped that everyone would be too busy to notice her.

It was as it always is after the heavy rains: the street was full of children wading in the shallow water that overflowed from the big gutter. Seleena gazed longingly at them. She longed to take off her shoes and socks and play in the water with them, but she knew that she could not. She was no longer a part of them; she did not belong.

She watched them revelling in their carefree actions. They seemed so childlike; and inside, she did not feel at all like a child. Even if she could muster the courage to try to join the other children, there was the problem of her Mama Sage finding out that she came to the neighbourhood without going to see her.

Just then, she caught sight of her three sisters standing at the side of the street with her Mama Sage, her Aunt Reevah, and her cousin Sayshelle. She stared at them as they stood together. They held their shoes in their hands, their skirts hiked up above the knees, as they allowed the swirling water to go all the way up to their calves.

Seleena's eyes brimmed full with tears, and her heart felt as if it would burst. All of the despair of the two years of living without her family washed over her. She felt a rage burst inside her at the sight of her Mama's hands resting lovingly on the shoulders of her sisters.

As she watched, her Mama Sage's fingers caressed their heads and then returned to embrace their shoulders. Seleena felt a shiver run through her; it was as if a cold hand gripped her spine and squeezed it. She did not stop to think. Just as the feeling washed over her, so she moved with it. It felt to her that this was what she had come there to receive. Now she felt a little spark move gently, softly, in the small of her back, just between her shoulder blades. It moved her into action. She slipped off her shoes and socks and put them neatly together under the *stinking-toe* tree. Then she walked to the gutter and took two big steps into the rushing water. She did not try to maintain her balance, but allowed herself to be pulled in, along with the pieces of tree-bark, empty Coca-Cola cans, cigarette butts, ripe and unripe *ginneps*, *stinking-toe*, raspberries all torn prematurely from trees, pieces of old newspaper, leaves, blossoms, and dead tree branches.

The water washed her clean, and she was glad that she was now as fresh as a newborn baby. She noticed with a little thrill of surprise that she felt no fear. The past two years were washed away from her as she became soaked to her skin. The rushing, greyish gutter water enveloped her, embracing her in the way she longed to be held by her Mama Sage...all this time.

She sighed. It was not her Mama Sage's arms, but it would do. She relaxed even more, letting the water cover her over. She knew that she would reach the sea as dead as a door-nail, for she could not swim, and no one would be able to rescue her in such deep, gushing water.

Her head bobbed above the surface as she rushed past her whole family. She registered the horror of recognition in their eyes and was glad that her hair fanned out in two big plaits behind her. She knew that her Mama Sage would be the first one to know that it was her daughter, Seleena, just from seeing her hair.

She was right. The moment she caught sight of the long, reddish hair, Sage recognized Seleena. The plaits floated out around the small head atop the light-blue billowing fabric of her school uniform. Sage let out a wailing cry and rushed to the edge of the gutter, but it was too late; Seleena was being pushed farther and farther along.

Sage ran down the street screaming: "Seleena! Seleena! Seleena! Somebody help me, my child drowning! Seleena! Seleena!" For a moment, Seleena felt a great well of compassion rise up in her for the grief she could hear in Sage's voice. Then it was over. The water gushed up to cover her face for the last time. She felt her body pulled down deeper and deeper, to the bottom of the gutter. Two large pieces of tree trunk rolled on either side of her, wedging her in, hauling her down with them. Her school uniform got entangled in them and suddenly she was being pulled much faster towards the sea.

A great sigh of relief escaped from her, rippling out of her lips, as the water pulled her down the street. Seleena knew that soon she would no longer hear her Mama Sage's lament.

No one had seen Seleena wade into the gutter. It was only when Sage screamed that they saw the figure in the light-blue uniform. Joyling ran alongside her mother in the road, shouting "Seleena! Seleena! Come out a'the water! Come out a'the water! Swim, Seleena! Swim!"

She knew that Seleena could not swim. None of the children in the family ever learned how to swim. When they went to the beach, they just played on the sand where the waves met the shore.

The whole family ran alongside the gutter: Sage, Ruth and Naomi; then Reevah, Sayshelle and Joyling. The only members of the family who did not witness the drowning were Juniper Berry and Clifford. The heavy rains had kept them at home.

It was later that they found out that at the same time that Seleena was drowning, Juniper Berry had a flashing image of Seleena's haunted eyes peering into hers. It was an image that came to her three times in all, and she had acted on it, making a telephone call to Sage at Reevah's neighbour's house. When she got no answer, she wondered if they had all gone for a walk to Tanner Street. She relaxed then, thinking that she would speak to Sage the next day and see what new tactic they could take to try to bring Seleena back home.

None of the men who could swim wanted to risk trying to rescue Seleena. They rightly guessed that the speed of the water could drown a body, easy-easy. And that is how Sayshelle always thought of the way Seleena drowned: "easy-easy, while the whole neighbourhood and her family watched helplessly from the street."

Seleena had seemed to be neither struggling nor crying out. One moment her eyes were staring at them as her head bobbed above the water. The next thing they knew, she had disappeared altogether. After a moment, the only sign left of her presence in the water was the fabric of her light-blue school uniform billowing out around her as she floated out to the bay.

Sayshelle would always remember the way Seleena's school uniform hooked her to the tree trunks and carried her off. It was like some eerie, malfunctioning floating device; it helped her to drown, instead of rescuing her.

Chapter Ten

The rainy season came again and rain fell heavy-heavy for days on end. Big Pond, also known as West Pond (the people still called it both names), swelled the gutter to an even greater height than on the day of Seleena's drowning. Soon everything was washed clean-clean; and only memory knew that there was ever any rubbish in the gutter. It was in memory, too, that Sage could see Seleena lying calmly in this same greyish gushing water, rolling out of sight, and out of their lives.

During the rainy season, she walked to Tanner Street to look at the overflowing gutter. Sometimes she would stand as lonely and forlorn as the big *stinking-toe* tree, her eyes fastened on the rushing water. Other times she sat at the foot of the *stinking-toe* tree, the very spot where Seleena had carefully placed her shoes and socks.

It was days before the funeral that she had walked as if she had been led to that spot. And there, resting neatly under the tree, were Seleena's shoes and socks. She needed no one to tell her that they were Seleena's. She took it as a wonderful sign between her and her daughter, for there was no body to bury...nothing of Seleena from that last day; but here were her shoes and socks, nestled under the tree, waiting for her mother to claim them.

Early on the day of the memorial service, Sage buried the shoes at the site of the headstone. During the service, she planted a beautiful *snow-on-the-mountain* tree at a spot just above the headstone. She thought that it was the least she could do for her daughter; and it felt good for her too.

One day, after she had spent a whole afternoon looking at the water, she went to speak with Reevah. She said to her sister, as if they were continuing a conversation, "It is as if God wash the place clean-clean; and my little Seleena just get wash away with all the rubbish and the dirt. It is sad to know that she leave in that way...to just go in the water with all the dirt, and wash herself away to the sea." Then her tears fell.

Reevah thought that the tears, like the rain, were a blessing taking place in the Spirit. She said to Sage, "In truth, there is a special blessing in that kinda all-day, stop-and-start-again, heavy-and-light rain. It fall like that when Sayshelle born and it fall like that when Emmanuel died. And is so it fall for Seleena and continue until we bury her. It is as if God wash the place clean-clean, including our lives. That is all. The poor child just did what came to her Spirit. And now, we must let her go; mourn her and release her; say good-bye."

Earlier, Sage had refused to mourn her daughter, seeing her death not as a thing to grieve over but as a piece of life's journey, designed just for her. It felt to her that she would release her sadness by looking in the water. She wished that the feeling would go from her as quickly as Seleena rushed past in the gutter, but sometimes it was a constant companion.

Now this day, for the first time, she spoke to Reevah of Seleena's passing. Her sister held her as her tears came, glad that Sage was finally saying good-bye to this most beloved daughter.

Reevah came to think that Seleena's drowning changed Sage so completely that even her face was different. Her eyes moved to a deeper shade, and they seemed to glow, like two *flambeaux*.

The biggest change, though, was in her body. Reevah tried to explain it to Juniper Berry. She told her in a voice filled with wonder: "All the while that day, as the police were dredging the bay for Seleena's body, Sage had pain in her hip so 'til she could hardly walk. But soon after we have the service, that pain seem to leave her altogether. This time, it leave her as if it is a thing that she *will* her body to heal for good."

It was right after the memorial service for Seleena that Reevah noticed that Sage walked with a new upright stance. It was not like it used to be in all the years that she managed the pain. In those days, even after the pain would leave, Sage still carried the memory of it in her body; but now, it was different.

She had a spring in her step that Reevah never saw before. Her hip was so healed that she stood erect for the first time. She moved from being the same height as Reevah to towering over her by a good two inches. She was now almost as tall as Juniper Berry.

It seemed to Reevah that from the moment Sage sang the first hymn and threw that first sod at the foot of the headstone that marked Seleena's passing, she released some of her grief. The tears were just the final release.

It was as if through the act of symbolically burying this beloved daughter she came into some kind of revival. She had a new life to live, and she just seemed to pick herself up, clean-clean, and move forward.

Sage not only looked different, she *was* different. She became fiercely independent and got a job very quickly, cleaning three business places in the heart of town. She refused offers from Rogain Dimitrius to assist her financially; and she rejected his offers to help with the cost of Seleena's memorial service. She preferred to accept the money in a loan from her uncle who made the offer.

As a final act of exercising her own power over Seleena's life, she had put her own last name —Simeon—on the headstone at the gravesite. For she did not want her daughter to continue to be associated with the name "Dimitrius."

She shuddered when she thought of how proudly she used to let everyone know that she had a child with a Dimitrius. Now she was ashamed of the association; ashamed of what she had allowed to be done to her body for the sake of a few pennies, really. For she was never even paid properly by old Mr. Dimitrius for the work she did in his yard. He was always shaving money off her pay on a whim, deciding that the work was not done clean enough.

She muttered to herself, recalling how sometimes he even accused her of stealing his figs off his Arab fig-tree. Apparently he had Arab blood in him; so he brought this Arab fig-tree to Antigua. It was a real fig-tree, bearing real figs; different from the bananas that they had in Antigua that were also called "figs."

Sage recalled how she did not even like the fruit; he gave her a fig the first time the tree bore and she ate it in his presence because he insisted on it. She had pretended that she liked the taste, but of a truth, she had wished that she could have spat it out, there and then.

Sage even refused old Mrs. Dimitrius's offer of financial help, although she did so with much more grace than she managed with Rogain Dimitrius. She was not rude to him, but she felt herself tighten up inside whenever he tried to speak with her. She felt that it would take years for her to overcome those feelings.

She was grateful that he had the good sense not to approach her at the memorial service, although she saw him in the church and at the cemetery. In fact, the entire Dimitrius family attended Seleena's memorial service; they even provided the largest wreath.

Sage accepted their condolences with grace, knowing that they never rejected Seleena. In her heart, she sought forgiveness for them, for not having taken the time to give her daughter the love she so craved.

It came out after Seleena died that she went home at odd hours and Mrs. Dimitrius just assumed that she was at school playing the piano. Sage was sure that she would not be so careless with her own daughters. She found it strange that up to five o'clock, none of the Dimitrius family had been out looking for Seleena. It was her uncle who went to the Dimitrius house and informed Rogain Dimitrius and his wife that Seleena drowned in Tanner Street gutter.

Sage knew that forgiveness would arrive in her heart when she was ready. Her uncle wanted her to sue Rogain Dimitrius for wrongful death; but Sage felt that she had had enough of that man. She was not his judge; and she knew that she would not be able to touch any money that came from him.

For now, releasing the pain of the loss of Seleena took all of her attention. And besides, she had a feeling that the whole Dimitrius family needed to be loved and did not know how to give love to each other. So how could her poor daughter have got what she needed from them? She worked hard to forgive herself for not going to court to fight for Seleena—or simply grasping her and forcibly bringing her home to be with the rest of her family. She had done it the way she had thought best, and she had been wrong. Who knows what is right? No one...not even Sage; and she loved her daughter more than life itself.

It felt good to Sage when she could say: "I am wrong. I make a mistake and it cost me my daughter. Forgive me." She asked forgiveness of God daily. She did not know whom else to talk to. She felt so guilty in everyone's eyes; even those who cast no blame made her feel guilty, for their great love for her made her feel unworthy to receive it.

It was a hard-hard walk. And just like everything else in her life, she faced it squarely. It was her walk, after all. She started it all. This was no time to lay blame. She took responsibility.

The week after she cried for Seleena, Sage took the fathers of her other three children to court for child support. Her lawyer sent a letter to her ex-husband Junior Tobias to the address on a sympathy card that his parents had sent her from New York. She wrote them a note apologizing for having to involve them with such matters. They were always very kind to her and their granddaughter Joyling; so she did not want them to think that she was using them.

She also put an advertisement in the newspaper asking for "anyone with any knowledge of Junior Tobias, or his whereabouts" to contact her lawyer. Soon Junior phoned the lawyer from the U.S., and so he too was included in the court case.

The next thing Sage did was rent a house at the bottom of Prince Klass Street, just a few steps from Reevah's house. She cleaned it from top to bottom, painted all of the rooms, cleaned the yard, and planted a small flower and vegetable garden.

She piled the rubbish and dead leaves into a heap and was about to burn it when she suddenly remembered the bull-pestle. The same words that she heard when she was leaving Rommel popped into her head: "Take the bull-pestle with you and burn it."

As before, Sage obeyed the command. She went to Reevah's house and fetched the bull-pestle from the bottom of her suitcase. For the first time, she spoke about it to Reevah; and as the words tumbled out, the tears fell hot and scalding on her face.

Reevah held her as she cried and then went with her to her new house to help her burn the bull-pestle. It felt so right to burn it there in the yard of her new home. She stood with Reevah and threw the bull-pestle on top of the pile of dead things. As she lit the fire, her face flushed with a sudden rush of freedom and a great wave of relief. She was overcome by a feeling of exhilaration. She knew that she had now thoroughly cleaned her life.

When all was ready, Sage and her three daughters moved into the house. One room of the house was turned into a small child-care centre which Sage named "Seleena's Playhouse."

Reevah and Juniper Berry were relieved to see Sage come into her own. As they watched their sister speak about her child-care project, they felt the joy well up in their hearts. For they saw in her a vitality that had disappeared soon after the rum had taken hold of her.

Sage's voice sang with passion as she said: "It is to help me say I am sorry to Seleena for leaving her...not once, but twice." Within a few weeks, she was ready to receive her first charges: Juniper Berry's twins.

Book Two
Song of Sayshelle

Chapter One

Exactly two years to the day after the birth of Aunt Juniper Berry's twins, I received my landed immigrant papers for Canada. The application process had dragged on for a year, with pieces of paper dribbling back and forth between Antigua and Toronto. Then one hot-hot Monday morning, the post-woman opened the gate with her usual cheerful call-out to Mama Reevah. "Mistress Hughes! Mistress Hughes!" From my seat at the window, I could see a broad smile peeping out of the sweat dripping down her face. Mama Reevah knew the post-woman very well; and she had told her that we were waiting for "one last envelope."

I heard it in the post-woman's voice and could see from her smile that the last envelope had come! I leapt to my feet and bounded out of the house to meet her.

"Mama Reevah isn't home," I began. The post-woman did not let me get any further. She whispered conspiratorially, stringing the words together as if they were actually the name of the brown envelope she held out to me: "One-last-envelope is here."

Without knowing why, I whispered too. "Thank you."

She whispered again. "I will find out what is inside of the envelope tomorrow." Then she lowered her voice even more. "You don't want to let people know your business; that's why I am whispering. Don't turn your head too fast; but look up the road at the corner-house." And she shifted her eyes to the side, indicating that I should look up towards Cross Street.

I almost burst out laughing at the sight of Harty-Di, our neighbour from Montserrat. She was peeping at us from behind a slightly parted curtain at her window. I must have looked at her too directly, because she quickly moved back from view.

The post-woman didn't understand that the people on my street hardly ever bore malice or made mischief against each other. She also did not know that Harty-Di was one of the first people that we *would* tell my good news. Harty-Di just could not help herself from peeping; everyone peeped at everyone from behind closed curtains in Antigua. And according to Mama Reevah, the only time that peeping had hurt anybody on our street was when the policeman had used Harty-Di's house to peep at Papa Emmanuel working in the yard.

Besides, contrary to the post-woman's caution not to tell people my business, I wanted everyone to know the good news: I was going to Canada to live with my great-aunt Helen. It was exciting, thrilling news and I wanted to shout it from the rooftops.

After Papa Emmanuel died, his Aunt Helen, who lived in Toronto, had written to Mama Reevah and offered to sponsor me as an immigrant to Canada. She had suggested to Mama Reevah that I could later sponsor her; but that idea was not received with enthusiasm. Mama Reevah said that she had no intention of leaving Antigua in her "old age." Seeing the disappointment on my face she said, rather unconvincingly, that maybe she would think about the idea again later on.

We both knew that that was not really going to happen. Mama Reevah was now comfortably ensconced as an aide at Aunt Sage's daycare centre; and she was having the time of her life. It was a relief from doing domestic work and boarding the two policemen from Dominica. I could see her joy in the way she sang as she got dressed in her street clothes to go to work every day. She said that she got a lot of satisfaction from hearing the children learn their ABCs and from watching them play.

The daycare centre was going to become fully licensed and would move into larger premises as soon as Aunt Sage received her certificate. Mama Reevah was excited at the prospect. She had even begun speaking with a lady at the university's extra-mural campus about taking the same child-care certificate course as Aunt Sage. That way she would be able to work with the children and not just cook and clean up after them.

Mama Reevah immediately told Aunt Sage and Aunt Juniper Berry the good news of my landed immigrant papers for Canada. She invited them to come for lunch on Saturday to celebrate; and she cooked her usual *pepperpot and foongie* that she made every Saturday.

As soon as she entered the house, Aunt Juniper Berry took my face in her hands with rejoicing. She told me that she valued the experience of travel and was happy that I would be broadening my horizons. "I can't wait to see you walking to that plane," she said, hugging me close.

Aunt Sage was less expressive, although she too told me that she was glad that I was going to be able to "better" myself. She was a much quieter person than Aunt Juniper Berry, but I could see her joy at my news nonetheless. She told me that she was glad that she had got to know me so well of late. I had become very close to her and to my three cousins. I knew that I would miss Joyling in particular, as we spent a lot of time together. We promised that we would write to each other often.

Every time my aunts or Mama Reevah spoke of my emigrating to Canada, they said how good it was that I would be "bettering" myself.

They all described "bettering" myself as going to school and getting a good job; either in Canada or in Antigua, if things changed. It was only from Aunt Juniper Berry that I heard that to "better" myself meant "to grow in any way that you-yourself identify."

She made a point of telling me that I would experience a feeling of freedom from a lot of things and reminded me that it was important to remember that freedom was also freedom to do a lot of things. "Embrace as much as you are able," she said, looking into my eyes and holding me by the shoulders. I laughed inside, but I listened to what she had to say, for it made good sense to me.

As we discussed my travel arrangements, I realized that I already missed them. It also hit me like a punch in the belly that after this, I would be the only person making decisions for my life. Maybe Papa Emmanuel's Aunt Helen would take over the role of my aunts and Mama Reevah, but what of the space I was leaving in Antigua? Who would fill it? Would I be missed and replaced?

I was glad that Mama Reevah and Joyling lived so near to each other. Maybe Joyling would fill at least *some* of my space; then Mama Reevah would not miss me too much. She could plait Joyling's hair and tell her stories...different from the ones about Papa Emmanuel. Those stories were mine, to be stored up as Mama Reevah had handed them to me: dusted, aired out, and tied up again in blue ribbon for safe-keeping.

Except for the fact that I would miss my family, I wanted to leave Antigua: to see other places, meet people, go to school. I was looking forward to living in a place that was bigger than a small island. I had seen movies with street-lights and television and trains running underground and I thought that it would be wonderful to experience all of those things. In the movies, people hardly walked about; and they spoke to each other on the telephone. I could see myself living in a place like that.

I also wanted to go to school, although I had not decided what I would study. I just knew that I would study *something*; if only to make Mama Reevah and Papa Emmanuel proud of me. Mama Reevah said as much to me as we sorted out my clothes, deciding which ones would be too "tropical" and which ones would suit the more sombre mood of a place like Canada.

My beige, grey, black, brown and white clothes were considered "decent enough" for Toronto; all of my brightly flowered dresses were stored in Mama Reevah's trunk. "For when you come home on a holiday," she said. And it occurred to me for the first time that I would be coming and going, just like the tourists who came and went from Canada and America.

"You know, Sayshelle, from your father's point of view, higher education is everything. We did not get to go too far; but you will. Then if you decide to come back home to live, the government would not be able to pretend that you are not qualified for any job. When you are educated, even if they block you, your qualifications will make you able to get a job in private industry."

I heard her release me from feeling that I *had* to return to Antigua when I finished going to school.

I focused all of my energy on appearing strong and resolute with my family and with my friends. From the time I knew that I would be leaving, and we began to pack my clothes, I felt a constriction in my throat. My laughter sounded forced and high-pitched even to my own ears, and my speaking voice came out of my mouth in a hollow imitation of its true fullness.

In my voice was my heartache at the thought of leaving all whom I held dear. And I knew that everyone else around me felt the same way; but we all acted as if the upcoming separation came easily to us...as if our hearts were not breaking.

How would I breathe so far away from Papa Emmanuel's essence? I did not know if I could sustain that feeling all the way in Canada. Where would I find a place to put the agony of living so far away from the garden that Mama Reevah and I watched over so closely? And where would I look when I wanted to see Mama Reevah's face, outlined in the last slice of twilight? What would I do when I wanted to hear her talking to me, combing my hair, making my head ache from the tight-tight plaits?

During my last week in Antigua, I was like a pining lover in one of the romantic novels I used to read. I spent the time grieving over the separation that was to come; and my family's presence was as painful as the thought of their absence. I dreaded the upcoming parting so much that I was unable to be happy in the last moments with them and with Antigua.

I was sure that while I was in Canada I would yearn for a visit to Papa Emmanuel's grave and Seleena's grave. I would long to run my fingers over the lettering of their names while I spoke with them.

Mama Reevah and I had planted a *snow-on-the-mountain* tree at Papa Emmanuel's gravesite. It was from a cutting of the one that Aunt Sage had planted for Seleena. We kept it free of weeds and as if in gratitude, it matured into a large, spreading, thriving tree. It flowered at any given time, refusing to stay in concert with its family, intentionally defying their rhythm.

Whenever I looked at the abundant white flowers of the *snow-on-the-mountain* tree, I remembered Mama Reevah telling me of the blossoms on the pumpkin-vine announcing Papa Emmanuel's passing. It felt comforting to know that he had flowers with him all the time.

The last Sunday before I left Antigua, Mama Reevah and I visited Papa Emmanuel's and Seleena's graves. I watched people placing flowers on their loved ones' graves and wondered if they missed them in the way that I missed my loved ones.

A group of people who resembled each other were visiting a nearby grave. They were all crowded together, sitting on top of the gravestone of their loved one. A few of them sang hymns, while the others continued talking and laughing. The noise of their blended voices was like the clamour of a market. And yet it was something more: a feeling I had that they were intentionally raising their voices all at the same time. There was sadness; but no one was crying.

We watched them for a while, then Mama Reevah said, with a little tinge of criticism in her voice: "It sound as if they making a party for their loved one." And I understood then why I could hear the sound of forced merriment, even as the sadness was still moving in their throats.

I wondered if Papa Emmanuel wished us to make a party for him. Unlike the other family, we did not sit on the grave of *our* loved one. Mama Reevah said that it was not a good idea. "The stone is cold; and besides it is not respectful; we would be sitting on top of your father."

Although I readily accepted her decision, I felt that I was missing out on some important experience. I stood, as did she, at the head of the grave, right next to the *snow-on-the-mountain* tree; and we said a prayer for the repose of Papa Emmanuel's soul. As we stood and prayed, I wished I knew what secret ritual had crowded a whole family onto a small, cold slab of stone. Maybe they were anxious to make contact with their loved one. Or maybe they were sending their loved one warmth through their bodies.

I touched my fingers to the fine lettering on Papa Emmanuel's headstone, appreciating the simplicity of the white letters on the black background. Mama Reevah had chosen it, explaining that it reminded her of the classy look of the letters on her bottle of Chanel No. 5 perfume. She said that she used to wear that perfume whenever she was with Papa Emmanuel.

In loving memory of Emmanuel Livingston Hughes;
beloved husband of Reevah and father of Sayshelle
1898–1958

As I touched the inscription, I wished that I could see Papa Emmanuel's face just one more time...see his eyes light up as he smiled at me just one more time. A whisper formed itself on my lips: "I am going away Papa Emmanuel. I am going to make my life in Canada...going to see what I am to be. I will make you proud. As you always said: 'From my loins, I will be vindicated.' You will see the result of your labour in me Papa Emmanuel." I kissed my fingers and touched them to his name.

Mama Reevah took my hand and we walked to the spot in the cemetery where Seleena's time with us was recorded. It felt odd, knowing that she was not in the grave; but I spoke silently with her anyway, the way I always did. Although Aunt Sage had buried her shoes next to the *snow-on-the-mountain* tree, they could not take the place of a whole body.

I told Seleena how sorry I was that we had not rescued her in time. I asked her to forgive me for not helping her while she lived in her father's house. Too soon, it was time to leave. I whispered, "I bid you a fond farewell, Seleena."

Tears flowed freely down my face. I could not say good-bye to Seleena without crying. Every time I visited her grave, I left in tears; whereas with Papa Emmanuel, I would always leave with a feeling of peace. Visiting Seleena's grave brought sadness and a feeling that things were not completed. The fact that her body was somewhere else left an open space in my good-bye.

It always made me think of the song that I had learned in school: "Adieu, adieu, adieu...I can no longer stay with you; I will hang my heart on a weeping willow tree and may the world go well with thee." I would feel the tears well up in my throat at the way I had not had a chance to say "adieu" to Seleena.

Mama Reevah put her arm around my shoulders and it was then that I saw that she too was crying. We left the cemetery then, making sure that we brushed the graveyard dirt from our shoes before we began our walk home. Mama Reevah said that it would not do to take home a *jumbie* with us. She was meticulous about this. Just before we went inside the house, she insisted that we take off our shoes and hit the soles together, as a last safeguard against bringing a *jumbie* inside. Mama Reevah said that she did not even want Papa Emmanuel following us home. Then she laughed, saying, "It is enough that I meet him in my dreams."

On the walk home, my heart was full of memories of Seleena. Whenever I would see her at school, I used to wish that I could hold her hand. I would look at her longingly, putting all of my love for her in my eyes. I had not wanted the difference in the colour of our school uniforms—the knowledge that it was a great cost for my mother to send me to this school—to keep us apart. It was bad enough that she lived out of our neighbourhood, with people other than our family.

Her light-blue uniform made a statement of separation in terms of our station in life. My dark navy-blue jumper with its inner light-blue blouse and navy-blue bloomers, plus a slip, made for a heat-producing combination. Seleena's one-piece light-blue dress was much more appealing in the heat; but it was not available to me because of my dark skin colour.

Seleena and I would smile at each other when we met at school, and we would speak shyly about nothing in particular. I could see that she had become someone I hardly knew. Her eyes were different somehow. They held stories beyond her years, and they looked as if they were drowning in pain.

Her eyes always seemed to plead with me to allow this space between us. It was as if she was using them to say: "Please don't ask me any-thing...and please don't tell me to go back to live with my Mama Sage."

The look in her eyes reminded me of the one I had seen in the eyes of a dog that Aunt Sage had had years ago. When she first got him from a neighbour, his eyes had a wounded, broken look. Aunt Sage took him in and named him Dog. "Because," she said, "he has the eyes of a real dog: hurt and wounded."

Uncomfortable in our shyness, Seleena and I would part, saying an awkward good-bye, knowing that the next time would be the same. And this shy ritual of ours continued until her drowning.

I hoped that while I lived in Toronto her Spirit would visit me. I wondered if she would make the journey with me to help me to be strong. It was a feeling that came to me on the plane as I waved good-bye to the rest of my family; and it stayed with me during my settling-in period in Toronto.

Throughout the early time in Toronto, I held my family's songs close in my heart. It was the music of my departure and my arrival. I sang them all together: the songs of my mother, my aunts and my cousins. I sang them over and over again, until they melded into one litany...like the sonorous mass in the Anglican church of my upbringing. After a while, they shifted to an entirely different tone as they settled into a place of safe-keeping in my heart.

There was no longer a deep bass drum thumping out the familiar life-path and rhythm. There was no more sand, pliable under my feet; no more wild heart beating, marking time. Instead, I felt a *reverb* as I ricocheted from my life in Antigua to the unknown world of Toronto. And the jarring lasted, shaking my body and my soul for some time.

The first time I heard John Coltrane's music in Toronto, I understood at last what was going on inside my head and inside my heart. The bleat-bleat-bleat scream of his saxophone filled up the Colonial Tavern on Yonge Street.

I sat riveted to my seat; I could hear all that I wanted to say in his music. It contained my story and my journeying and my feelings and my heart's desires and just about everything! It contained my scream. It spoke my passion. It lit up the pain in my heart and replaced it with joy and hope and peace.

Coltrane stopped screaming so I could breathe, and he stopped for the silence, present even as the rhythm of the drum and the percussion went on beating in step with my heart. He noticed. He nodded. He smiled. I smiled. It was a moment of recognition of a way of hearing life.

The voices of my friends faded into the background as an epiphany lit up my body. His smile was an end-note to the music. It transported me to that last visit to Papa Emmanuel's grave, when I had listened to a family mourning in talk and in laughter. I heard them again through the sieve of Coltrane's horn. Their hearts had screamed just so, expressing meaning in percussive form. I understood at last that they had crowded onto the grave so that their bodies could make a grounding with their loved one.

I had watched them, filled with wonder at the creation of a painting with sound and sight. I had not known what to make of what I had seen; but it had mattered to me and I had stored it for safe-keeping in my heart. I retrieved it in the music of Coltrane.

Chapter Two

My great-aunt Helen was Papa Emmanuel's oldest surviving relative. She was someone I had never seen before; for she left Antigua in the 1920s to marry her childhood sweetheart. He had worked on a ship that sailed to Canada. One year he "jumped ship" and stayed in Montréal. Later, when he obtained immigrant status, he sent for his fiancée and married her. He had died several years before my arrival, and he and Aunt Helen had not had any children. I wondered if they had chosen to be childless, but could not ask Aunt Helen the question. It would have been considered rude to ask about such a private part of her life.

In the first months in Toronto, my head whirled with the books that Aunt Helen pressed on me. She found my knowledge lacking in the area of Black writers and things about Black people. She introduced me to all of her dog-eared copies of books by Frantz Fanon, W.E.B. Du Bois, Zora Neale Hurston, Langston Hughes, and C.L.R. James. Aunt Helen read everything that she could put her hands on by and about Black people; and she made sure that I did the same. In the evenings, we would curl up with books, or watch a show on television. It was not the same as my evenings with Mama Reevah, but it was close; and I enjoyed them.

During the week, I worked at a bank, having secured a job as a clerk, where I took down details of applications for loans. On weekends, I danced to calypso and ska and soul and funk music with the new friends I met in nightclubs and at parties.

The first friendship I made in Toronto was with the granddaughter of one of Aunt Helen's friends. She was my age, and was a school teacher and a very nice person. She told me a lot about the university system and the kinds of courses that I could take. And she introduced me to the night-clubs that she and her friends went to on weekends.

Although she was not from the Caribbean, she liked going to Caribbean nightclubs, as they were among the few places where she could meet groups of young Black people. We would dance until the wee hours of the morning and then make our way home to tumble into bed and sleep until late-late the next day.

We became a tightly knit group of friends and talked on the telephone in the evenings. I figured I was living like people lived in the movies; for I was talking to people on the phone instead of walking about. It was not as fascinating as I had thought it would be; in fact, it felt rather alienating and lonely. I missed my family and friends and glad noises and sun and twilight and the smell of the sea.

I tried to find the smell and sounds I longed for in the music of the voices, in the words and in the faces of the people from the Caribbean whom I met. A lot of women from the Caribbean had come to Toronto as domestic workers and had sent for their families later on. There were also many Caribbean nurses who had come from England. And there were others, like me, who had left high school and come to Canada as immigrants.

Their presence, like Aunt Helen's, eased my feelings of being un-grounded and dislocated from my centre. But I could not duplicate all that my heart longed to hear, all that my eyes yearned to see. I did have memories *longer than who* and I called back as much as I could from the corners where I stored them for safe-keeping. It was a way to manage newness, loneliness, the cold, and the blues that had begun to seep into my life and take up residence deep inside of me.

Some days, I felt as if my head was turned to Antigua at the same time that I had my eyes focused on Toronto. It was a kind of anguish I lived in: being in one place, with my heart in another. Sometimes I felt as if I was marking time, just hovering around in my life, not really present in it. I wondered if that was how Seleena had felt, living life away from those she loved and who loved her.

During the evenings when I went out with my friends, joy would grudgingly come to the top, pulling itself from among the ruins, the ashes of all of the feelings that were not bright and beautiful.

A few months after I arrived in Toronto, Aunt Helen became ill with a heart condition and complications of high blood pressure. She asked me if I would continue to live in her house and pay the same small rent that she had been charging me. She would move into an apartment in a fully serviced senior citizens' building, for she could no longer manage to look after herself in a three-storey house.

She asked only that I not bring anyone to live in her house, as she had never considered having tenants. That was what she said; but underneath it I heard a warning not to take a boyfriend to live with me. Aunt Helen was very prim and proper and it would have been against her principles to have that kind of living arrangement going on in her house, whether she was living in it or not.

I tried to convince her that we could manage by finding someone who would take care of her during the day while I was at work. Aunt Helen would not hear of it. She did not want to deal with a person in her home all day, she said; that was too risky.

"And besides," she said, "there are activities at the seniors' apartment building; and there are other people my age to talk with and play cards. There are trips here and there; and to tell you the truth, I would enjoy those trips. They go to lunchtime plays and sometimes to hear a speaker and so on. It sounds good; I checked it out a few years ago. It is a very well-run apartment building."

I had thought that she was putting herself into a "home," but the building she described was not a "home." She would have her own apartment, with a kitchen and bathroom, and she would have the choice of eating meals in a common dining room. This arrangement sounded more acceptable than a "home." It had been a shock to me to discover that people in Canada did not always look after their elderly relatives. Some of them shunted them off to a "home" as soon as they became old.

I gave up trying to talk Aunt Helen out of her decision to move to a senior citizens' building. I believe that she worried about being a burden to me and I tried to make her understand that I did not see her that way. Finally, I accepted the offer she made and thanked her from the bottom of my heart for her generosity. My salary barely allowed me to pay the rent she charged me and provide my other very simple needs, since I was also trying to save money to go to school. It would have been a great hardship to suddenly be confronted with regular apartment rent.

Aunt Helen in turn thanked me for being in Toronto at the right time to be a companion to her. I loved her company. Sometimes we talked for hours and hours; or rather, Aunt Helen talked and I listened, for she was full of stories about how things had been for her when she first came to live in Canada.

She and her husband had lived first in Montréal and then moved to Toronto after they retired. He had been a builder and Aunt Helen had been a school teacher. She had gone to school and received her teaching certificate soon after she came to Canada. At first she had worked as a scullery maid in a big mansion for a rich white family in Montréal. Then she had saved for the fees to go to school.

She told me that she had not realized that people still engaged scullery maids. She had thought that it was only in the novels she read that such a job existed. "And 'scullery' it was too, child. I worked in the pantry."

At my surprised look she said: "Oh yes my dear; there was a pantry and that is where I worked, day in and day out. I polished the silver and I set the table and I made sure that the trays of food were filled...and...you know, took a damp cloth and kept the gravy spills from the edges."

There was a thoughtful look on her face. "You know, I would never hire people to look after my whole life like that. I would feel so babyish. Those people could not even boil water to save their life." She laughed a deep, infectious belly-laugh that made me laugh too.

They had had friends in Toronto then, Aunt Helen and her husband. She told me in a sad little voice: "Most of them are all gone now." Some had gone home to the Caribbean, others like Aunt Helen had stayed and experienced a great loneliness. Most of their relatives were in the Caribbean, in other North American cities, or in England.

When I first arrived, Aunt Helen told me that she had two Black women friends who were born and bred in Toronto. I thought that she meant that they were black-*skinned*. I was surprised, when I met her friends, to see that one of them was brown-brown, and the other was light-skinned. I was reminded that in Canada, "Black" was the word that was used to refer to all who looked like me, regardless of the shade of their skin.

In Antigua, there had been white people and there had been all of us. I never knew that I was Black. This realization was what had prompted Aunt Helen to assail me with books about who I was; so that I would see myself as a member of a group larger than just my family. My head and heart had to stretch to accommodate this new group identification and membership.

Aunt Helen and her two friends got together once a week for breakfast at Fran's Restaurant at St. Clair and Yonge. "We talk over old times and laugh and cry in our coffee," Aunt Helen laughingly told me. She invited me to join them each week; but I felt that I would have been intruding to go every time. I went once soon after I arrived, just so Aunt Helen could show me off to her friends.

It felt like a kind of old ladies' show-and-tell. Her friends showed me pictures of their grandchildren and their great-grandchildren; and they asked me questions about my goals. Those were tricky questions to answer, but I repeated some of the things that Mama Reevah and my aunts had said about going to school and finding a good job, and bettering myself. It must have been the right thing to say, because Aunt Helen's friends nodded approvingly; and Aunt Helen looked pleased and proud.

After Aunt Helen moved into the seniors' apartment building, I visited her one evening during the week and every Sunday. And Saturday was a permanent, well-rehearsed arrangement with us. We went to Kensington Market and sought out the ingredients to make Antiguan *pepperpot and foongie*. Then we cooked the *pepperpot and foongie* in the tiny kitchen in Aunt Helen's new apartment or at her house; and we ate, seated on the couch in the living room, while we watched television.

The first time she came back to her house, I watched Aunt Helen walk around the living room, touching everything, as if she was greeting her things. I suggested to her that she take more of the figurines and pictures off the wall, even if they cluttered her new apartment. "You can put them in a cupboard and then sometimes change the ones you keep out," I suggested. She welcomed the idea; and I realized just how hard it was for her to be away from all of her memories.

After that, I made sure that we spent more Saturdays at her house than we did at her apartment. Sometimes Aunt Helen would stay with me for the entire weekend.

Whether we spent Saturdays at Aunt Helen's apartment or at her house, we followed the same routine. We ate our dinner sitting on the couch with trays perched precariously on our laps. While we ate, we watched *Soul Train* on the old television set that looked like a piece of antique furniture. It was encased in an oak cabinet with elegantly carved legs. Its black-and-white picture was clear as day and Aunt Helen took pride in it, saying that she had no intention of getting a colour television set.

When the dance segment of the show began, Aunt Helen would say in a voice filled with consternation: "But these people don't have no bones in they body!" She said it every time with the same degree of incredulity. And I laughed every time.

The Saturday *pepperpot and foongie* ritual was something Aunt Helen had always done; ever since she came to Canada in the 1920s. She had roped me into doing it with her as soon as I arrived in Toronto, saying that I made her feel connected to Antigua.

Aunt Helen told me that when she was growing up, she and her mother used to go to the market every Saturday morning and buy the ingredients for *pepperpot and foongie*. Then they would return home, cook the *pepperpot and foongie* and serve it to the whole family. It was the same kind of Saturday that I was accustomed to having with Mama Reevah; and so I found it comforting to have it recreated, without fail, every single week.

I used to wish that Aunt Helen's memory of my Papa Emmanuel had not been so fleeting. She had *some* memory of him; but more than forty years had passed and she had never returned to Antigua for a visit. When I told Aunt Helen that I wished there had been more of my Papa Emmanuel in her memory, she patted my hand and said: "I wish so too child. I wish so too."

Were it not for Aunt Helen, those first immigrant-months in Canada would have been like living Seleena's life, a life lived away from love. I was a shy-shy girl and spent more than a healthy amount of my spare time pining for my family. While I had made quite a few friends, friends could not replace a person from my family who knew me and loved me for me.

When Aunt Helen died, I felt a sense of desolation that I could not explain to anyone. Friends asked how it was that I felt so connected, so close to someone whom I had only known for a short time. I shook my head, unable to explain the enormity of my sense of loss.

Aunt Helen left me all of her life's savings, as well as the house and all its contents. I was so overwhelmed at the reading of the will that I stumbled out of the lawyer's office onto the sidewalk, my eyes filled with tears.

I thanked Aunt Helen in my heart; but I would rather have had her with me. I wished that she had told me about the contents of her will, so that I could have thanked her properly for being so good to me. I knew, however, that given what I had seen of her generous spirit, she would not have wanted to hear my thanks.

I buried Aunt Helen in a gravesite in Mount Pleasant Cemetery with a headstone that carried her particulars. I asked for the lettering to be the same as that which Mama Reevah had chosen for Papa Emmanuel. I wished for a *snow-on-the-mountain* tree that I could plant, but there were none in Canada. Aunt Helen would have liked that reminder of Antigua. She would have to be satisfied with my second choice: a beautiful silver birch tree.

It had intrigued me to learn from Aunt Helen that the silver birch tree, which looked so serene, could wreak havoc with its roots. She told me of a neighbour who had to repair the foundation of her house when a silver birch tree damaged the concrete structures in its path, deep underneath the soil. Aunt Helen said that she had always wanted a silver birch in her front yard, but her friend's experience had stopped her in good time. Now she would have one with her throughout eternity.

I chose a gravesite that faced the traffic, because I thought that Aunt Helen would have liked that; she enjoyed activity and action. She liked peaceful nights too, and each evening, when the traffic eased, there would be peace and quiet. But her days would be filled with the hustle and bustle of the cross-town traffic on Mount Pleasant Road.

As I left the cemetery, I remembered how I had delighted in watching Aunt Helen as she danced a few halting steps with me. She had often played calypsos on her decrepit record-player. Its needle was so old that it sounded like a nail scratching on the vinyl; but Aunt Helen did not care. So long as she heard the words of Sparrow and Kitchener and Melody, that was sufficient for her. They were the three calypsonians she remembered from her young days and she had quite a few of their albums. She would sing along lustily as we danced: "The creature from the black lagoon is your father!"

Lord Melody was the calypsonian she liked best of all, "because his voice is raucous and he tells it like it is," she said. She believed that the way he told it was exactly how Black people felt about their own colour and their big noses and thick lips.

Whenever we danced to Lord Melody's last chorus of "The Creature From the Black Lagoon is Your Father," Aunt Helen would drop into a chair, saying, "That is for you young people." I would smile as I continued dancing; for I understood that it was her invitation to me to entertain her with my dancing. I knew that she liked to watch me dance and it was easy to oblige her, because I loved to dance. I enjoyed hearing the music that used to ring in my ears and my heart day in and day out in Antigua.

I had danced a lot in Antigua. Mama Reevah was not partial to dancing; Papa Emmanuel used to try and drag her up whenever there was a calypso on the radio, but she would pull away from him, saying, "Emmanuel, you know I don't like to dance. Teach Sayshelle to dance." He would pull me up then, and teach me the intricate steps that he used to do when he went to dance-halls. I would dance with him, happily watching as he twirled and twisted and swung his waist.

I missed Aunt Helen very badly and thought that it would help me to continue our Saturday *pepperpot and foongie* ritual. The trip to Kensington Market without her was wrenching. However, I returned home and resolutely recreated the *pepperpot and foongie*; but the food tasted bad in my mouth. It had lost its joy without Aunt Helen's company.

I turned on the television set and tried to watch the *Soul Train* dancers. They looked ordinary now; without Aunt Helen's voice commenting, all the magic of their contortions was gone. I said her words out loud: "But these people don't have no bones in they body!" And I laughed for the first time since the funeral. I got to my feet and danced with the

Soul Train dancers. I could almost hear Aunt Helen say: "But you don't have no bones in your body!"

Chapter Three

Months passed into years, and still there were moments when a great longing for Aunt Helen would take me over. It would suck my breath away, leaving me gasping for air. A longing for her essence and her presence would arrive with a sound, or a memory, or the smell of something that she had liked. *Florida Water*; or *Lavender Water*; or English pork sausages sizzling in a frying pan; eggs waiting on the side. It would come too with the sight of large slivers of rind in orange marmalade; and on days when the rain came "non-stop," as the weatherman said.

One such rainy day, I went outside, just to smell the air and look at the clean-clean plants and the leaves that had been washed off of the trees. I said good-bye to Aunt Helen in a more final way than I had ever done; for the rain had stopped...and everything was new...and fresh...and washed clean.

There was no gutter overflowing into the street in which to dabble my feet after the rain, so I satisfied myself with walking through the Humewood neighbourhood that was my home. All around me, I saw other people who looked as if they were having some version of my experience. They had said good-bye until eternity and were as far away from their families as I was.

They too sought ways to live without their Mama Reevahs; their Papa Emmanuels; their aunts, cousins, families; their navel-strings buried under a backyard tree without so much as a by-your-leave. Like Aunt Helen, they faced being buried here, far away from the land and the sea and the sounds that they held close in their hearts...still, after so much time.

The snow falling in the middle of winter gave me that same feeling that everything was being cleansed. The sun made little highlights on the top of the waist-high snowbanks along both sides of St. Clair Avenue. It was a pretty picture, and reminded me of the Christmas cards that Mama Reevah used to hang on a string across the bookshelf in our drawing room. When the time came, I too hung Christmas cards across a bookshelf in the drawing room of Aunt Helen's house. It was one of the things I did to keep my Mama Reevah's essence close. It took some effort to remember that in Toronto, there was a "living room" and not a "drawing room."

Mama Reevah's essence came in letters every week. I loved receiving her letters. She wrote joyfully of familiar things, and of political events that saddened me. "There are accusations of corruption in government, accusations of corruption in the elections. Things are worse than your Papa Emmanuel could have ever imagined. I am so glad that you are over there in Canada, away from it all. Your father would have been happy to know that you are making a good life for yourself somewhere else, instead of being trapped here and prevented from advancing in your life." I did not want her to worry about me. She had had enough worry in her life, I figured. I turned my eyes to Toronto and looked toward trying to make a life for myself.

The Toronto of my dreams was sweet-sweet and soft-soft: feeding squirrels in the park, resting easy in my mind, working hard by day and at peace at night, welcomed in society and offered equality. The Toronto of my immigrant-life was a different reality. In this-here space, in this-here place and in this-here time, I struggled to breathe, and I walked my own ground with my head held down, my chin on my chest.

I felt a relentless fear taking hold inside me that I would never catch my breath if I let it out. For white people would snap it up and prevent me from *being*. I could see their intent lurking in their eyes; especially when the headlines screamed of Black people in the U.S. demanding equality in all areas of life. I could feel them breathing in and out, wondering: "When will they do it here?"

It was present, too, in the way they sidled away from me in the subway trains, on streetcars, on buses, in supermarkets. I joked with friends that it was great that no one sat next to us on the subway; we got two whole seats to ourselves.

Toronto moved through my life, drying and hardening into my bones. I felt crisp and petrified, like moths and mosquitoes stuck on a kitchen door screen.

I thought of how women like me were still running home from the attack of men who were not like me. I thought of "sailor-pickneys" in Antigua, doomed for life to bear the mark of the scandal of their mothers. And I winced at the numerous men like me whom I saw in Toronto rushing headlong, seeking women who were not like me. There would soon be many "pickneys" of another hue. I wondered what Canada would look like in a hundred years.

When night came, I hurried home, away from the Toronto streets, for none of my friends had cars. We were too newly arrived, my friends and I, to do more than submit to the discomfort of stares on public transportation.

The rain came as I walked and dreamed Toronto. My feet were damp at the ankles, despite two pairs of thick socks and lined knee-high boots. In the wetness of the streets, the lamp-light shone brightly on the puddles, so I could avoid them. But instead of walking around their ragged circle, I stepped over them, consciously breaking my Mama Reevah's taboo:

"Don't step over water at a cross-roads. Evil people throw out their sickness at the cross-roads. It could be somebody's dead-water; or worse yet, their sore-foot water; or even worse still: their throw-way-pickney water. Then for sure, your insides going need to be cleaned from all their sickness."

In the shimmering water I saw grotesque images of the silenced candle-flies and mosquitoes, smashed against mesh screens. All life was dead and gone from them, except for the fear. The fear was preserved forever.

Wanting to prove to myself that I had evolved from the prohibitions of my growing-up, I pretended that I did not know that in big-city life people do not go to the cross-roads to throw their sickness onto the street. I pushed away the knowledge that no one looks after their sickness at home in this new place. I let myself act as if I had forgotten that everyone has running water in their homes; so that bath-pans filled with sickness are things of the past.

I did not miss the closeness of sickness that I had experienced in Antigua. It had filled up my nostrils and my senses in childhood. Besides Papa Emmanuel's time of sickness, I still held a disturbing memory from when I was very small, of the scent of the antiseptic in Granny's dead-water. Despite myself, I had listened for the drip-drip sound of the drops of dead-water falling into aluminium buckets placed strategically around the dead-board. The ice was an attempt to preserve her body. I would walk past her room with my head averted at least twice each day: once in the morning to leave my bedroom, and once at night to go to sleep.

Her body waited for people to arrive to see it before the minister would sing hymns and make a sermon and speak of our loved one. I had made sure that I did not see her body laid out in the coffin in church. And I resented those who walked past the coffin and made comments under their hands; as if they thought that we really could not hear them.

"But she look good-ee? Like say she just sleeping. Is how old she is? They write her age on the programme? Is how come she look so *likkle* an' shrivel-up? They shrink her, or she shrink by herself? Her shroud look good-ee? I wonder if is Mistress Hughes make it, or if she did give it out?"

These people who viewed Granny, all beautiful in her silk-lined casket, had not seen life through her eyes: cold, with a pin-point of blue at the centre of the blackness. They could afford to enjoy the tableau of the white shroud on white saint, the arranged smile, the silken, blue-black hair, serene, not a strand out of place. And all was dry.

In Granny's day, unlike in Papa Emmanuel's, there were no funeral homes to prepare loved ones for burial. Working silently, women removed bucketfuls of dead-water...reeking of antiseptic. They were careful not to spill the dead-water on the inside of the house, for that would have required scrubbing the floor even more carefully afterwards. And there was still the bedding to be burned.

The women did not take Granny's dead-water out to the cross-roads. They simply tipped it over into the trench leading out of the yard, and the water ran to meet the green slime in the gutter-water in the street. Then Mama Reevah threw bucket after bucket of fresh water behind Granny's dead-water. She stood on the back step and looked behind it as it was washed away from our lives.

As I stepped over a puddle in a Toronto street, I felt a little tug of fear, a moment of unease at what I had done. Shaking off years of memory, I boldly loosened the hold of Mama Reevah's words. I felt as if I lost something precious as I broke the sacred taboo. For I liked the mystical nature of it; liked knowing that I had been handed something. It had been passed on with as much seriousness as the ritual of my Anglican confirmation.

Life in Toronto did not exactly smack me in the face in the way moths and mosquitoes slammed into a screen door, but it did not exactly embrace me either. I felt that it was more correct to say that life had taken me over, chewed me up and spat me out in small pieces. All of my pieces felt as if they were being stuck back together in the wrong places.

I did not write that in my letters to Mama Reevah for fear that she would think me crazy. And maybe she would be disappointed that I was not full of glowing reports of a life being well-lived with enjoyment and peace. I wrote long-long letters that said in small emotions: "I miss you."

I still desperately missed Aunt Helen; and I still excluded that fact from my letters to Mama Reevah, and from my letters to Aunt Juniper Berry and Aunt Sage. I wrote lovely little letters to my three cousins. And at night I cried, missing them all so much that my belly hurt, right where my navel-string would have connected me with them. I remembered that I had left my navel-string buried under a tree in the yard and had not even said good-bye.

I worked at my job; I did household chores; I spoke to people who spoke to me; I did things that seemed necessary to enable the rest of my day and my life. I lived uneventfully from day to day, taking up space, marking time, like the bark of some weathered tree. At the end of each season, I was like the aged tree: still standing, no taller, and yet much more come-of-age in the space and time that I occupied. It was a narrow existence.

I did not notice just when it was that the sound of the song of my family moved itself to a more distant place inside me. When I reached to embrace it, there were only faint strains playing in the distance. I feared that eventually the song would leave my heart altogether. I also knew that I would need to hear it again; when things changed; when time passed; and when my ears were clear of the clutter that I had allowed to take over.

All things moved through me in a slow, jangling kind of passage. It seemed sometimes that the descant of my life was heard through grooves that were etched long-long ago. Although joy was a constant hum in the foreground, there were many yesterdays in the background marked by tears and sorrow.

I dared not make prognostications for the future, but I knew that there was a cool-cool spot awaiting me. In that place, flames would take me breathless by the hand and clear the way through my heart's bad-lands. I asked myself if it was worth the promise of treasure waiting under the covers of the cool-cool forest and the rushes.

The answer was clear: through streams of pure heart's desire, tempered by truth, I would find that cool-cool spot, untouched by human hand; caressed only by soft breezes. The promise of the taste of the joy that would come made me breathless.

Days slipped into nights as gently as the spinach leaves showed themselves in the mornings in Antigua. Nighttime would close with just a few leaves curled on the vine. Then morningtime would arrive and reveal four leaves unfurled, fresh as the new day; a drop of dew nesting here and there, testimony to freshness.

As my Toronto-days drifted into months, then into years, tears became the hallmark of the quality of my life. I cried rivers of tears; they fell on me and around me. There was no gutter to catch them; they overflowed and washed the street.

I consoled myself with the thought that time was a material construct. Observed, it offered only limitations, frustrations, and even hope-lessness. Spirit, on the other hand, was ethereal. Acknowledged, it brought freedom, liberation, celebration of moments that appeared tem-poral. In essence, Spirit's markings were far more permanent than the limitations that time sought to impose.

I came to see that Toronto made my Spirit poor. I did not want to be who I used to be. I found myself struggling to remember the girl I was, the girl who was hurtled into Toronto-life; chilled to the bone in winter; overheated in summer; unable to fully embrace springtime; devastated by the fall.

I searched in the people around me for all that I knew as normal from my growing-up in Antigua. My Mama Reevah's song, my family's song; both grew more and more elusive. Not even memories of Saturdays spent with Aunt Helen's *pepperpot* and *Soul Train* eased my heart. The essence of my life had been inexorably changed; it was forever divided into two halves: "before I left Antigua" and "after I came to Toronto." It was as simple as that.

My life had other defining moments, but none could compare to the hollow in my heart that had been made by immigration. I told myself that that was what it was: a big hole that nothing would ever fill up again; no love, no hatred...nothing could fill the space that leaving Antigua had made...nothing.

Chapter Four

I had witnessed the disruption that change can cause in a person's life and I was frightened. It seemed that the only way to deal with change was to change myself to accommodate to the newness. But I was not prepared for so much change. I could not yet manage the leap from being Antiguan-Sayshelle to being a member of a group of people who looked like me. Black-Sayshelle. The space in which I knew myself was a space where all that I was could be found in those from whom I came. Now my life was leading me away from the closeness of these stories, and it was painful. Nothing had arrived to sufficiently fill the empty space they left inside me. Then the Black Power Movement was upon me and I was forced to understand the notion of *blackness*.

Two policemen shot a man in Toronto as he knelt inside his house under the watchful eyes of his two little daughters, aged nine and eleven. Black people in the U.S. had been killed and were being killed because they were Black and because of the Black Power Movement. But this man in Toronto had been killed just *because* he was Black, everyone felt; he had not even joined a protest movement. He had simply waved a garden tool and shouted in his own house.

I felt as if *they* had come for me and I was not ready! I could easily have been that man, kneeling at the bottom of my stairs, holding my garden shears, shouting, being shot. My heart hurt. For the first time, I felt moved to march and protest about something.

The Staple Singers' "I'll Take You There" helped me to cope. "*I know a place, where ain't nobody dying...ain't nobody worried...ain't no crying faces...*" The words made my heart sing just as deeply as when I had felt James Brown shouting deep in my belly: "*Say it loud: I'm Black and I'm Proud!*" His words spoke directly to me:

> *I say we don't quit moving, until we get what we deserve.*
> *We'd rather die on our feet, than keep living on our knees.*

I could relate to this much more than to Chubby Checker's "Let's twist again, like we did last Summer!" The Supremes filled in some gaps and the Jackson Five burst onto the stage. They did not ease my pain, but they entertained my feet. Music fed me in those days; I listened to music as sustenance for my soul. And I continued to read books that opened up my mind.

At the Town Tavern on Yonge Street, Thelonious Monk made everyone listen to him while wearing his hat. He would leave if ice clinked too loudly, or if conversation drowned out his heart's notes on the piano. And King Curtis made us dance in our seats at Le Coq d'Or until we finally stumbled out onto Yonge Street with daylight to spare on a Saturday afternoon. They were enough; and if they were not, there were many, many more.

The Temptations sang about how *"The only person talking about love my brother is the preacher...The only person interested in learning is the teacher."* The words hit me in the gut. I bought the record and listened to it over and over. At one point, I felt it became a substitute for Mama Reevah's voice, for it resonated so much with her way of looking at life.

I wanted to spin around and create another focus, the way Mama Reevah had wanted for Papa Emmanuel. I wanted to look at the extraordinary things that ordinary people had done and were doing, instead of focusing on the despair that was falling all around me. That was the way Papa Emmanuel had lived and it was not what I chose for my life.

I told myself that we were not all made of the stuff that wars called for. The force that the white establishment unleashed against Black people in the U.S. was more like a genocide than a war. The Black Panthers' headquarters was under surveillance and had been riddled with bullets. Those Panthers who were not killed were arrested. People demonstrating for the right to vote were sprayed with fire hoses and spat on. And some if not all of this was carried out by the forces of the state.

Some of my friends watched this war and filled their hearts and their tongues with it. I realized that I was not prepared to fight to the bitter end like Papa Emmanuel, my hair grown long on my head in protest, my comrades in arms, dead around me.

There seemed to be more jail cells and bullets for martyrs than I had the stomach to manage. I went to community gatherings and I listened to what was being said. I volunteered in community projects. I focused on my job in the bank. I went to school at night during the week; and on weekends, I went out with my friends and danced.

Being a part of the Movement would have been the natural thing for me to do, as natural as my parents' engagement in Antiguan politics. But my heart beat to a softer drum than that. I collected newspaper clippings about Black people in the U.S., in Toronto, Halifax, and Montréal. Beaten. Assassinated. Arrested. Threatened. Killed. Spied on. Spat on. Lied to. Hiding. Invaded. On trial. Jailed. Tired.

It was becoming impossible to have a community meeting, or a rally, or a celebration, without being watched by the RCMP or the CIA, or a combination of both. In one instance, a white man rented a house opposite a Black community centre and spent his time watching us as we came and went. We couldn't see a camera, but we could see a shadowy figure camouflaged behind a curtain.

I was glad that I did not have a car because the police delighted in stopping Black drivers, especially Black men. A friend of mine had even been stopped one night walking home and was asked to produce a piece of identification with proof of his address. Another friend was picked up while jogging one evening. When the police asked for his identification, he pointed out that he was wearing shorts and a t-shirt and had no pockets. He was only two streets away from his apartment, but he was taken to the police station and locked up until his wife arrived with his driver's license and his passport.

These things fired the spirit of revolt in me in a personal way. I felt frustration and a lack of real power. As more martyrs fell to the brute force exercised against them in the U.S., people just seemed to go inside their houses and close their doors.

I felt as if the Movement went to some place where I could not even see its pulse beating softly, gently, like a heart under skin. It was as if weariness from harassment took hold of its very centre and stopped its pulse some place within; some place where the martyrs were forgotten and cultural icons and heroes and heroines shifted in perspective. And sometimes, the media and the market would hype them back into recognition, as a commodity, as icons; with everything from handbags to umbrellas made of Royal Kente cloth.

Then, as suddenly as the storm of voices was raised in anger and heat, shouting down Jericho's very walls, so it rapidly turned to a calm numbness. A fire scorched the land, but had been quickly burned out; lashed into submission by repression, making for a great shift into the numbness of daily life. It was like switching from John Coltrane to Duke Ellington. A smooth ride on the black and white keys of the oh-so-cool-A-Train numbing the strident reach of Coltrane's horn.

Chapter Five

It was at the tail-end of the Black Power Movement that I met Cicero Finley.

One night, walking home, I was contemplating the idea that I was ready to love someone. It was not a hunger that I had, but it was a strong feeling that it was time. I was lonely. I lived in a house by myself and I did not have to play by Aunt Helen's rules. But I did not want to just live with someone; I wanted to get married.

I was enjoying walking in the rain, my head bent low, reading pictures dancing in the puddles. Each raindrop fell with a rhythm, making music, creating a pulse beating in the centre of the water.

My steps slowed as I watched the raindrops rippling out gently from the pin-point centre in the puddles. My wistful longing to love a man properly and be loved properly by a man swirled inside me. I felt that my centre, my heart and my soul, needed to be touched, the way the raindrop touched the water.

I was almost finished my formal education at night; I had made Mama Reevah proud of me and made myself bored. I finally decided what I wanted to do in school and had completed a business degree at night and in the summer. The bank agreed to help me pay for the courses and that was a factor in my choice of study.

I had expanded my cultural horizon, and I was active and involved with my community. These things had come as naturally to me as drawing breath; but loving this man or that man was difficult. It was big-big work and I just never got beyond a second date before pulling back from closeness. I had not met the right man and I was not going to settle for anything less than the right one.

And then I met Cicero Finley. I met him just as I wondered if I ought to stop seeking the kind of happy peace that my Mama Reevah had known with a man, or the joyful celebration of life that I had seen my Aunt Juniper Berry embrace.

It was as I walked with my head bowed low, my eyes cast on the ground, that I met him. The lamp-light shone brightly on the darkened street, and I could clearly see other people passing me by. I was concentrating on seeking the light glistening in the puddles, and did not notice another set of feet in my path.

When the feet sidestepped quickly to avoid colliding with me, I looked up and was greeted by the loveliest pair of eyes I had ever seen. They were light brown and while not particularly large, they were striking in their intensity. The thick eyebrows that framed round-round eyes met in the middle of a broad forehead. He had an intelligent face.

He smiled at me and I decided that I liked his lips too; they matched the shape of his eyes. I noticed that his mouth had a weak curl to it, but I decided to minimize the importance of that. I looked instead to see if his face was also round. It was not; he had a long, angular face, set on an also long neck. It was a graceful neck, unusually graceful for a man, I thought. The way it was set on his shoulders made me think of Audrey Hepburn or a swan.

As he stood in front of me, his body seemed to hold itself taut, as if he was ready to run away. There was a certain air of stealth in the way he hunched his whole body forward. I judged him to be an athlete. Much later, he told me that he was athletic, but was not an athlete by profession. By then, we were sitting at a table in a coffee shop on St. Clair Avenue.

I could not believe it when I had heard myself agreeing to go for coffee with a total stranger. Even though Black people in Toronto all spoke to each other when they met in the street, I had never been brave enough to do more than say "hello." I had accepted his invitation to go for coffee only because it was a public place. And besides, the coffee shop was just around the corner from my house in a very well-lit and busy neighbourhood.

On the street, he had stood and smiled at me, trying quite unsuccessfully to open a conversation. First he chided me for walking with my head buried in the ground. He had asked teasingly, clearly expecting an answer, "What were you thinking about?"

When I did not respond, he prompted, "Were you far away from here?" As I nodded, still not speaking, he said into my silence, "Your eyes still look lost and far-away."

I blinked, trying to find my voice. I was quite shaken at being confronted with a live man in my path. I resisted the temptation to laugh out loud at the ridiculous way he had suddenly materialized. I told myself: "Things don't happen that way."

I smiled at him. "Yes, my thoughts were miles and miles away. Sorry I walked into you; it really shook me up."

"Don't apologize; I am very glad that you walked into me. It has given me a chance to speak with you. I have been watching you for a couple of weeks, ever since I moved into that apartment building."

He gestured to the building that had grown up next door to Aunt Helen's house.

I felt a little uncomfortable at the thought that this stranger had been watching me "for a couple of weeks," as he said. I got right to the point. "How is it that I've never seen you and you have seen me?"

He hastened to reassure me. "Oh, don't worry," he said, patting my arm. "I was not stalking you. It is just that you walk right under my balcony every day when you are going for a walk, or going to work. I see you at least twice a day. You don't see me because of the way the building is shaped, but I have not been spying on you. You don't have to be so paranoid."

I felt embarrassed that he was defending himself from my unspoken inference that he was stalking me. I had not intended to communicate my discomfort so clearly. I flashed what I hoped was a brilliant smile at him and said: "You know, women can't be too careful these days. It's not that I'm paranoid."

He laughed, showing white-white teeth that almost gleamed when the street-light struck them. "You're right," he said. "I am sorry I said it that way."

He put out his hand and covered my hands which were resting on the table. "I was happy to see you and not be seen," he said. "That way, I got to admire you walking past me. And now I will have to stop doing that as you will be uncomfortable, won't you?"

I nodded and moved my hands under his, indicating that I did not want him holding them for so long. The thought that he had watched me walk from the rear now caused me not fear, but embarrassment. I looked at him carefully. "But what if you are really a stalker at heart? How would I know? I don't know anyone who knows you."

Again he laughed. "Well, you are very bad for my ego; I thought everyone in Toronto knew me." I studied his face. As far as I could tell, I had never seen him before; yet he seemed vaguely familiar.

"Are you an athlete?" I was not embarrassed to ask the question; I had absolutely no interest in sports beyond the political issues that surfaced in them from time to time. I did not think that I would recognize anyone besides Cassius Clay, who had only recently renamed himself "Muhammed Ali."

The drop-dead-gorgeous man who sat across the table from me shook his head. "No, I am not an athlete. We have met before; my name is Cicero Finley." I smiled and told him my name. It now bordered on the comedic, because his name was completely unfamiliar to me. "You don't recognize my name, do you?" he asked. I thought that his voice sounded hurt and so I searched desperately in my memory for some way of connecting his name to something I knew, but could not.

"Cicero Finley...Cicero Finley..." I muttered under my breath. I hoped for some revelation to come to me, but none did. Finally he said, "I work with the same community group for Black kids that you do," and I immediately remembered that I had seen him at the end-of-summer celebration of the project.

Now I was really embarrassed, because he and I and five others had been singled out and honoured as committed volunteers of the project. I had also seen him at a performance of Derek Walcott's play *Dream on Monkey Mountain*. I remembered that he had come up to me and said "Hello" and I had not remembered who he was then either.

I apologized, but he did not seem the least bit concerned. That registered with me; I thought that it showed that his ego was not involved. In fact, he seemed embarrassed as he said, "I just thought that it might have helped me to curry favour with you, that's all." I decided that I liked his sense of humour. And I thought that his shyness was sweet.

He said in an earnest voice, "I don't lay any store in accolades, except for what they can help me to do in my life and others' lives. I just thought that it would put you at ease if you knew that you were with someone who is of your community." And he smiled disarmingly at me, showing those white-white teeth again.

I smiled broadly at Cicero Finley. He tapped my hand playfully and I noticed that his fingers were long and thin. He took my hands and stroked them as he held them captive in his own.

I surprised myself by suggesting that we go to a restaurant and have dinner together. He quickly agreed, and thus began my close-close friendship with Cicero Finley.

From the day I met him, I framed time in a different way. Whereas I had previously defined everything in terms of "before I left Antigua" and "after I came to Toronto," now my perspective changed completely. I measured time as "before meeting Cicero Finley" and "after meeting Cicero Finley." It was not that he took over my life; it was simply that knowing him completely changed the rhythm of my life.

It felt as if I had lived in black and white until the day I met Cicero Finley. He brought colour into my life, beginning with Aunt Helen's house. He helped me to redecorate it so that it became my house and no longer "Aunt Helen's house." He encouraged me to choose bright colours for the walls and even for the plates from which I ate.

I put away Aunt Helen's good dishes with their subtle, pale sprays of rosebuds, and I made her everyday dishes my good ones. Then we went shopping for heavy and serviceable bright royal-blue plates and cups and saucers so that I could entertain my friends without worrying that they might break one of Aunt Helen's good dishes.

Chapter Six

My political understanding of the world and my surroundings was still shifting. It was impossible not to notice that Black women were second-class citizens twice: in the white world and in the Black world. Yet no one said anything about it publicly. I knew that I was not the only one who noticed. I found myself looking at Black men and their attitude towards Black women with a highly critical eye.

The rhetoric of white feminism provided the language for my frustration, but something was amiss, for at a deep-deep level, I did not want to be in conflict with Black men. I found myself torn between wanting to accept and be accepted as a member of the whole community of Black people; but being concerned not to play a Mama Reevah role to any man. I recalled her description of how she had allowed Papa Emmanuel to do things that affected her life, even when she did not agree with him.

I thought of my family often, so safe, so protected in their little cocoon of every-day-being-almost-the-same-as-the-day-before. They could even rely on the corruption of the government in Antigua being the same. Nothing was going to suddenly change and right all of the wrongs and ills that had taken place in Antigua—these things had gone on for so long that they now had a predictable life of their own.

The issue of men and women and who got to speak for the whole group was not something with which Mama Reevah had ever had to concern herself. She had allowed Papa Emmanuel to handle their lives, and in the end, she still spoke of him with what I now took to be hero-worship. It was a set way of being; it was orderly and consistent; nothing ever came up for review.

In Toronto, there was no such normalcy on which I could rely. My life was no longer my story; it was a political entity, a beast which had to be fed. I *had to* pay attention to things political to live life in Toronto. It was the only way I could feel as if I was exercising some power over my life.

There was a time when I considered climbing onto a BWIA plane and "just land-up right back in Antigua." It was only the presence of the great love in my life that stopped me. In the early days, I stuck it out because I did not know how my mother and my aunts would take it if I were to suddenly arrive to reclaim my navel-string. Often, though, I wished I could just give myself over to the feeling that I could not do this immigrant life any more.

I worked in a white space every day, and then tried to catch up on my *blackness* in the evening and on weekends. My double life went like this: Afro played down by day in the bank; demure head-band in place; filling out forms; checking records; writing letters to customers; speaking with customers. Then at night and on weekends: Afro picked up and out; heart feeling free; mind able to focus on what brings clarity; community events; community work; friendship; dancing; laughing; *feeling* free, even if I was not really free.

The head-band-by-day had come into being because one day, the bank manager asked me if I could "do something" with my hair. I had answered: "Like what? What exactly do you have in mind that I should do with my hair?"

The answer came back with a whole lot of attitude strumming the words: "Maybe cut it!"

I bristled; even though I was normally a peaceful person, I wanted to reach out my arm and yank her long hair. Instead I had simply said, "Your hair grows down, mine grows out." I saw understanding register on her face, but it did not alter her request. "Do something about your hair ASAP; *your* hair gets in the way, *mine* does not."

And with those words, she flicked her hair to move it out of her face so that she could look me in the eye. Strands of her hair latched themselves on to the brooch pinned to my collar and pulled her into my chest. She had just proved her statement to be a lie!

The expressions that crossed her face and mine were so comical that we both doubled over with laughter. It was really too funny for words. Then she became serious again. "Okay, so my hair probably gets in the way too...I will pin up my hair if you pin up your hair...deal?" I nodded, feeling scammed; I wanted to show that *Black is beautiful* every single waking moment of life. It had become nothing short of an expression of all that there was of me.

After that, to avoid hassles from my supervisor, I started putting a *Kente* cloth head-band around my Afro, pretending to myself that it was some-kinda-African-princess-hairstyle. But in my heart of hearts, I did not like that I was compromising my very body. I felt the unfairness of it acutely when I watched white tellers toss their heads and hit customers in their face with their hair. I would be so vexed and think: "At least my Afro doesn't hit the customer in the face when I toss my head."

I felt that if you were Black in Toronto, you just could not live life in a casual way. Within white society, you walked on eggshells. And if you wanted to belong in the Black community, you had to be seen doing the right things.

I no longer just walked into a supermarket and bought groceries. First I checked to make sure that I did not buy any products that were produced by companies that were on a banned list because they operated in South Africa. All over the world Black people had begun to observe this boycott; it was a way to put some economic pressure on the system of apartheid operating in South Africa. I also did not buy beer or wine from just any company; some of them had holdings in South Africa. It was the same with cigarettes.

There was a list of Black entertainers who were on the banned list because they had accepted the invitation of South Africa's white regime to perform at segregated concerts. I did not buy their records either. Sports figures, including cricketers, were also condemned for this lack of integrity. Everyone talked about these people for weeks and weeks, mourning their betrayal.

I thought that these things were much worse than the things that went on in Antigua, the things I had seen my Papa and my Mama fighting against. It was one thing to be in Antigua and hear of apartheid by reading about it in *Time* magazine. It was quite another to hear Nelson Mandela speak about it with the passion of his voice resonating like a drum-beat. I was sure that I could never live life in a shallow way again after hearing him speak just before he was arrested. One evening at a community meeting someone brought a film of his last speech at an African National Congress rally and we had all listened to it with rapt attention. He spoke of things I had never heard of before, about the monstrous treatment of Africans in South Africa at the hands of whites.

I felt the same way about Malcolm X and Martin Luther King, Jr. After hearing these voices of truth, there was no way to just "keep on keeping on" as if nothing was happening in the world around me.

Before I met Cicero Finley, I had dallied with two other men who were involved in the Movement; but here for the first time was a man whose behaviour seemed to have the promise in it of a healthy relationship. He was committed to the freedom of Black people, speaking about it with every breath he took. I saw him as my comrade, my brother-in-arms, even though we never took up arms and I was not formally a part of the Movement in the way that he was.

Cicero Finley was from Montréal and he had recently come to Toronto to go to law school on a full scholarship. He talked the right talk, walked the right walk, and wore the right clothes. I was not so interested in his walk and his clothes, but I was impressed by his talk.

I never got bored talking to him, because he had taken the time to notice what my particular interests were. Although he had a different focus, he listened when I talked about my passions and contributed to the discussion in a knowledgeable way. I appreciated his taking the time to honour me by listening to me as closely as I listened to him. My gratitude was huge; I was a very lonely person.

Most days, Cicero Finley came to meet me for lunch. We alternated between Chinese food, Indian food and Canadian greasy-spoon food. I had a penchant for open-face chicken sandwiches, a dish that Cicero Finley said turned his stomach. He would look at me digging into slices of chicken and green peas on top of white bread, all smothered in a thick, suspicious-looking gravy. "I cannot understand how people eat that stuff; it is peculiar to Canada, you know," he would say. He had travelled a lot, and so his palate was much more sophisticated than mine.

Cicero Finley read the same books that I read; most were written by and about Black people: Chairman Mao's *Little Red Book*, Marx and Engels's *The Communist Manifesto* and Sun Tzu's *The Art of War* were probably the exceptions. When he spouted quotations from them, I would turn my eyes to him and watch him. He did public readings of poetry, although he never wrote any; his writings were all political essays, or speeches for rallies.

In his voice, Langston Hughes was magic; Zora Neale Hurston a thing of beauty. He would read me their words and laugh at my ecstasy. I loved hearing him perform the words as if they were finely-tuned scripts, written just for him. His Montréal accent sounded very American and so he pulled off Zora's language wonderfully. And so he wooed me.

Cicero Finley seemed to know everything about the Movement all over the world, and particularly in the U.S. He had visited the Black Panther headquarters in Oakland, California; and I listened to the things he had to say about Huey P. Newton, Bobby Seale, Kathleen Cleaver, and Eldridge Cleaver.

Others watched Cicero Finley the way I watched him, admiring his energy and the way he had of breathing fire and brimstone. He would speak for hours on the Black Panther Party's platform. He would quote Stokely Carmichael and Fanon and Elijah Mohammed and Malcolm X and H. Rap Brown and others who had written and spoken about the wave of revolt against racism that was shaking the U.S. power structure.

He lumped all of his sources together, creating a synthesis of revolutionary talk that could wake up a dead body, easy-easy. My body was not dead, but it had been sleepwalking, taking me woodenly through a daily existence that had numbed me by its sameness. And now, the right man had come along and stirred the embers waiting to be stoked into life.

Cicero Finley knew the sisters and brothers in the Movement and this was a relief, for they were all people whom I knew from working in community projects. It was important to me to know that he was accepted by my community, and I looked to see how others regarded him. I was satisfied with the responses I got to my tentative check on him. Hard as it was to believe, several paid government agents buzzed around the Black community, and I was not adept at identifying them. Even though I was not a part of the Movement, I did not want to be connected with a person whom the Movement considered a "plant."

I was told that he was considered, by all accounts, to be what he appeared to be: a law student from Montréal who was committed to the Movement. He knew all of the right people in Montréal. He had gone to the Congress of Black Writers in Montréal in 1968; he had also participated in the Sir George Williams Affair in 1969 when a group of Black students held a sit-in to protest a professor's racist conduct. Cicero Finley said that when the students began the sit-in, he was not present, but he had gone to support them as soon as he had heard about it. He supported their protest over the racism in the grading of students. He said that he had no idea how the computer centre was set on fire; and none of them were claiming to have done it. He believed that it was done by provocateurs in order to implicate and arrest the leaders of the sit-in. He even produced a photograph showing him with the key people who were involved in the incident. And he showed me a Montréal magazine with an article about himself and several other students on the day of the incident.

In the months that followed, I liked all that I saw in this man who had landed right in front of me as if in answer to my prayers. I enjoyed the closeness and I enjoyed our arguments about politics; about whether Canada would allow racism to take hold even more acutely than it already had. I felt a hope he did not share—that Canada could benefit from the example of its neighbour to the south. He had lived here longer, "for five generations," he said.

He often told me that I was full of bourgeois sensibilities and that they would lead me nowhere but to a reactionary lifestyle. "A house in suburbia and a two-car garage," he said.

"And what's wrong with that?" I would ask, bristling at his assumptions about me. They were true; but I did not see anything wrong with wanting a house and a car and I did not like being so accurately typecast. The only thing that was not true was the business of the suburbs. I liked the Humewood area where Aunt Helen's house was, and had no intention of moving to suburbia. I saw no virtue in being poor and in my view, reaching for material comfort did not mean that I was reactionary.

Our arguments sometimes became so heated that Cicero Finley would pound his fist on the kitchen table while I would stand with my hands on my hips, shouting my counter-arguments at the top of my voice. I noticed that when he was genuinely angry, Cicero Finley's accent sounded more American than Canadian. I told him this one night, saying that he ought to stop trying to talk "Yank." A lot of people I knew tried to speak like Black people in the U.S., as if it made them somehow more Black.

Cicero Finley laughed and said, as if it had just occurred to him, "Well, I *did* spend a lot of time in the U.S., as I told you, going to rallies and so on. And I hang out with the guys dodging the Draft who live here."

I could not understand why he claimed to "hang out" with Americans in Toronto who were dodging the U.S. draft, because he did not. I thought, rather, that he seemed to avoid them. I had one very close male friend from San Francisco, and I noticed that whenever I tried to invite him over to have dinner with us, Cicero Finley would balk at the idea. He did not want to bring "the shop" home, he would say.

One night, as we argued about the CIA take-down of *Ramparts* magazine, which had recently occurred, Cicero Finley became more incensed than he had ever been during any of our arguments. All playfulness was gone; he seemed so personally involved that I could not get through to him on a *reasoning* level. He pounded his fists on the kitchen table a little louder than usual, and I too raised my voice a bit higher than usual. Suddenly, the police arrived.

A neighbour who had only recently moved in next door had told the police that there was a violent fight going on and that a woman's head was being knocked against a hard surface. He claimed to have heard a woman scream.

When the doorbell rang, Cicero Finley and I were laughing at the fact that he had lost the same argument twice in a row. The laughter was still on my lips as I smiled at the policemen. I opened the door with the sounds of Aretha Franklin's "You make me feel like a natural woman" wafting behind me. The policemen insisted on coming inside to see that there was no one being hurt.

Afterwards I said to Cicero Finley, "Do you realize that we are so different from white people that even our way of speaking is misunderstood as war?" He nodded silently. He seemed to have been transported somewhere else; but he did not divulge the location of this place.

Chapter Seven

I told Cicero Finley about the two relationships I had had with men. I made a point of explaining how betrayed I had felt when I discovered that they had other relationships going with other women. I had been particularly upset because I knew the women from my work in the community.

Cicero Finley took his cue; he "tut-tutted" with me about how bad that was; and he looked into my eyes when he said that he had never understood men who did such things. It sounded as good as a promise that he was not promiscuous and would honour any relationship in which he became involved.

It did not take long for us to develop a deeply intimate friendship. Most of our evenings were spent working with children in the community, going to meetings about community issues, or participating in events of celebration and camaraderie. Cicero Finley had become even more active in the Movement; at the same time, he had revived my lapsing interest. He wrote and gave speeches, and sometimes he chaired meetings. I ran off fliers and typed his speeches; and along with the other women, I cooked and cooked and cooked whenever the men visited our homes.

It was months before Cicero Finley and I kissed, although we held hands that first day and continued to do so every time we met. It felt natural to hold hands, and we never questioned it. One day, as we walked home from the movies, I tucked my hands into my coat pockets to brace myself against the raging winter wind. Cicero Finley pushed his hand into my left pocket and held my gloved hand firmly with his.

"You can't take back your hand from me," he said jokingly. Then he added: "May I have your hand forever and ever?"

I laughed, thinking that he was joking, trying to keep my mind off the cold. He asked again, "May I have your hand forever and ever?" Again I did not respond, but only laughed. He stopped walking and, turning to face me, got down on one knee on the pavement in the cold and said: "I mean it Sayshelle Livingston Hughes...will you marry me?"

Still I laughed, assuming that he was extending the joke, especially as he had used my elaborate name and had gotten down on one knee. Then something about the serious tone of his voice made me stop laughing and look at him. I did not answer; I silently pulled him to his feet and put my arm through his as we began to walk again, battling the wind.

Finally, I asked him: "Are you serious?" I think I still half-expected him to laugh and say, "Just joshing you," the way he always did when I did not realize that he was making a joke.

"I am really serious," he replied, and then he turned to face me, so that we stood still again on the sidewalk. I noticed with relief that there was no one else near us, for Cicero Finley put his arms around me and kissed me full on the mouth for the first time!

I reeled in shock and pulled my head back from his to look at him. His eyes were brim-full with tears. "I mean it seriously, Sayshelle; will you marry me?" First I asked him why there were tears in his eyes and he said, "I just wish that I had met you years and years ago...my life would have been so different." I nodded happily then, saying yes to his proposal. I was certain as I did so that I had taken leave of my senses. I had agreed to marry someone who had just kissed me for the first time. I felt as if I was living a life that was much more chaste than anyone I knew!

It did not occur to me until much later how little I knew about this man I had agreed to marry. I just knew that he felt good in my life. His politics were the same as mine. He smelled wonderful. His hands matched mine. His feet were warm. He rubbed my back when I felt stressed. He was beautiful to look at. He held me right. His kiss had just taken me into heaven. He was mine. I was his. It was as pure and as simple as that.

I lay in bed that night after our first kiss, hugging the sweetness of it around me. His kiss made me think of chocolate ice-cream warmed by a raging fire. He had not tried to go beyond the kiss, and that had endeared him to me. I did not want to be rushed.

I thought of Mama Reevah and Papa Emmanuel. I remembered that just before I had left Antigua, Mama Reevah had told me about how she used to go and visit Papa Emmanuel. She had talked about "loving this man Emmanuel" from the day she first saw him, and loving him even when he could not move to love her back, and loving him still, even after death.

Mama Reevah said that she thought it was time to tell me these "big-woman stories," because I was going to be alone in Canada. She felt that I needed to know how to conduct myself when I was ready to love the right man. She had painted a picture of herself as a wantonly hot young woman, yet she had held out for the right man. By her example, Mama Reevah taught me that it was not a good idea to hop into bed with a man until you knew for sure that he was right for you. "And in your soul you will know," she had said. That is exactly how I felt about Cicero Finley. It was in my soul that I knew that I loved him. And it was with my body that I felt that the fire he ignited in me would never ebb or die. It would flow from me to him forever, even after death.

Mama Reevah had also cautioned me about acting the way she had, going to Emmanuel's house when she was just a girl, seventeen years old and still in school. "For whatever it is worth, it is my life, child, and I can do no less than to say to you: here is how it went for me, and here is what I learned from it. I know better now, so I want you to have that knowledge. Besides, you will be meeting people you don't know. So pay attention; and take good care of Jesus body."

And it was only now, with the wisdom of my lived experience, that I understood why Mama Reevah had cautioned me against being too free with my sexual favours. I had really not looked after "Jesus body" very well, for I had already bedded with a man and had almost bedded with a second before meeting the love of my life. I made a decision then and there that Cicero Finley would be *the* man in my life, forever and ever.

Here in Toronto, I did not know the families of the men I had held in my arms; one had been from Antigua and the other had been from Nevis. And now here was Cicero Finley from Montréal, a place I knew next to nothing about. In Antigua, Papa Emmanuel would not have dared to love Mama Reevah and then leave her, the way men were free to do in Toronto. The way they had done with other women friends of mine. They did not have to answer to anyone.

I remembered Mama Reevah's description of the evenings when Papa Emmanuel walked her to the top of her street, mindful of her parents' waiting for her to come home. Here in Toronto, I had no parents for men to fear or respect. In comparison with Mama Reevah and Papa Emmanuel's evenings, mine were quite immoral. I did have my suspicions about what had gone on behind closed doors in Papa Emmanuel's little house, but I had not dared to ask Mama Reevah the question: had they really just talked and touched each other's faces?

It felt very natural to sleep in the same bed with a man even though we were not married. It would never have occurred to me to say to a man with whom I was having an intimate relationship that I did not want him to stay overnight in my house. The severe loneliness of immigration created the need in many of us for hastily constructed "replacement families" that did not always work. Mama Reevah would never have understood what it was like to be alone in a whole house in a strange country by yourself. Still, I felt a sense of shame when I broke this second taboo handed down to me. The thoughts would run through my head almost nightly as I lay next to Cicero Finley: "Imagine Mama Reevah and Papa Emmanuel's daughter Sayshelle living in sin with a man!" For we were almost living together.

I felt a little guilty about being the only one in the family who was not "living right," as Mama Reevah would put it. Aunt Juniper Berry was safely married, and Aunt Sage had left her live-in situation with Rommel. I sought, but could not find, a way to reconcile how I was living with who I knew myself to be. Yet it did not occur to me to do anything but love this man Cicero Finley in just the way my heart directed. I did not even consider an alternative.

Cicero Finley said one evening that he appreciated that I demonstrated that I had a brain and was not just a woman for "womanly duties." I wondered what those were, but I said nothing. I *knew* what they were: cooking and washing and cleaning and sex, and in his case, typing his speeches and his articles.

As he was leaving the next morning, he kissed me and smiled saying, "Sister Sayshelle, what a joy you are." I forgot my irritation over the words "womanly duties." I shelved it, along with the fact that he had a weak mouth. It was so much easier to bask in his parting compliment. His words sang in my heart all day as I interviewed people about their collateral and suitability to get the bank's money.

When I came home that evening and freed my Afro from its restraining head-band, I thought of Cicero Finley's Afro and wondered how he handled it in law school. I made a mental note to ask him about that, because his Afro climbed the highest mountain and scaled the widest walls. It was big-big, sticking out around his head; besides Kathleen Cleaver's Afro it was the biggest one I had seen up close. When we made love, I wrapped my fingers in it and pulled his head close to kiss him.

We got married at City Hall with only a week's planning and two witnesses: a friend of Cicero Finley's and this friend's wife. I had no relatives in Canada and my best friend, Aunt Helen's friend's granddaughter, was not able to attend as she had gone home to Windsor on vacation. Cicero Finley said that he was estranged from his parents and did not have any siblings. His cousins lived all over the world, he said, so there was no time to contact them.

A few weeks later, I wrote home to Antigua, telling my family of my marriage. I sent them pictures of us on our wedding day. I selected several shots of the whole wedding party: Cicero Finley and I were resplendent in our African clothes. He wore a long robe made out of *Kente* cloth that he had borrowed from a Ghanaian friend. My wedding outfit was an elegant gown made out of African fabric, with a matching head-tie. The couple who were our witnesses wore regular Canadian suits.

In the letter I asked Mama Reevah for her forgiveness for having got married without her presence; but I promised that we would have a proper wedding in a church in Antigua, one of these days. I did mean that; but even as I wrote it, I knew that it would be unlikely to happen for a long time. It was not something I had even raised with Cicero Finley. We were caught up in life in Toronto, and a trip to Antigua for a church wedding with all of the frills was not on our agenda.

Cicero Finley said to me on our wedding night as we lay in each other's arms in Aunt Helen's house: "Your lips are like the wine-dipped petals of a thick, red rose, and your hips move in a heady rhythm that makes me scream." I believed him, for with him, I felt beautiful and alive and sensual...like an opening had been made to my soul that I could not close, even if I wished it.

I fell headlong, in a plunging kind of movement, into loving Cicero Finley even more deeply. I dismissed little things like his ineffectual responses to my questions about his past life. For he filled up my space and my house so much that I was too busy being happy.

Those parts and those places that were my reserves of energy, time and money were used up by Cicero Finley too; they seemed to flutter in his hands, like feathers. I told myself that it was not that he was deliberately using up my energy and resources; he was just not cognizant of things in the material realm. I understood him, for it was the way I would have liked to have been, if there could have been someone like me to pick up the pieces and pay attention to the tangible details.

He took up a lot of space and used up a lot of resources, it seemed, and I, not wanting to be mean-spirited, said nothing. He offered no money for groceries, but ate like a horse. It was not that I was so grateful for his presence that I put blinkers on about everything. I simply made a decision to take the bad with the good. And the good was very, very good. Pure and simple; I was head over heels in love with him.

Chapter Eight

It was puzzling to me that even though Cicero Finley said he was estranged from his parents, he went to Montréal frequently. Try as I might, I could not get a straight answer from him about why he travelled there so often. He spoke of estrangement, yet there were mounting telephone bills including collect calls from Montréal. I recognized the area code. There were three separate numbers; but only one number was called almost daily. And I wondered how it was that calls from Montréal only seemed to arrive when I was not at home.

Cicero Finley told me that he did not understand why I had a problem with this, seeing that he paid all of his bills promptly, but my curiosity got the better of me and I made a note of the three numbers that he called in Montréal. I picked the most frequently called number one day and dialled it. When a woman answered, I asked her name and she said "Mrs. Finley." I thought: "This is too trite...way too predictable...this is my life, not a soap opera." I apologized, claimed that I had the wrong number, and hung up quickly. I told myself that it was his mother, and I even had the grace to feel ashamed of having called up his mother.

Then early one morning, I woke up with a strong feeling that Seleena was present with me. My head was full of a strange pull of energy on the left side. It had happened that way before and I had phoned and asked Aunt Juniper Berry about it. She had explained that it meant that I ought to pay attention to whatever I was doing and reach for the guidance that was being communicated in the realm of Spirit. "Either that, or Seleena's spirit is really with you as a protective energy."

That had sounded good, but nothing was becoming clear this morning. I decided that it was just Seleena's spirit reminding me that she was with me. However, just in case Aunt Juniper Berry's other explanation for this feeling was valid, I listened to the radio more carefully that morning. I expected that I would hear some news item that was of interest to me, because hardly a day went by without some calamitous thing happening in the world.

I had set the table for breakfast and was trying to decide what we would eat that morning when the shocking news of the death of Jimi Hendrix was broadcast. I was not a Jimi Hendrix fan, although I had listened to his music, if for no other reason than to understand what all of the hype was about. He was way outside of Pharoah Sanders and John Coltrane, and I had already done some stretching to be so deeply into their music.

"Jimi Hendrix is out on another *tip* altogether; it is a far-out *tip*," Cicero Finley had remarked one day as I was listening to Jimi Hendrix's rendition of the American national anthem. I told him that I was listening to his music to try to understand if he was really creating what the media claimed: "an important, new form of music." I did not like that it was mainly white hippies who listened to his music.

"I find his music interesting," Cicero Finley had said, "but not as wonderful as the folks at *Ramparts* magazine used to claim." It struck me that Cicero Finley was very preoccupied with *Ramparts* magazine.

The radio reporter said in a deadpan voice that Hendrix was dead; it was thought that he had been cut down by mixing drugs with alcohol, but this could not yet be confirmed. I shouted up to Cicero Finley to turn on the radio in the bedroom, so that he could hear the news. It was his birthday and I was planning a surprise party for him. I thought: "What a thing! From now on, Cicero Finley's birthday will be associated with Jimi Hendrix's death."

Just then there was a knock at the door. I opened it to find a woman standing on the steps smiling brightly at me. She was holding the hand of a little girl who looked like she was about four years old. I stood and stared at them with my mouth hanging open. I could not take my eyes off the child. Her resemblance to Cicero Finley was so strong that it made my head reel. My eyes took in her colour: *light chocolate brown*; and the woman's colour: *white as driven snow!*

The woman was speaking. I knew that, because her mouth was opening and closing, but I had lost my capacity to hear her. She spoke again and I concentrated hard, resisting the temptation to turn back into the house and close the door behind me. Then I could have convinced myself that this was not real; this was not happening.

"Hello. I'm Cicero Finley's wife, and this is his daughter, Sasha. Is he at home?"

I looked at her blonde hair...the golden yellow curls cascaded down to her shoulders. She smiled at me with a hint of something maternal that I have come to recognize as a liberal's attempt to be non-racist.

"Bet she thinks I'm the maid." No sooner had the thought crossed my mind than she said, albeit politely, "Do you work here?" I noticed that she avoided asking directly if I was the maid or the helper.

"So she *is* liberal," I thought, as I struggled to close my mouth. "Well, she would have to be...she is married to a Black man and has a Black child." I stood as if frozen, with the doorknob gripped in my hand.

As I looked at them, my mind grappled with the thought that it was not just Cicero Finley's birthday that would be joined to Jimi Hendrix's death. I knew that if someone asked me: "What were you doing when you heard about the death of Jimi Hendrix?" I would not be able to answer without remembering how loud the other question rang in my head that morning: *Do you work here?*

I nodded, but I did not speak. I was glad that I had managed to close my mouth. The radio upstairs squawked some more about Jimi Hendrix. I said Cicero Finley's name in a strangled little voice and he shouted back, "I'm hearing it! Jimi Hendrix is dead!"

Mrs. Finley stepped inside, uninvited. The child ran past me to the foot of the stairs. She was excited. She had heard her father's voice. "Daddy!"

I gathered my wits about me and managed to say quite clearly: "You have some visitors!"

In my head, I told Aunt Helen that I was sorry for messing up my life in *her* house. It had become her house again, for I had soiled it. This was more life than Mama Reevah, Papa Emmanuel, Aunt Juniper Berry, and Aunt Sage could muster together!

Cicero Finley came bounding down the stairs. He stopped midway; shock then fear registered on his face. Then I saw embarrassment set in, and watched that change into love as he hugged his daughter. I thought: "My eyes are witnessing this man manifesting the chameleon that he is."

I watched him try to avoid Mrs. Finley's embrace, but she was not having any of it. She cornered him, kissed him roundly on the lips, and hugged him tight. "Will you stand still so I can kiss you? You'd think that we see each other every day! Oh, I have missed you so much. We just had to come and surprise you for your birthday." She looked up into his eyes while the little girl hugged them both around their knees. I thought: "This is soo-oo domestic!"

While she still held him, she said: "I had to tell the lady my name, but I was glad she didn't tell you who it was that was here to see you." I blinked, still watching Cicero Finley. Now his eyes registered fear. My mind raced. She means me! I am "the lady." She still thinks I am the maid.

And then she turned a dazzling smile on me. I did not think my face could form itself into a smile, but I tried feebly. I felt faint. I could hardly hear her. I looked into Cicero Finley's desperate eyes as he returned Mrs. Finley's embrace. My right hand twisted the rings on the third finger of my left hand: the wedding band and the diamond engagement ring of which I had been so proud. It was the first time a man had bought me anything, let alone a diamond.

Cicero Finley's eyes darted this way and that, and I realized that he was desperately trying to direct me to remove our wedding photographs. They sat in silent condemnation on a little table that we had bought just for the display. There was a photograph of us cutting the cake in the restaurant; another of us dancing; one picture was of us kissing; and another photograph was the whole group, including the Justice of the Peace and the two witnesses.

There was a white ribbon with the date of the wedding draped over the top of the frames, creating a little shrine-like cluster. I had had the ribbon made especially at an Italian wedding-supply store.

I considered a knock-down drag-out confrontation, using the shrine of our wedding to show Mrs. Finley that her husband was married to me. Then I thought of the child and hastily picked up the photographs while I kept a watchful eye on Mrs. Finley's back. I managed to take them to the kitchen and stuff them into a drawer just as she turned around to look at me.

I had the distinct impression that she knew that I had put something away, but that did not bother me. After all, I was a total stranger to her, and only the maid. I told myself: "No one pays attention to servants."

Suddenly I remembered that our wedding certificate was prominently displayed above the fireplace. It stood accusingly behind Cicero Finley, right in Mrs. Finley's line of vision. When she turned her head away for a moment, I caught Cicero Finley's eye and pointed at it. As he went over to the fireplace and stood in front of the certificate, I almost laughed out loud at the idiocy of it all.

Casually, I walked around them and removed the certificate from its treasured spot. As I walked up the stairs with it, my eyes filled with tears. "What is going on in your life Sayshelle Livingston Hughes?" I missed Papa Emmanuel then more than ever. I needed to feel his eyes smile at me, to hear his heart beating under my head as I rested it on his chest.

As I splashed water on my face in the bathroom sink, the mundane kicked in: I had planned a surprise birthday party for Cicero Finley. I shuddered, and picking up my handbag, ran downstairs and mumbled something about "some errands." I left the house.

I had to work fast to cancel the party, and I only had a few hours to do it. It did not even occur to me that I had eaten nothing all day, not a glass of juice, not a cup of tea. I had been confronted with Cicero Finley's past before I had even got a start on my day. His past had chased me out of my own home.

Later that afternoon, I went to the neighbourhood restaurant that Cicero Finley and I frequented. I bought a newspaper and coffee and settled down to read about Jimi Hendrix. I did not want to go home to deal with the family that was now ensconced in my house. I had not been in the restaurant for more than a half-hour when I looked up and saw Cicero Finley hurrying down the street. I wondered where he had deposited Mrs. Finley and the child.

He came into the restaurant, looked around, waved at the bartender and called out: "Thank you!" Then he sat down at my table. He explained that he had asked to be called on the phone if I came into the restaurant.

He talked and talked, and I listened. Eventually I asked, "Are you divorced from her?" He shook his head and averted his eyes. I said nothing after that. I could not look at him; my eyes hovered on his neck and chin and then came to rest at last on his left shoulder.

I focused on the striped pattern of the shirt he was wearing. I gave a little start as I recognized it as my birthday gift to him. I had given him the shirt early that morning while still in bed, saying: "This is part one of your birthday gift."

He noticed my scrutiny and said, "Oh yes, I am wearing the shirt. Thank you; it is really nice." I felt like ripping it off him. He had a lot of nerve, wearing my birthday gift when a wife and a child had just materialized on my doorstep.

For a moment, I felt light-headed, as if I was not in my body. I had used all of the adrenaline that the morning had created to call everyone and cancel the party. I had managed not to give any explanations; I simply said that some family business had come up and it would be inconvenient to have the party. I promised another party later on.

I looked at Cicero Finley. I bared my teeth at him in what Antiguans called "a roast-dog grin." It took effort to restrain the laughter that was threatening to come bubbling up. He took my grimace for a real smile and seemed to bolster himself somewhat. He told me that his wife was dying of cancer, and that he had known of this when he left to come to live in Toronto. "We were separated before the baby was born, I just did not want to hurt her by asking for a divorce."

I stared at him. "And you had not even thought to tell *me*, the second Mrs. Finley, about *the first* Mrs. Finley when you made such a big show of asking for my hand in marriage?"

With a desperate look in his eyes he began, "How can I apologize to you...?" His voice trailed off.

I felt as if I were living a modern version of *Jane Eyre*. I could not resist my laughter any longer. I laughed until tears ran down my face.

"You are a crazy man," I said finally, looking at him in wonder. "You are like Mr. Rochester in *Jane Eyre*...People don't do these things in real life. What were you thinking? How long did you think you could get away with it...especially as you gave her your address? What did you think would be the future? That we would just carry on after she died? What about the child?"

And I laughed again when he said, "I was going to tell you eventually. I was just afraid of losing you."

"That weak mouth," I thought. "That weak mouth is an indicator of this weak behaviour. I have chosen a weak man." I cried a little then, but only inside. I cried for who I was, for what I had lost in a moment.

Cicero Finley talked while I plodded through the breakfast I had ordered. The eggs were overdone and rubbery, the toast was limp and the coffee cold by the time I remembered to sip it. I used orange juice to wash down the food.

Mrs. Finley (Salome, he said her name was) had not only come to wish him a happy birthday; she had also come because she wanted to tell him that she had had a bad report from her doctor. The cancer had taken a turn for the worse, and she had not wanted to tell him about it on the telephone. She was going into the hospital in Toronto to receive treatment from a specialist. She lived with her parents, but she did not want to leave the child with them as they were too old to manage a young child.

I could not believe what he was asking. "Can Sasha live with me...with us, while Salome goes into the hospital for treatment? Otherwise I will have to drop out of law school and get another job." When I did not answer, he pressed on. "It would only be until the summer when I can work full-time. Of course I will pay more for the use of utilities and the use of the guest room." He had it all worked out.

I looked at the place in which I found myself. I saw us lost together, for through my silence I had been complicit in his deceit. I had never been firm about my suspicions about the frequency of his telephone calls and trips to Montréal. I had not allowed memory to impose itself onto my knowing, for it would have been like leaping backwards over a cliff of betrayal. I had accepted the feeble excuses made by a man who showed love except in loving me properly, with trust and integrity.

I pushed all of the darkness and sadness underground, and decided that I would look after this innocent child. I reasoned with myself that I could throw Cicero Finley out and take him to court for bigamy, but what good would that do? How would it help the child to have her father in jail? She would end up as a ward of the state, because Cicero Finley's parents were not able to look after her either.

Besides, he had never made peace with his parents, he said. He told me at last that the reason for their estrangement was their anger with him for marrying a white woman. I was never quite sure about that—it did not have the ring of truth and I felt sure that he was telling me this story to win me over.

I could no longer pretend that I did not know about the hazards in dirty puddles of water, no matter how illumined they were by the light. It was not an easy thing, living through being lied to good and proper in the name of love, commitment, and loyalty. I told myself that it was love, commitment, and loyalty that would allow me to keep on cooking for him after that, to keep on sewing his *dashikis*, to begin sewing little-girl dresses for Sasha, and to keep putting on a brave face, despite it all. I would tell no one, not even my closest friends. I would explain Sasha's presence by saying that she was from Cicero Finley's first marriage. I laughed wryly inside, because that was indeed true.

As I sat in the restaurant, allowing Cicero Finley to make his defence and his plea, the great crash of the revelations lay like a heavy stone inside me. I worried about it becoming a cancer, like the one that had grown inside Papa Emmanuel. For now I could see myself in him, in the way I made a commitment and followed it through to the end. I did so even if it looked foolish to other people. Commitment would keep me silent, allow me to tell people that Cicero Finley had been divorced from Mrs. Finley before he met me. So it was that we could keep on keeping on.

I had fought white racism, but had succumbed to Black male oppression in the guise of sweet love. How could I possibly consider myself a whole person? There had been so many unanswered questions about this man; and I had allowed them to slide, carelessly entrusting my heart to him. And in his dishonesty he lived with me in sin in Aunt Helen's house. In my view, it was worse than living in sin, because there was dishonesty in it; if we had agreed to live in sin, at least we would have been in an honest relationship.

I acknowledged to myself that I loved Cicero Finley, despite what his mouth indicated. I watched his lips tremble as he waited to hear my answer. Then his lips settled into a tremulous line as he whispered, in answer to my question as to his family's present whereabouts, that they were indeed installed in my home. He had no place to put them and no money to rent a hotel room. It was in-between the monthly stipends from his scholarship fund and he was broke; in fact, we were both broke.

"Besides," he said, and he claimed my hands between his, the way he had done the night we first met, "I was hoping that you would agree to allow Sasha to stay with us until Salome comes out of the hospital."

I went home with him and took Mrs. Finley's hands in mine. She greeted me warmly, saying that she knew now that I was not the maid. I told her that I would look after Sasha while she was in the hospital. I declined her offer of money, and she clasped my hands tightly and refused to accept my answer. She said that Cicero Finley would be able to draw on her account, as she had given him power of attorney over her affairs. She also said that I would be paid for the work I had undertaken.

She spoke too fast, I thought, as if she was hastily trying to make everything clear. I confirmed the lie Cicero Finley had explained to me in the restaurant: that I was his landlady, and that I rented out the basement to students, and Cicero Finley was the latest student.

She seemed embarrassed for having mistaken me for the maid. I smiled wryly and thought: "Well, I guess landlady is better than maid." In order to explain his moving into my house, he had told her that because I offered it as a university residence, it was cheaper than the apartment he had first rented.

I smiled silently, thinking, "Sure it is cheaper; he pays me exactly half the rent he paid for the apartment." I did not begrudge him this; I had set the amount and I had been fair. Besides, his monthly rent came in very handy.

Mrs. Finley was a nice woman; I could not bring myself to be anything but nice to her. She explained that she was dying and her parents were elderly. She did not say that a part of her story was that she had a husband who had not done right by her. He had not done right by her much more than he had done right by me. And there was Sasha. Mrs. Finley said that she was sick with worry about her and hoped that I would agree to help Cicero Finley look after her while she was in the hospital.

I watched the family of three carefully from behind the shield of the lunch I had offered to prepare for us. I thought wistfully of the catered food I had cancelled.

It was clear to me that Salome loved Cicero Finley, and I could see that he was a father who paid attention to his child. However, it was clear that Cicero Finley did not love Salome, and she obviously knew this.

She fought desperately for his attention every time she opened her mouth. Cicero Finley paid attention to her and listened to her, but there were no embers between them.

Every now and then, he would catch my eye and there was in them a pleading I knew I could not resist. I knew that I would help him and this woman and this child. I would make a decision about Cicero Finley and the fact that he had committed bigamy at a later time. Under my breath, I whispered what was fast becoming a refrain in my head: "I love him still; bigamy, child, weak mouth and all."

Salome did not eat lunch. She said the doctor had told her not to eat anything before her treatment. "Not even water has passed my lips since midnight. I'm very prepared." She got ready to go and check herself into the hospital, insisting that Cicero Finley not come with her. When I offered to accompany her, thinking that another woman would be helpful, I saw her eyes fill up with tears. She thanked me, but refused my company as well.

There was a resolute set to her jaw; she was clearly determined to be alone. As she stooped and kissed Sasha, she touched her fingers, ran her hands down her cheeks and over her shoulders. Then she bent down and caressed her feet; it was as if she was trying to commit her daughter's body to permanent memory.

It was a moment before I realized that I recognized the movement of hands over body like that. It was the way Mama Reevah had said good-bye to Papa Emmanuel in the last days before he had died. She had touched his hair and his head and his feet with her hands, loving him good-bye, over and over again.

Salome repeated the loving caress of her daughter's hair and her head one more time, then she whispered "Good-night" in her ear.

The tears were wet on her face when she stood up and turned to

Cicero Finley. My heart went out to her and I moved away, taking Sasha with me. I thought that the least Salome deserved was some privacy with Cicero Finley.

Later she came into the kitchen and sent Sasha to her father. Then she surprised me by hugging me closely again, saying, "Please take good care of my child. I know you love Cicero Finley. It eases the pain a whole lot. I see that you love him enough to love his child. Here is a note for you to read tonight after Sasha is in bed. Could you please do me the favour of not opening it until she is tucked into bed?"

There was a strange, wistful look on her face as she added, almost as an afterthought, "I will likely be resting peacefully by then." I looked at death approaching in Salome's eyes, for despite her talk of treatment, there was about her a feeling of the embrace of death. It had shone in her face and in her eyes when she had said "Good-night" to her daughter and caressed her.

She thanked me again profusely and I assured her that I was glad to be able to help her out at what must be a difficult time for her. I promised to look in on her at the hospital and she smiled, seeming pleased and surprised. She thanked me, saying, "You are so kind."

Deep behind my decision to help look after Sasha were memories of my Aunt Sage. I thought that this must have been how it had been for her when she left her children. Salome was not chasing rum and a man, she was seeking medical attention so that she could be well for her child. However, I had heard Aunt Sage say that the craving for rum and Rommel had the same kind of power as someone seeking food. I now also understood Aunt Sage's craving for a particular man at a particular time, for when I met Cicero Finley I had felt just the same. I would have followed him anywhere.

I told myself: "Take it or leave it, I love Cicero Finley." I could not turn off my heart's connection to him with the snap of my fingers. I had always known that he was not perfect; now I knew that he had a large wart. His dishonesty was now manifest all over my life.

Looking after the child felt like the best outcome from the whole situation. I wondered what shape Salome would be in after her treatment. And where would she go to convalesce? I had a hard time digesting how quickly my house had moved from oneness, to a couple, to a polygamous family with a child. Despite my resolve, I felt overwhelmed as I said good-bye to Salome. The enormity of what I had agreed to do had begun to sink in. Even though it was only going to be "for a week or two" as she had said, it would be a big change in my life.

I asked her questions about the treatment she was about to undergo and she answered with a stream of medical terms that I did not understand. As she rattled them off I thought that they sounded rehearsed, as if she had taken the time to learn how to pronounce them. I was impressed that she had taken such a great interest in what was being done to her body.

At first I had called her "Mrs. Finley" to embarrass Cicero Finley; and it had stuck. In the late afternoon, just before she left for the hospital, she touched my hand and asked if I would please call her "Salome." I smiled and nodded.

When her taxi arrived, Salome looked peaceful and happy. She smiled at the way Sasha hung onto me saying, "I am so glad that she likes you." So was I; she was a very well-behaved, bright child. I looked forward to the time that I would spend with her.

Cicero Finley started making calls to the hospital to check on Salome at about seven o'clock that evening. However, the telephone operator at the hospital said that there was no information on her and that perhaps she had not been formally checked into a room yet. Salome had said that she was not going to undergo treatment until the next day, so he expected that she would have been in bed, reading or watching television.

He had given her one of his precious old copies of *Ramparts* magazine, and told her that there was an interesting article on the Black Power Movement in it that he thought she would enjoy rereading. I thought that it was odd that he had not shown me any such article, seeing that it was I who was Black, not Salome. I consoled myself with the thought that they had shared radical politics while in university together.

It was almost with regret that he said that he had not been able to stay in love with her. He said that his whole perspective on life had shifted when he joined the Movement and he could do nothing about keeping things the same.

His consciousness as a Black man had made it impossible for him to feel happy with a white woman, even if she was the mother of his child. I did not answer as he spoke his story that night; I still felt as if I was only able to listen. I could not bring myself to speak the volumes that lay inside me.

It was while we waited for news of Salome that we remembered that we each had letters from her "to be read after Sasha is tucked in." So when her bedtime came, Cicero Finley read her a story from one of the books her mother had left for her and then he kissed her good-night. Sasha was fast asleep moments after she was tucked in. She had had a long day. She had travelled to Toronto by train, and had not taken a nap, either on the train or in Toronto. She had been too excited to see her father.

I did not open my letter right away. First I went to the kitchen to make us peppermint tea. I heard Cicero Finley gasp with shock. "Salome has killed herself," he tried not to shout, but his voice was high-pitched and frightened... "When she left here she didn't go to the hospital, she went to jump over the Bloor Street viaduct." He was dialling the police as he spoke. "She says people have been jumping there since 1919...she thinks that their spirits will help her." Then he mumbled under his breath. "Crazy white bitch...I don't know what I was thinking of, having a child with her."

A few moments ago he had been acting like a concerned husband. Now Salome had become a "crazy white bitch." I thought his reaction was callous, but I did not say anything at the time. I was too shocked.

As I made tea I tried to focus on Cicero Finley's voice reading Salome's letter. I was too scared to read my letter. I had taken a peek at it and had seen the salutation: "My dear Sister Sayshelle..." I had looked over the first page and noticed that it was full of ellipses. "It looks as if she was taking deep breaths as she wrote," I thought. The ellipses had disappeared by the time she had reached page two, so I guessed that her emotions had evened themselves out the more she wrote.

"Poor Salome," I thought. My heart went out to her; for with much less on my plate, I had once considered doing away with my life. It was my memory of Seleena and the feeling of her spirit close around me that had kept me from succumbing to such a drastic response.

Cicero Finley agreed to meet the police at the Bloor Street viaduct as they needed him to identify Salome's body. I heard him telling them of her cancer, then agreeing that she was not in high spirits. He held me close as he got off the phone and hung onto me. I had a feeling that he was afraid of being by himself, but we both knew that I had Sasha to look after and could not accompany him. Our lives were changed; we were no longer free agents.

After Cicero Finley left, I began to shake. My feet pulled me to the kitchen to finish drinking the tea. Although he would not likely be back for some time, I made Cicero Finley another cup of peppermint tea: his favourite. He had gulped down the first cup while reading the letter from Salome to me. I wished he could have stayed until I read mine.

She had not been too kind to Cicero Finley. The first sentence of his letter spelled out everything about the suicide: the place, the point along the bridge, the reason she was doing it. It went on: "Please do not hate me for doing this. It is the easiest way for me. Please find a way to tell Sasha gradually, as she grows older. She is very comfortable with the concept of death. I have prepared her well for my passing; she just needs to be cushioned from knowing the way I chose to do it. I've prepared her by telling her that I am going to a place for treatment (I did not want her to think of hospitals as bad places) and that my body may not return, but my spirit will always be with her."

Salome also asked Cicero Finley to have her body cremated and the ashes kept until Sasha was deemed by him to be old enough to make a decision about where she wanted to have them scattered. She asked that Sasha sing a song, or read a poem, or just speak...say anything she wanted in a little ceremony to say good-bye to her as she scattered her ashes.

The letter had shocked Cicero Finley; but he understood how carefully she was instructing the police about the nature of her death. He took the letter with him so that the coroner would have evidence that it was a suicide and not a murder. She had arranged her death in a most tidy way.

I had returned my letter from Salome to its envelope. I was unable to keep it in my hands. It even felt strange holding the envelope. I set it down on the table, thinking, "She touched it just before she left to jump." It made me shudder. I poured a capful of brandy into my coffee, wishing I had a cigarette. I had not smoked in five years.

Cicero Finley called me from the police station to obtain the telephone number of Salome's parents. For the first time, I saw the inside of his briefcase and his address book. Under "Campbell" I found their telephone number. I recognized it as one of the three numbers I had seen on our telephone bill. I also saw Salome's number listed under "S. Finley." I recognized the number I had called. I winced inside, wondering how much, besides telephone numbers, this man had kept hidden away from me.

I went back to the phone and gave him the telephone number. Then I reminded him that I had asked Salome why she was taking a full bag of clothes to the hospital with her. I had even offered to keep the suitcase until she came out of the hospital. He said that he remembered her replying, "No, I might as well keep all of my clothes with me. I might need more than the one outfit."

There was sadness in his voice, but I heard relief as well. As soon as I rang off, I remembered that this was his birthday—the day that Jimi

Hendrix died—now the day that Salome had died. This was the day of Cicero Finley's birth.

Chapter Nine

My dear Sister Sayshelle,

I am writing to make sure that you know that my death has nothing to do with your relationship with Cicero...I am aware that he committed bigamy...by marry - ing you...I am sure that you did not know that I existed...let alone that we were still married...I saw the photographs...after Cicero left the house to go and meet you...I went seeking...and I found the lovely wedding photographs...I had noticed that there were wedding photographs when I first entered the house, but without my glasses, I had no idea that they included Cicero!

I want you to know that I had the baby...to try to hold on to Cicero...He and I were in love during our first two years in university...Then he found the Black Power Movement and it was as if the scales fell from his eyes...While I believe that he still cares for me, he just could not feel the same way about me any more...He grew and that meant that he outgrew me.

These things happen and I do not bear him any malice...I insisted that he leave to pursue his studies. For we were no longer living together...In fact...we separated when I was still pregnant...He agreed to stay close to his daughter...and he has. By now, you must know that your man is weak. He is not the soldier he pretends to be. So I am hoping that you will forgive him. He is fallible. I cannot tell you what to do; I love him so much, I only want for him what he wants for himself. And I see that he wants you.

In the beginning, Cicero tried to hang in there with me, but it was eating him up inside. Before I understood all that was going on with him...I figured if I got pregnant...he would not leave me...You see we had only been married for a year when he changed... I still hold the memory of how happy we were in the begin - ning...But...I wanted him to leave by the time I was pregnant because I could not bear to live with his unhappiness.

I would watch him cringe away from me...and feel so upset...I thought it was bad for the baby growing inside of me. So we agreed that we would separate. He looked after me, however, all through the pregnancy and the delivery and the after- care of Sasha. He is a wonderful father, as I am sure you can already see.

I am writing this letter to you for the sake of my daughter, but also for Cicero's sake. I watched you with Sasha and I watched you with him and I can see your heart. You are a kind and gentle person. I am begging you to see it in your heart to be co-guardian to Sasha, if anything should happen to me. I watched you look at

Cicero when you thought I was not looking and I can see that you love him. When he looks at you, I see a depth in his eyes that I have never seen before; not even when we were young and in love did he look so at peace as when he rests his eyes on you.

Sasha is looked after financially by a trust fund set up by my parents...I have put Cicero's name as the recipient. My parents have agreed. He was very close to them; he still is. I have also left a will with my lawyers and a copy for Cicero out - lines these things. I am really hoping that you will agree to my request. It is a lot to ask of you, but I am hoping that your love for Cicero and your kindness towards Sasha will help you to do what I ask.

I hope that my arriving on your doorstep did not cause any disruption in your relationship with Cicero. I am sure that you can see that whatever love he had in his heart for me has long since turned into appreciation of me as the mother of his child.

So, Sayshelle, kiss my daughter good-bye for me. I am not brave. I will kiss her good-night, but cannot explain that it is a good-bye kiss.

I have given Cicero a letter to be read to Sasha now and another that is to be given to her when she is twenty-one years old.

With deep appreciation of your kindness and friendship, though brief.

Peace and love and sisterhood.
Salome Campbell-Finley.

My head ached. I was glad that Sasha was asleep. I did not feel like seeing a reminder of her mother at that moment. It occurred to me that if she and her father left my house tomorrow, my life would be uncomplicated, simple, and uncluttered. If this is what my house felt like, I would rather revert to Aunt Helen's house. I went to put the kettle on to make a cup of Aunt Helen's favourite *noo-noo* balsam tea.

I lit a candle to say good-bye to Salome, for I did not want her spirit or her essence with me anymore. I was glad that she had taken her bag of clothes with her. As soon as possible, I would throw away Sasha's clothes and buy new ones. I would purge her mother from my physical and spiritual space, though not from her daughter's memory. I would never do that.

Now I felt oppressed by a Black man and his white woman. "Lord have mercy, Mama Reevah, what a to-do!" I thought of calling her or Aunt Juniper Berry on the telephone, but I balked at explaining the whole situation. There were no words I could have found to explain how the man in the wedding photograph had already been married when he married me.

Chapter Ten

Not long after I had agreed to marry Cicero Finley properly, I started hearing disturbing rumours that he was in fact a "plant." We were about to put into motion a church wedding in Antigua, with my whole family in attendance. I had not yet written to Mama Reevah to tell her the good news; but I planned to do so very soon. We would then have been legally married in at least one legal system. We had not yet figured out what would be done about the false marriage we had had, complete with wonderful photographs in front of the beautiful building of Old City Hall and a marriage certificate that had disappeared. Cicero Finley said he did not know what had happened to it and neither did I.

The rumour was that Cicero Finley was working in the Black Canadian community as a deep-cover agent of the CIA and the RCMP. At first, I ignored the rumours. I laughed about them and thought that they were the fantasy of some jealous person. But when Cicero Finley and I were excluded from several small gatherings at different people's houses, I wondered if there was any truth to the stories. Before the rumours, we were always at every event, just like everyone else. There was a core group of people who saw each other at every party, every picnic, every meeting.

Now we only seemed to hear about things after the fact, and in a rather by-the-way kind of talk, with no details. Within a month, it was clear to me that we had been ostracized by the inner circle of the Black community. Cicero Finley brushed it off, saying, "Maybe they forgot to invite us."

I did not believe that, for in the past we had never been forgotten. I decided that I would make a point of getting in touch with my friend Rashaan, who was someone in the know, and ask him to tell me what was going on. It was almost as if he heard me call his name, for that very evening I received a phone call from him. Rashaan and I had gone out briefly a few years previously, but had parted company. He was one of the two men with whom I had dallied before meeting Cicero; the one with whom I had not had an intimate relationship.

I agreed to meet him the next day for lunch, knowing that it would be hard to wait through the night for the morning to arrive. If Cicero Finley was not to be trusted, I needed to find out for myself, first-hand, whether it was true or not. The fact that he had chosen to ignore what was happening disturbed me and pointed, in my view, to the possibility of his being guilty of what was suspected.

That night I watched Cicero Finley as he read a bedtime story to Sasha. I found it hard to reconcile this image of the good father with that of a man who would sell out his own people for a few pieces of silver. I made sure that I went to bed much earlier than he did, so that we would not have any more conversation that night. My head ached from so much life.

The next morning, I got up earlier than usual and dressed for work while Cicero Finley was attending to Sasha. He always dealt with her in the mornings—bathing her, feeding her, and taking her to the daycare centre. I kissed Sasha good-bye as she sat in her high chair eating oatmeal. She asked me: "You're not eating breakfast Momma?" Cicero Finley and I had taught her to call me "Momma." She had called Salome "Mommy" and we had not wanted to confuse her with the same name.

Sasha was accustomed to our routine: usually I came downstairs in my dressing gown and ate breakfast while Cicero Finley cleaned the leftover pieces of food off her face, from her hair, off the table. I always made a joke of the routine, saying: "No toys in my breakfast please...who put all of this toast on my chair? Who did it? You, Sasha? No? You, Cicero Finley? Daddy did it! You're bad Daddy...you put toys in my breakfast and you put toast on my chair."

This would bring peals of laughter from Sasha each and every morning. I always thought that it was amazing how much children were able to repeat the same action, or say the same thing over and over and over again. She loved continuity, regularity, the familiar. I wondered how she would cope with any change in our household. For I had already begun to think of how our living arrangement would change if the worst possible thing were true.

Had I jeopardized my friendships with people in the community by harbouring Cicero Finley, by marrying him? I had clearly given him an opportunity to penetrate the community more deeply than he would have been able to on his own. If Cicero Finley was an agent, it meant that he had effectively destroyed my status in the community. And my community was my family. What would I do for a sense of grounding...of belonging? I knew that I could not survive the loss of another family.

Somehow I managed to get through the morning at work. Rashaan arrived for our lunch meeting with his face full of doom and gloom. He had asked me to meet him at Bonny's Place because of the confidential nature of what we planned to discuss. Bonny was a part of the Movement and she had converted her basement into a little bootleg restaurant cum meeting place. You could reserve the space a day in advance, Rashaan told me. I had only been there once before and it had been so long ago that Bonny did not recognize me.

Bonny cooked a different meal each day of the week. It was Friday, so it was stewed fish. After that day, whenever I smelled stewed fish, I remembered watching Rashaan eat as my world fell apart. He got to the point as soon as his lunch arrived. He was using the time to the best advantage, he said. There was a lot he had to tell me and a lot I needed to read, plus there were photographs.

I had had the good sense to order only bush-tea. From the look on his face I knew that I would not be able to eat. My pot of tea arrived at the same time as Rashaan's meal and I was grateful for the strong aroma of the Caribbean bush. I had chosen *noo-noo* balsam, needing the sense of comfort that the familiar, healing aroma would bring me.

Rashaan took a large brown envelope from his briefcase. He said that he had obtained permission to convey to me the information in the Movement's possession concerning Cicero Finley. "It is time for you to be apprised of the situation. At this time, if Cicero Finley also knows what we know, it is all right. We have taken the appropriate steps to safeguard ourselves. And now we are concerned about safeguarding you. Even though you are not in the Movement, you are of the community and you work hard for our community. We have to look after you."

When Rashaan said those words, I burst out laughing. He looked hurt; I knew that he took things very seriously. So did I, but I was nervous and needed the laughter to help me cope. Feeling as if we were in the middle of some cloak-and-dagger operation, I fell into the spirit of things. I looked around as I opened the envelope. Bonny had discreetly gone upstairs and left us alone in the room.

The contents of the envelope were shocking. Not only was Cicero Finley a mercenary in Toronto, it was also believed that he carried out the same role in the United States and in England. He was thought to be an international undercover agent whose assignment was to keep radical social movements under surveillance.

He had been a writer at *Ramparts* magazine in the U.S., and had been recruited by the CIA as a part of their taking-down of the magazine. *Ramparts* magazine had published articles indicating that the CIA had funded the National Student Association through a number of front organizations. The CIA set out to close *Ramparts* magazine down.

When that operation had been exposed, Cicero Finley had been kept on the CIA's payroll as an undercover agent. He had never been formally outed as an agent, but people suspected that he had been feeding information to the CIA for his last two years at *Ramparts* magazine.

The CIA had then sent Cicero Finley to investigate the Movement in Canada, especially in Toronto, Halifax, and Montréal. His cover included the story of parents in Montréal from whom he was estranged.

I had not yet met Cicero Finley when the story about *Ramparts* magazine broke; he came to Toronto after the Sir George Williams Affair in 1968 and had left *Ramparts* magazine in 1967. At that time, I had not even taken a cursory glance at the articles that talked about the CIA shakedown. It had all seemed far away and unrelated to anything that was going on in the spaces of my life.

Of course, my lack of knowledge about events in the U.S. made me a perfect target. I would not have caught on to Cicero Finley's cover as easily as another American, for example, or a more informed Canadian. I did not know many Canadians and the only Americans I knew were effectively kept away from us by Cicero Finley's avoidance of them. I had noticed that he had a proclivity for things American, but not for Americans themselves. I had never understood why he did not hang out with the Black Americans who were dodging the U.S. draft; they were about the same age as him and were focused on the Movement in the U.S. So many things that had seemed odd to me now fell into place.

He used to get up early on Sunday mornings and go to a particular newsstand to buy the *New York Times*. Whether it was snowing, raining, or hot as hell, he never missed a week. I thought that it was an incredible commitment to a U.S. newspaper, but then I began to enjoy reading it myself and so thought nothing of it.

It was hard to swallow the fact that along with gathering information on the Black Power Movement all over the world, Cicero Finley had also been instructed to incite riots so that the police could step in and shoot and arrest people.

"He was in it for the money," Rashaan said. "He was a mercenary, not an ideologue." In one skirmish at which he was present in the U.S., the police and firemen had used dogs and fire-hoses on Black people who were demonstrating for the right to vote. And there was Cicero Finley's handsome face in a photograph, peering out from among the leaders of the protest, who had been ravaged by dogs. He had managed to be in so many scenes of conflict, but he had never been shot or mauled by dogs. He had always been forewarned about where to go if things got out of hand.

It came to light that Cicero Finley was not Canadian at all. He was American. There was a picture of his real passport, complete with photograph and signature. I winced as I looked into the face that I had held so often between my hands and glanced at those treacherous lips that I had kissed with sweet abandon.

Rashaan pointed out that unlike the usual hangers-on around the Movement, Cicero Finley seemed too polished, too right for the role...everything was just too conveniently in place. Cicero Finley's game had struck some people in the Movement as being too superbly fine-tuned. He never tried to be connected or to get close to the inner circle in Toronto. His game was designed to keep him in a holding pattern on the edges of every political hotbed.

A check on him revealed that he had been present when too many events went down. And he had been photographed with too many key players. It didn't matter whether it was in Montréal, Toronto, Chicago, New York, Watts, Baltimore, or England; he was always present. It was as if he was creating evidence of a life that he was not actually living.

"And no one thought of warning me?" I asked. Rashaan assured me that I was warned as soon as they knew for sure...and so this was the day to tell me. Apparently, I too had been suspected of being an agent.

"Did you vouch for me?" I was surprised to hear how small and vulnerable my voice sounded. Rashaan smiled reassuringly at me. "Sayshelle, you know you are my girl. Of course I vouched for you; from the very beginning, I said that your being an agent was a ridiculous notion. You are not in the Movement, but we had to protect you as well as ourselves." Then he paused and said jokingly, "You dropped me for Cicero Finley, but you are still my girl."

I could not bring myself to reprimand him for calling me "girl." And I did not bother reminding him that I had dropped him long before I had met Cicero Finley. I had dropped him because he had been romancing another woman in the Movement. I was well aware that he meant "girl" as a term of endearment, and I knew that he wanted me to know that he was available for support. So I smiled back.

"You know, Sayshelle, when we were dating, I was young and foolish; I was untutored about how to love a woman." I looked at him with amazement; he sounded so sincere and earnest. He must have taken my look for one of disbelief, because he reiterated that he was much changed.

Then he added, "I know you are involved with Cicero Finley, but if you pick up your shoes and run from him as fast as you ought to, then maybe you will give me a chance to make amends...to show you how much I care about you. I'm not trying to rush you, and I mean it when I say that you are my girl. You have stayed in my heart."

He brought his face close to mine and took both my hands in his. "I am here for you Sayshelle...I was not able to tell you anything before this. As soon as I knew that it was all right to tell you, I called you. So know that I am here to support you."

He then pretended to sing to me. *"Call me...don't be afraid, you can call me."* I laughed, glad for the relief from the seriousness of our meeting. The photographs with Cicero Finley's face loomed out like sharp reminders of the state of my life. I did not respond to Rashaan. I smiled and clasped his hands tightly, then released them. I sighed and turned my attention again to the material on the table and the thoughts churning inside me.

My head was spinning as I tried to recall all of the places Cicero Finley had told me that he had been. Besides the Sir George Williams Affair, there had been an incident in Halifax where community activists had been watched by the police. He had just happened to be in Halifax that very weekend. Those were almost the very words he had used when I had remarked that he always seemed to be in the right or wrong place at the right or wrong time.

It was members of leftist political groups in England that had started to investigate Cicero Finley. He had run from London when he discovered that they were on to him. It had taken them three years to track him to Toronto. I also knew that Cicero Finley had been present in Trinidad during the abortive revolution of 1970. I always thought that odd, because he had no ties to Trinidad. I never understood why he had chosen to go there alone and stay in a hotel during a time of social unrest. I chalked it up to his commitment to the Movement. That is what he had said and I had accepted it.

He said that he saw struggle as a global, international concept and not as something that could be viewed in isolation. I had rather admired that about him, even though I recognized that I was not so committed as to travel to participate in conflict. I felt that there was enough within Canada's borders that needed attention. The information I had in front of me showed that he had spent the last ten years of his life going from conflict zone to conflict zone. I lost count after the number rose to ten.

There was even a photograph of him taken in Paris in 1968. At that time, according to him, he had just become a father and had had no money. His being in Paris was as bizarre to me as his having been in Trinidad in 1970. There was a whole package of photographs that showed him in places I had never even known he had visited. Clearly he had reported the details of his life to me and to others quite selectively.

As my fingers nervously flicked from photograph to photograph, one in particular caught my eye. I picked it up and stared at the date written on the back in shock. It showed Cicero Finley at a meeting in London, England. It had been taken at a time when I had thought him safely tucked away in his parents' home in Montréal for a week's holiday.

He had made a big deal of going home, saying that perhaps this time he would make peace with them. I remembered that he had even phoned me, and had put me on hold while he took a cup of tea from his mother. I distinctly remembered the incident, because I had thought it a good sign that they were making peace. When he had returned from that trip, he had told me that "things were hopeful." It was not just the date and his face in the crowd that caught my eye; there was another face that stood out. I noticed this face because there were so few white faces in the room. It was Salome.

Shock rippled through my body. Rashaan stopped speaking; I thought that he must have realized that there was a lot for me to take in all at once. My head reeled. I recalled all the other occasions when Cicero Finley had said that he had gone home to Montréal, always on extended weekend trips. Sometimes he would be late getting back; he would call me from Montréal (he said) and give me explanations that I used to grudgingly accept. I always had a nagging feeling that there was something else going on, but my worst suspicion was that he was with other women.

"What God is he serving then?" I wondered. "The god of money? But he does not have any...or at least, he *says* he doesn't have any." I realized that everything had to be held up to scrutiny now.

I had always believed Cicero Finley about everything. Since I had found out about Salome and Sasha, I simply thought that his trips had been to visit them. I had never bothered to ask him about them, because it had all seemed unnecessary once I knew that he had a child whom he visited and phoned. And Salome had said that he spent a lot of time with his daughter. My fingers raced back through the other photographs. Earlier I had barely glanced at them long enough to find Cicero Finley's face. Now I looked for another face: the white face of Salome. And there she was, smiling in several of the photographs, right there alongside Cicero Finley.

"It was a meeting of the Radical Left Caucus," Rashaan said of the group in London. He explained that Cicero Finley and Salome were members of the group, and had been recognized as undercover agents for a number of years. They had been allowed to appear to infiltrate some groups, just so the spy-plate could be filled and the group could then get on with the business at hand. If they had known that their cover was blown, then along would come another agent and the group would have had to check them out all over again.

"Even their marriage was a part of their cover. She is from Montréal, so that facilitated his living there." Rashaan's voice sounded full of sympathy. He touched my hand. "I am sorry, Sayshelle." I appreciated his concern; I was glad that I had kept him as a friend. I could not have taken this information from just anyone in the Movement.

"However, the child came from the wilful act of Salome, and it almost cost her her job as an agent. She fell in love with Cicero and seduced him from time to time, trying to get pregnant. She figured that seeing as they already had a marriage certificate, it would be convenient.

Their employers, the CIA and the RCMP, were not happy about this. Oh, and they are not aware of the fact that you two got married. They were not watching Cicero Finley; Left political groups were. The Left found out that he committed bigamy and figured that they would leak it to the police and get him arrested for that. We in the Movement are concerned about you, however, so we struck a deal. They will threaten him with the bigamy charge in order to get him to leave town, so to speak." He laughed. "Sounds like the wild, wild West, doesn't it?"

He continued. "It is very likely that he will accept the offer. His employers were banking on his presence here not being discovered by the police. This is partly the reason that he tended to lie low at first. Then things changed and he was ordered to step up infiltration of the Movement and also destruction of the Movement, by framing people and so on.

We believe that he was just about to start that kind of activity and we are concerned about how he would implicate you, or use you. He needs human resources, because he is on his own; there is no cooperation from the police on this project. It is deep-deep-cover...underneath *their* cover...kinda like a mission impossible."

Rashaan looked at me with concern in his eyes. I was thinking of how over one short lunch, my life had become nothing but a cover for an undercover agent. I was also thinking of how I had loved Cicero Finley so much and so well. A little vicious part of me wanted to see him suffer. I soon let that thought go; it could hardly be worth it to invest any time and energy in revenge.

Black people in Toronto were known to border on being paranoid about undercover agents. So Cicero Finley had been given a hard task and he was working his way into it in the deepest possible way, laying down roots, working on community projects, getting close to someone in the community. He was really worming his way in quite nicely.

Cicero Finley had asked his employers for permission to marry me properly. He had confessed to them that he had fallen in love with me and committed bigamy. He had suggested to his contact that such a marriage was a good way of solidifying his cover, because he was a widower, they had no problems with it, from a legal standpoint. They promised to look after erasing our first marriage certificate from the files at City Hall and had advised Cicero Finley to destroy our copy of the certificate.

At last I had a reason for the destruction of our framed marriage certificate. I had long decided that Cicero Finley felt embarrassed and ashamed of himself every time he looked at the certificate. It had been merely another lie that I had added to his package of lies.

Rashaan told me that Cicero Finley and Salome had had no separation, for they had had no *real* marriage, even though they had been legally married for their cover. They had both simply told me their cover story about meeting in university and so on. So there were no years spent together at Sir George Williams University, although Cicero Finley had made sure that he was present to be photographed with the students during the Sir George Williams Affair.

Salome had lied to me as well...but why? "She lied," Rashaan explained patiently, "because she was also an undercover agent. She was making the best of the situation. She wanted to die knowing that her child would be well looked after."

"And she had chosen me as their Mammy?" I was feeling manipulated and used. "Sure sounds like slavery to me!" Then I remembered that we had even taught Sasha to call me Momma!

Rashaan's information was impeccable. I thanked him for meeting with me and I thanked him for his concern. I *did* appreciate his concern, but I told him that I still felt betrayed. For I wondered why no one had attempted to warn me, why gossip had been leaked all over the community instead.

Rashaan explained that one person had leaked the information before they were sure enough of it. As soon as they had received reliable information, he had been asked to contact me. He was also to help me sort things out with Cicero Finley, help me to get a lawyer if one was needed.

I was frightened and did not know what to do. Rashaan advised me to ask Cicero to leave my house immediately. In the meantime, he would continue to keep me informed. "And what will you do about the child?"

he asked, his voice full of concern.

"The child did not ask to be born," I said, proudly quoting Mama Reevah. He looked at me with surprise. "You're going to keep her?" I nodded. "If I can."

I did not have a sense of whether or not Cicero Finley would voluntarily give his daughter over to my guardianship. I did not want joint custody with him; I wanted full custody of Sasha. I would then adopt her. It was a wild idea, but it came to me as clearly as if I had thought about it for a long time.

I had proof that Cicero Finley had spent very little time with Sasha; even now, the only time he *did* spend with her was in the mornings and afternoons when he happened to be in Toronto. For he had continued to travel up until the last week or so. I had even been thinking of hiring a private detective to find out if he was having an affair. For now that Sasha was with us, I could not figure out why he had felt it necessary to visit the parents from whom he claimed to be estranged.

I thought that I could have him declared an unfit father in a heartbeat, and then I could hold that threat over him. I had Salome's letter, didn't I? And if I moved fast and was clever, I would soon have his letter from Salome, plus a copy of her will. I knew where they were kept and I would be able to gather them up and give them to a lawyer.

As we walked out of the restaurant, a ray of sunshine hit me straight in the middle of my forehead. I looked up at the sky, grateful for the warmth; in that moment, I knew that I would definitely look after Sasha.

Salome's letters made more sense to me now. Cicero Finley had labelled her a "crazy white bitch," but she did not seem so crazy to me. She seemed to have known *exactly* what she was doing when she had deposited her child and her letters on my doorstep. When all was said and done, I appreciated her as a mother of her child. She had looked after her daughter's life in the long-term very well.

I did not even need to get divorced from Cicero Finley. It was good, too, that he had always paid rent as a tenant in my house; so in the legal sense, I had been merely his landlady. I could separate myself from him quite easily, but my emotions were another matter.

I hoped that Aunt Helen was looking on and smiling with me. It would be good to go home after work and reclaim my house...yes indeed.

Chapter Eleven

I returned home in the middle of the afternoon and as I stepped out of my car, I walked right into Cicero Finley. He said he had been hoping that I would come home early. I wondered why he had not called me at work. I said nothing; I just wanted to get our talk over and done with. I also realized that there were only three hours left before we had to pick up Sasha at the daycare centre.

I could feel my knees buckling; I was shaking with fear mixed with rage. When he asked, "What did you hear about me?" he had the grace to look genuinely worried and unhappy. I used as few words as I could to tell him that I had heard and seen enough to know that he was a liar, an undercover agent, an impostor, and so on, and so on.

Halfway through my tirade I simply stopped myself and said, "I will be back in a few minutes with my lawyer, so you might as well begin thinking of where you are going to rest your head tonight. Sasha can continue living with me, if you would like. In fact, I would be happy to continue looking after her. I will honour my commitment, for she did not ask to be involved in all of this."

He seemed grateful to hear about my intention to continue looking after Sasha, and it occurred to me that maybe the business of Sasha would be easier than I had anticipated. I did not want to talk with him any more. I just wanted him out of my sight as soon as possible.

He did not confirm or deny anything, but the alacrity with which he agreed to move out and leave Sasha with me spoke volumes to me about his guilt. It was not necessary for him to confirm things, but he would have gone up a notch in my estimation if he had offered an explanation of how he had comfortably lived as a traitor to his people.

I felt that it was in my cousin Seleena's name and memory that I would take care of this child for as long as was needed. And I would give her love. She was not of my family but she was of my human family. In fact, she was a part of my extended family. After all, I had married Cicero Finley in good faith and this was his child, although it was not for him that I would mother her. It was through him, however, that she had arrived for me to acknowledge and honour her by helping. Yes, it was for

Seleena's sake that I would be mother to Sasha.

Through all of this, I had flashing memories of the nights I had held Cicero Finley in my arms, loved him and listened to him. There were some nights when he had not been able to sleep and I had stayed up with him. One night he had cried tears while he talked about how much the white man trampled on the Black man.

I felt now that those were all crocodile tears. "Or at best," I muttered to myself, "they were tears over how he had his own foot up the Black man's ass. Lord have mercy, how could I have been so trusting? That man could have killed me in my bed." Maybe he had meant those tears. For guilt must have hit him in the gut from time to time.

All the way to the lawyer's office, I tried to remember what personal secrets I had revealed to Cicero Finley; but then I laughed at myself, because I did not really have anything to hide. My life was an open book on the personal level. And on the political level, I had not been involved in the Movement. In fact, I knew of no subversive activities that could be attributed to anyone in the Movement in Toronto. Everyone's activities were confined to community work, in particular, to working with children.

I wondered what Cicero Finley's reports to his superiors had contained. How did he justify their spending money, sending him to law school, paying his rent, for his food, his clothes, all of his expenses, to spy on a community of people doing their normal living? All of that money had been used to keep tabs on hard-working Black people in Toronto. Sometimes there had been peaceful demonstrations. And there were protests against police shootings of Black people, and against apartheid, and to remove "Little Black Sambo" books from school libraries, and against the police raiding a fundraising event for the legal costs of those Black people who had been arrested in the Sir George Williams Affair.

These activities hardly warranted undercover agents; but clearly, just as people in the Movement were careful, so too were the CIA and the RCMP. They obviously thought that it was worth their while to know everything that was happening.

The next day, Rashaan called early in the morning and asked me to meet him at a restaurant for breakfast. I felt dazed as I got ready to go to meet him. The night had passed uneventfully, but I still reeled in shock from the turn of events.

Sasha had not reacted to her father's departure with any emotion. She had been used to seeing him come and go throughout her whole life, I figured.

At breakfast, Rashaan told me that things had moved swiftly. He had received word late in the night that a decision had been made to leak the news of Finley's status as a CIA agent to the press. "It is being done as a self-protective measure," he said. He did not explain the precise reasons, but I figured that they had decided the way to get rid of Cicero Finley was to expose him publicly. That way, the backlash would be minimal.

If the Movement decided to do nothing about him, they would have had to continue to maintain the elaborate ruse by which they had been feeding him the wrong information. They had essentially been having two sets of meetings: one that included him and the *real* meeting at someone's home without him.

Rashaan told me that Cicero Finley was virtually under a kind of house arrest. He had been given forty-eight hours to leave Toronto before the story about him being an undercover agent would be leaked to the media. The inner circle of the Movement had also threatened to expose his bigamy to the police. He was instructed not to use the telephone and to book himself a ticket to the destination of his choice. His every move was being watched; one of the men from the Movement was staying with him until it was time to go to the airport. He had moved into the YMCA for the night.

I asked: "But what about Sasha and me? How will we escape news reporters?"

"I am coming to that," Rashaan said. "With your agreement, we would like to help you and the child to leave town on an impromptu vacation." He explained that they had arranged for us to go to his home in Nevis and stay with his parents. "You can cool out there for as long as you want to," Rashaan said. "My parents will not be advised of what is going on. You will be described as a widow...your husband was a white American who died in the Vietnam War. That will explain his absence and Sasha's skin colour."

He looked worried, as if he thought that I would resist the plan, but I liked the idea of taking Sasha away from Toronto until things had calmed down. It would prevent her being sullied by the media hype that was sure to take place. I was worried about money, however, because even given Sasha's monthly cheque from her trust fund, I knew that more money would be needed while we were staying in a strange country. I also had to maintain my home in Toronto.

Rashaan explained that one of the "brothers" worked for the airlines and would be able to obtain discount tickets for us. In addition, he offered to pay for our meals while we stayed at his parents' house, so the only money that I would need would be for transportation to and from the airport.

Thankfully, Sasha was young enough that her sudden absence from the daycare centre would not be considered unusual. Getting away from my job was a little more difficult. I knew that if I wanted to keep the job, I had to make a reasonable excuse to my supervisor.

I did not want to return to Toronto from an unplanned holiday without a job. True, I had no mortgage or rent to pay, but I had living expenses and I had taken on the care of a young child. So I explained to my supervisor that my husband's ex-wife had committed suicide and left her daughter with us.

I watched her face as it went through contortions. She worked hard at holding the muscles of her face taut, so that, I suppose, she would not say things like: "Whaa-aat? Are you making this up?" I suspected that I had given her enough to talk about for a long time.

"So as you can imagine, I have a bit of a family crisis...I was thinking of asking you..." I had not quite worked out how much time I could reasonably ask for, but Mrs. Jenner did not allow me to get any further.

"Would you like to take a month off and get her settled?" I had my mouth open to continue speaking, but I closed it. I did not know what to say. A whole month! Then I figured I had better ask for even longer. "I actually hoped to ask for six weeks, or even two months," I said. She easily agreed to two months, saying, "It's our down time right now. If you had adopted a child, you would have been entitled to maternity leave."

I thanked her and felt tears of gratitude well up in my throat. I got up hurriedly; I did not want to share my tears. I hoped that the smile I turned on her was as brave as I tried to make it appear.

I appreciated the time off because an idea had been running through my head that I ought to sell my house. I would need time, after I returned to Toronto, to make it ready for viewing. I knew that I could not live in my house any more. Thanks to Cicero Finley, my address was in the CIA's files. I had seen it written in neat, printed handwriting on several pages from his reports to his superiors. It was a part of the identification of his reports...my address...Aunt Helen's house...*my house*.

Cicero Finley came to the house the next day and kissed Sasha good-bye. He had packed his things and moved out already and was preparing to leave the country. He tried to kiss me good-bye on my lips, but I turned my head and he caught me on the ear. We both laughed nervously. Then suddenly, on an impulse, I took his face in my hands and kissed him deeply, like a woman kisses her man good-bye. And he *had* been my man.

I had loved the warm heart I had known. I had seen flashes of it from time to time during our relationship, even though he had always seemed to be fighting against restraints that I had never understood. He had cheated us both out of the kind of love we needed.

He signed the papers that the lawyer had drawn up to give me sole guardianship of Sasha. I told him that whenever he felt that he wanted to see his daughter, he had only to let the lawyer know. As he said good-bye to Sasha, he told her that he would be in touch with her soon. We had agreed that he would always be able to write to her through my lawyer and that he would leave an address where letters from Sasha could be forwarded to him.

After that day, I had no trouble getting Cicero Finley out of my heart. I had effectively moved him out of my life, but I had been holding him in my heart...still. I remembered how weak his mouth had looked and how it trembled when he signed the papers from the lawyer. It trembled when I kissed it too.

The meaning of that mouth that I had seen on the very first night I had met him returned to haunt me. I could not have seen in his mouth that he lacked a conscience and that he would bring such emotional wreckage, but I might have paid more attention to his lack of openness about his background and his movements back and forth to Montréal.

As I sat by the sea in Nevis, I let the mist wet my face. When I thought of Cicero Finley, I saw little streaks of anger radiating out from me. Feelings of betrayal, humiliation, and guilt left me as well. It was as if I was letting memory cleanse itself in the fine spray from the sea.

I could not shake a feeling of vulnerability. My sense of security as a member of a community based on skin was shattered by this experience. I was not protected; no one was protected. We were at the mercy of all and sundry who claimed to be Black.

I had the nagging feeling that I was still not comfortable, not entirely, with the way Salome had manipulated me. Only the sight of Sasha's face, her eyes smiling trustingly into mine, and the way her hand felt small and vulnerable as she put it confidently into mine kept Salome's guile from swimming before my eyes. It had been there in her eyes, in the smile on her face, but I had been preoccupied. I had been blinded by the shock of meeting her, the cancer, the whole drama of it all. I reached for peace in my heart; I needed it, if I was going to be able to mother Cicero Finley and Salome's child with a pure, loving heart.

The hours and hours of sitting, playing with Sasha, and talking with Rashaan's retired parents provided much time for introspection. It was not a great complex puzzle, but it had all unfolded in a very short space of time, and I was still in shock.

I had ricocheted from Toronto to Nevis expecting that it would be a little while longer before my head stopped spinning. The beauty of the country was just what my heart needed and I felt blessed that Rashaan had suggested it.

Sasha was a joy to Rashaan's parents. His father played games with her endlessly, delighting in the repetition of things just as much as she did. He taught her to play draughts, saying, "I taught Rashaan this game when he was a child."

I watched, fascinated at his patience. He was a gentle teacher and used laughter to soften every hurt that she felt from losing. By the end of our stay, I too learned to play draughts.

Rashaan's mother also developed a close-close relationship with Sasha. After two weeks, they had settled into a routine of hair-combing in the evenings. The first evening that she set up the cushions in front of her and called to Sasha, my eyes filled up with tears. I heard Mama Reevah's voice as it had given me the same simple command: "Come!"

Sasha had arrived in Nevis with the bobbed head that her mother had created just before leaving her at my house. Salome had cut her daughter's hair for the first time, she had said, and the child had loved the freedom from the thick plaits that had, up to that point, swung on her back. The warmth of the sun seemed to be like growing food for her hair, and within two weeks it needed to be braided to keep it from becoming a tangled mess.

Sasha took to the ritual of having her hair combed in the evenings like a duck to water. I had waited anxiously for her to wince in pain, but was pleased to see that Rashaan's mother had a gentle way of plaiting hair that Mama Reevah never had. Sasha hardly seemed to be aware that her hair was being plaited, and drew pictures on a piece of paper while her head was turned into a beautiful design of "Congo." Nevisians called it "Cane Row" or "Corn Row," but the style was the same rows of plaits that Mama Reevah had created on me and called "Congo."

After watching the closeness between Sasha and Rashaan's mother, I made a decision that I would set up the same kind of circumstances for hair-combing in the evenings once we returned to Toronto. I envisioned calling Sasha to plait her hair in the evenings in just the way Mama Reevah used to say to me: "Come!"

Chapter Twelve

I knew that it was not self-interest that had made Rashaan suggest his parents' home in Nevis as a place for me to "cool out," as he put it. He said that his family home was ideal because of its location in the countryside, and I agreed with him. It was so peaceful that I could almost feel myself de-stressing as the clock ticked away the minutes and hours and all I had to do was make sure Sasha had a good time. Nevis was only a half-hour plane ride from Antigua, but I was not ready to make the trip home as yet. I was gathering myself together.

One day, I reclined in the hammock on the gallery, swinging gently, keeping my back straight so that I could watch Rashaan's parents playing with Sasha. They were all laughing as they chased an elusive butterfly. It was too idyllic a scene for me, and I closed my eyes to get away from it.

I laid my head back in the hammock and took myself out of the scene in the front yard. I heard the child's squeals of delight turn to sheer joy and I considered raising my head, but by then, sleep had begun to envelop me. Finally she called out to me, "Momma! Momma! Look who's here!"

I opened my eyes slowly and my first thought was: "I was not dreaming of Cicero Finley; why is he in my dream?" It was Cicero Finley in the flesh. All he said to me was: "How can anyone spy on a spy?" I stared at him with my mouth hanging open foolishly. I could not speak.

Finally my voice came in a cracked whisper. "Does Rashaan know you're here?" He shook his head. "No; no one knows I am here. They think I went to New York. I gave a grad student friend of mine the ticket and he travelled using my birth certificate. He's going to enjoy a week or two in New York. I paid his return fare too. Then I used my passport to come here."

He gave me a lopsided grin; he seemed to be very proud of himself. It occurred to me that he had spoken quite loudly and my thoughts went to Rashaan's parents. "What must they be thinking?" I wondered.

He tickled Sasha, saying, "Did you think I could just walk away from you, Baby? You are my family."

I tried to get out of the hammock too quickly and caught my foot in it. I pitched forward and Cicero Finley caught me before I could crash onto the floor of the gallery. He held on to me, and then he hugged me and kissed me after he helped me to my feet.

I did not resist his embrace, as I figured we were under the watchful eyes of Rashaan's parents. I could not even think. My mind was fuzzy...I knew that there were many things I wanted to ask him, but I could not seem to formulate a question. I got out of his arms and looked around for Rashaan's parents. They stood in the yard where they had played happily with Sasha a moment earlier. I did not try to read their faces; I was too embarrassed.

Cicero Finley talked and talked about how much he wanted Sasha to live with him. He had a job, and he was going to make his home in the same town as his parents. I noticed that he did not say which town that was and I did not ask but I registered that he was hiding it on purpose. It made a lie of his saying that Sasha and I would be able to be in touch all the time. I recognized his words as comfort for his child.

He spoke to me in between the kisses and hugs that he gave to Sasha. I stared at him without speaking. Inside I screamed: "He sounds soo-oo American!" I supposed that now that he did not have to pretend to be from Montréal, he had reverted to being who he was...as American as apple pie...*Black* apple pie.

Rashaan's parents looked from me to Cicero Finley. I could tell that they knew that I was not pleased. My mind was focused on how ashamed I felt of the lie that Rashaan and I had told them. For the husband that we had claimed had died in Vietnam was in front of them...in living colour!

Of course, it would have been a bigger lie if we *had* told them that I had a husband, for that would have implicated me in bigamy. I knew that they would now be wondering about the parentage of the child. It was obvious that Cicero Finley and I could never have had a half-white child like Sasha. "Maybe they will think that we adopted her and my white husband really did die in Vietnam." A lie had a way of tying you up in it.

I was saddened at how quickly we had lost the little bit of Eden that we had enjoyed all morning. Only Sasha's spirits seemed higher than before. And no wonder: her daddy had suddenly arrived to surprise her. Her world was whole. It was clear to me from how happy she was that this man and his child belonged together much more than she and I belonged together. He had probably realized that he needed her more than anything right now, so I hoped that that would make him stay put and look after his daughter. Either way, I relinquished my concern and involvement; it was *his* child; he would look after her in the way he saw fit.

Without thinking about it too much, I was ready to give up Sasha. It was as if I had been doing a noble deed and had suddenly been relieved of the need to do it. My ego was suddenly no longer involved. In addition,

Cicero Finley had shown me that as long as I had Sasha, my life would be never free of him; and by extension, I would never be free of the CIA and the RCMP, so long as he was still employed by them. And I believed that he still was, no matter what other fables he told me. I decided to release his child to him immediately and then look after the documents formally and legally when I returned to Toronto.

I went inside the house and packed Sasha's clothes and books and toys. I took her into the bedroom where we had stayed together and I spoke with her for a long time. I told her that I loved her very much, but that it made sense for her Daddy to be the one with whom she lived. And I tempered her father's lie by saying I hoped that she and I "would be able to be in touch all the time."

Salome had trained her daughter to say good-bye. She did not seem to consider good-byes as heralding long-term separations. I supposed that that was because she had been left so often, but never for long. I promised that I would visit her and comb her hair one day. And I reminded her of the time that we had spent laughing and playing on the beach in Nevis. I kissed her and smoothed my hands over her head, her shoulders, and her toes in the same way that Mama Reevah had said goodbye to Papa Emmanuel; and in the same way her mother had said good-bye to her. For I knew that I would never see her again.

Wisdom came at night, pretending to be a thief, so that I hardly noticed its arrival. And when the sweet joy of morning came, I was ready, my mind wide open and clear. I no longer wavered back and forth, my emotions strung out between Antigua and Toronto, my Spirit still in Antigua. I learned to call my Spirit back from people and places.

I saw life reflected in the mirror, then I reluctantly shifted my gaze to regard it in the flesh. I felt myself unwilling to pull my eyes from the mirror, so that I would not have to experience the real event. For it was more than I wanted to bear.

All it took was that brief moment—as I turned my gaze away from the mirror, my whole life changed forever. The reflection clung to me like a separate entity and made itself seen in my eyes. One day, I was unseeing; the next day everything was altered.

It was not as if I had never suspected that there was something to see, but seeing pierced a hole in my heart. What had been a nagging ache after the discovery of my fake marriage became a great, big gaping hole with the revelation of Cicero Finley's deceit. I thought of this hole in my heart as burrowing so deep that I felt I could not touch the bottom.

I tried filling it with tears and they soon created a wet-land inside me. They would not fill that deep gaping chasm of pain. Eventually the tears seeped into my body and just stayed there. I was weeping for the life I was relinquishing. Giving up Sasha to her father felt as if I was closing a chapter in a more final way.

Rashaan's mother treated me the way the ailing are treated in the Caribbean. She gave me coconut-water to drink. She made soup and insisted that I eat. She and her husband asked no questions and I told them no more lies. I simply said that there was an explanation that Rashaan would give them. I was sure that they did not even need an explanation. They could see that a drama was unfolding in my life and wanted to help me keep it from turning into a tragedy.

They fed Cicero Finley and Sasha lunch and then the three of us left for the airport in a taxi.

I know that Cicero Finley spoke pleading words into the silence to which I had retreated, but I did not hear him. Even if I had, we no longer spoke the same language, so I would not have understood him. When he picked up Sasha to walk to the plane, I watched his mouth open and close, still forming words that begged for forgiveness.

He hoped his words would be a salve for my aching heart, but they would not have been able to sap the wound sufficiently. He spoke about love and I heard him at last, but I thought about politics and my people...Black people, whom he had betrayed. The two were intertwined and I could not consider one without the other.

I said nothing to his words. Instead, I observed the silence that had come to me since I had last seen him. It soothed me. It bade me leave things unspoken. I could not bear to touch him. I had already given him the residue of respect and love that had been in me when I had kissed him good-bye in Toronto. It was final.

His lips touched my forehead just before he walked to the plane and I marked the spot, so that I could cleanse it later.

Chapter Thirteen

Nevis was a place of quiet after my quasi-family's departure. I took long walks on the beach in the mornings and in the evenings. It was a time to think.

My thoughts were full of all that had taken place. Even though I knew that I generalized my personal issues, I realized that they spread further than my one little life. So in this-here place, on this-here new ground, I heard the same call to integrity that had beckoned Papa Emmanuel and Mama Reevah. And I heeded the call, but I did it differently. For the ground was different, the protagonists were different, the political work was different.

Without a doubt, Black men and women in Toronto were different; certainly they were unlike Mama Reevah and Papa Emmanuel. And we lived life in an entirely different way from everyone in Antigua.

In Antigua, I was Sayshelle Hughes, the daughter of Mister and Mistress Emmanuel Livingston Hughes. I was the daughter of "Corpie," whom people came to visit when he was sick, bringing him ground provisions and blue party-cloth for his shroud.

In Toronto, I was simply *Black*. For colour of skin was what mattered. It was the new story that was wrapped around us all. And it was buttoned around us in just such a certain way. So even though I was learning about other Black people for the first time, it was assumed that we were all one and the same. And we were not. I enjoyed knowing them, but we were not alike. I missed my own story. For I did not know "Black people"—I had learned them while *dreaming* Toronto, and I had learned them in the reality of *living* Toronto. I had learned about a Black man who had sold his soul for money, selling out Black people so that his life could be saved. This was a new kind of creature in my world; an entirely unknown quantity.

If I was lucky, there were times when I was *Black* Sayshelle Hughes. With my co-workers, I was sometimes *Black* Sayshelle Hughes; but more often than not, I was simply *Black*. And no matter how long we worked alongside each other, that was the first definition.

It brought with it no shortage of responsibility for everything and everyone Black. Working at my job, I was consulted about every difficult Black customer, as if I were a vast repository of knowledge about all Black people, no matter where they came from. I longed to say that I had not been hired to be a "Black consultant" but I did not. I needed the job. It would be interesting if I now said that I had not even been able to differentiate between a Black man from Montréal and a Black man from the U.S.

I noticed that when my feedback about a Black customer was positive, it did not necessarily help the customer to secure his or her loan. My input was only used when it was negative. I came to understand what Malcolm X had meant about the responsibilities of "Miss First," for I was still the only Black woman in my bank. Malcolm X had warned that "Miss" or "Mister First" had to avoid being used by the white power structure. There had been a "Mister First" before me, but he had left to go to university, I was told. "He was from Barbados. Maybe you know him?"

Even as I felt the loss of my story, I sought and loved the vastness of blackness and the connection with other people who looked like me and who thought like me. For it was not just white folks who identified me as Black—I had identified myself as Black. Black was my fiction. I had woven it and stitched it full of all of the symbols that we had created about ourselves: Afro; Power To The People; Black Power; Black Is Beautiful; African clothes; African head-ties; Rosa Parks; *Ahmad Jamal at The Pershing*; Coltrane's *Kulu Se Mama*; Miles Davis's *Sorcerer*; Otis Redding singing "Fa-fa-fa-fa-fa-fa-fa-faa"; a good stereo system; a poster of Malcolm X...the one with him pointing a finger; a poster of Martin Luther King, Jr.; a poster of Bob Marley; posters of Huey P. Newton and Bobby Seale; a picture of a young lawyer, Nelson Mandela, speaking at a microphone; and a poster of Angela Davis with her afro large and lustrous.

These fictions of blackness allowed me to embrace the welcomed vastness that came with being Black, even as it brought me a feeling of loss. I had shifted another cell, let go cherished ways of being that had been with me forever. And so...I gained *blackness*.

A struggle came with it. For this larger family, this blackness, received persecution in the larger power-wielding society, based not on its ideology, but on its skin. It mattered not what heart beat underneath the skin, the skin *itself* was deemed unworthy. For it was on skin that all eyes first focused.

It felt almost like a cliché to even think of these things; they were too embarrassingly simple to speak. It was easier to pretend that I had emigrated to Canada wise and sage, knowing that the big stick of racism would hit me over the head...and that sometimes it would be a sledgehammer. And sometimes it would attack me where I lived, in the form of a man who was sent to watch.

And besides the larger society, the critics within the family of the Black community were harsh. You had to do the right thing, and be the right thing, and say the right thing, and be clear on everything...everything...even if you had only just seen it in you or outside of you for the first time.

Papa Emmanuel's voice was the strongest and most useful thing that I had to work with, to help me withstand the sledgehammer of the larger society and the rules of the family of the Black community.

Papa Emmanuel's voice was a big voice, but it had grown faint; and I was far from the corners where it lingered: in Antigua; in our house on Number One New Street, now renamed Prince Klass Street...which really ought to have been King Court Street; in the *snow-on-the-mountain* blossoms, whispering in their own life-rhythm on Papa Emmanuel's grave. I wished that I had made a party for him on that last day. I wished that I had sat on the gravestone and grounded with my loved one.

At this time, I needed to hear every chord of Papa Emmanuel's voice, standing up for justice against a great big machine that had eventually overtaken him. He had said that by the fruit of his loins he would be vindicated. And I was his only child.

I came to accept that it was not a question of whether or not I stayed in Toronto, but how I stayed in Toronto. My ambivalent way of being involved in my community had had dire consequences. From now on, I wanted to be right at the heart of things, for that was where it felt right to be. I wanted to be able to contribute in much more than the peripheral role to which women were relegated. I would not argue my way in; I would simply walk in, as if that was where I belonged.

Walking into such a male centre would require me to make several changes. I would cover my body in clothing that was purposely not enticing. Gone would be the short-shorts, the backless dresses. I would replace them with plain, loose dresses, reaching to the ankle, flowing into leather sandals or boots, depending on the weather. Sometimes I would wear African clothes with head-ties that matched the fabric of my dresses.

I had always made my own clothes and shirts for some of the men I knew. There were two or three women who could sew and who had sewing machines. It had seemed natural that we undertake this role. So much hard work had seemed so "natural." Now I would release all of that work, and move to do other work to which I was better suited.

And I would make a point of raising discussions concerning the distribution of labour...a phrase I had heard bandied about so long that I figured everyone would know what I meant. I would raise the discussion of the distribution of labour between women and men in the Movement.

I was not willing to tolerate being second to any man, even if he was

Black. Together, we were treated as second-class citizens by white society, but I did not even accept that position to which white people sought to relegate us. And even so, white society's perception of me and all like me did not give the Black man the right to put me in second place. That would make me a twice undervalued person.

The time had come for me to stop cooking for men. The preparation and serving of food was no longer in my sphere of interest or action. No matter what, I would refuse to be relegated to the kitchen. I decided that no meals would be cooked in my house for all and sundry ever again. When the question of food arose, I would just be silent. That is how the men handled it and so would I.

It seemed to me that it was inevitable that Black women would refuse the position to which they had been relegated. Why would the Black feminist movement not continue? Black women had always established their place in any society in which they lived. They had been feminist long before the word had come into vogue.

The struggle of Black women looked different from that of white women. We shared a simple demand for respect and equality, but we were not demanding to be moved out of the role of "shrinking violet." We had never been so privileged! I wanted Black men to stop having relationships with two and three women at a time. And I wanted our men to stop sleeping with white women, just because they *were* white women. I could not understand why it was that those who shouted loudest about "white crackers" and "white pigs" had slept the whitest.

I wanted Black women's feelings to be recognized as valid, so that it was understood that we were vulnerable like everyone else; we needed care and nurturing like everyone else. Black women were not, after all, super-women. We had feelings, and we would protest our roles in the struggle, and in our relationships as well.

I had come to despise the phrase "a strong Black woman" and the clichéd idea behind it. It felt like a curse, an open invitation to treat Black women as if they were workhorses with backs stronger than the plough. It sounded like slavery to me.

I was experiencing journeying: in the mind, in the body, in the spirit, in politics. I was engaged in an odyssey, undertaken not as a prescribed rite of passage, but as an exploration of the descent into degradation and my subsequent self-rescue out of it. The degradation I had felt acutely, because it was of Spirit and not of life conditions.

Much that was beautiful and maybe even idyllic in my heart had been destroyed. The destruction happened inside me where no one knew, no one saw, and so no one cared. I had heard it happening and had wanted to tell it to be quiet, but could not. So the movement began deep inside me and worked itself all the way up to my skin.

Chapter Fourteen

Lovely as Nevis was, its closeness to Antigua was more than I could bear. I had not wanted to go to Antigua, as I did not want to arrive there with my heart all broken and my spirit poor. But I was too near to my family not to be with them. I longed to hear my Mama Reevah's voice, feel her arms holding me. I longed to hear my Aunt Juniper Berry telling me how to love a man, and the thought of Aunt Sage and my cousins formed a lament in my heart.

I had my photographs with me; they were not sufficient, but they were all I had. Before I left Toronto, I had taken them from their place in my bedroom cupboard. They were in a white shoebox, tied together with a blue ribbon. The blue ribbon had seemed like the right colour to use and I had not even thought of its connection with Papa Emmanuel until I had brought it home from the store.

My face was already formed into a smile as I took the envelope of photographs out of my suitcase. I thought of the joy I would get from looking at all of my family's smiling faces. My longing was such that I even felt ready to look at the photograph of Papa Emmanuel in his dead-suit.

At first I looked at them and smiled, remembering. Then my tears came, even though I worked hard at stopping them. I did not want to cry.

Maybe I would cry in the sea in Antigua, but in Nevis, I had to stay strong, strong as the very trunks of the silk-cot tree and the mahogany tree. Loving this man had caused me great pain, but I could not let all of my restraints down yet. I did not want Rashaan's parents to be beleaguered by a heartbroken guest, sobbing her eyes out, day after day. I knew that if I opened the dam, it would all come gushing out.

Papa Emmanuel visited me one night in my dreams in Nevis. His presence seemed so natural, but the next day when I tried to reclaim the experience, I could not. I knew that the dream was connected to my reaching for something deep; some wonderful manifestation of what I was to do, to become. The dream had seemed to clarify it all, but upon waking, I could only remember that Papa Emmanuel had spoken softly to me for a long-long time.

It used to be that once upon a time, I had great faith in the "I-believe" of things. I could look backward and see my beginnings; if I folded my eyes to mere slits, I could see future versions of myself. But the present gave me trouble; for I could not find my way to freedom without leaving the imprint of the shame of not being there for myself.

All of my pain was rolled up into one small nugget of a feeling: I had to wrest the reins of my freedom back into my hands, become all that I had envisaged way back when...way back then.

The light I saw in my Papa Emmanuel's eyes when he looked at my Mama Reevah is only in a man's eyes when he has learned to be a loving human being and as pure as that light. I had seen that same light in Uncle Clifford's eyes when he looked at my Aunt Juniper Berry. I knew that it had not been present in the eyes of any of the men whom I had held in my arms. I despaired that I would ever see it, ever find it present in any whom I dared to love.

My life was led not by my heart as I had thought, but by a deep desire to feel that I belonged. Now I felt that my world was a broken world. I felt small, crushed, without a voice...weak and ineffectual. It was time to see my family. For I longed to hear someone say: "This is my beloved Sayshelle, in whom I am well pleased."

I was going home to Mama Reevah. I wanted to hear her voice speaking gently in my ears as she plaited my hair. The memory of the tight rows of "Congo," which had made my head ache, felt bittersweet. I even missed the pain.

I wanted to hear Aunt Juniper Berry's voice telling me that everything was all right and that I would heal; even broken hearts like mine would heal. I needed to look into Aunt Sage's eyes and say in my heart, even if my lips could not form the words: "I understand who you are now, more than ever. I have loved a man in just that same way that you loved Rommel and rum." And I wanted to take Joyling by the hand and say: "Girl, let me tell you how it was for me, loving this man named Cicero Finley."

I made a telephone call to my supervisor and resigned from my job. She wished me well, but sounded understandably puzzled. I did not give any explanation beyond saying that I was caught up in family issues. Then I called my lawyer and asked him what legal document I needed to send him so that he could list my house with a real-estate agent. I had decided that I would move to a new house, one that was not on anyone's list of houses to be watched.

Then I went into Charlestown and sent the necessary fax. My next task was to call Rashaan in Toronto and tell him about Cicero Finley's surprise arrival and departure; and that I was leaving for Antigua. I gave him a neighbour's telephone number in Antigua as Mama Reevah did not have a telephone. That was another hardship that the wrong party card had always brought: no telephone line was ever available to my family.

I then called our neighbour in Antigua and asked her if she could please call Mama Reevah to the telephone. She asked me, "Sayshelle? Is something wrong?" She was a very close family friend and knew that I did not call often. "No," I lied; everything was *quite* wrong, but I knew that she meant illness or death, and I could only report on a weeping heart.

When Mama Reevah came on the line, she sounded anxious as well. "Sayshelle? What's wrong, child?" I could not speak; at the sound of her voice, tears filled my throat and my eyes and all of my words slurred into two words, "Mama Reevah." I sobbed uncontrollably. I had only meant to tell her that I was coming home. After all of this time, I was coming home. "But just for a holiday," I reminded her. I did not want her thinking that I had failed at life in Toronto and was running home with my tail between my legs. That would shame her in the eyes of her community. I did not want her even thinking such a thing had happened.

Telling Mama Reevah the truth about my life was not an option for me. Learning that I had been involved with an undercover agent would have frightened her. I also did not tell her that for love and not for politics I had put my life at risk more gravely than anything that she could have ever complained about with Papa Emmanuel.

I stepped off the plane in Antigua, greeted my family, and lied through my teeth to Mama Reevah for two weeks. I told only Aunt Juniper Berry about all that I had been through. I told Mama Reevah that I had cried that day on the phone because I had been so happy to hear her voice. I lied about what I was doing in Nevis. I said only that I had gone there and stayed at a friend's parents' home for a holiday.

I could tell that they found it strange that I had not called from Canada to say that I would be in Nevis. And I know that they wondered why I had not called until the day before I left Nevis. I could not explain that I had not planned to visit Antigua at all; that I had been on a mission that had been abruptly curtailed. They assumed that I merely wanted to surprise them, and I did not deny what they assumed.

I had a wonderful re-entry to Antigua. The reunion with my family and friends was so warm and loving that I knew it would be hard to leave them again. This time, however, I knew that I would return again and again instead of allowing as many as ten years between visits.

Aunt Juniper Berry and Uncle Clifford promised to bring Mama Reevah with them to Toronto for a visit. Aunt Juniper Berry thought that it was the only way we would get her sister to travel. Mama Reevah said, when I asked her if she would ever come for a visit, "If your father was alive, I would have travelled with him; but now, I would prefer if you came to visit me, child."

I arrived in Antigua to find the country experiencing a drought. It was a shock to my system, because Nevis was green and flowering, with rain falling almost daily. There was a fine mist that used to caress my face every morning in Nevis. I thought that if I lived there, I would have wonderful skin.

Everyone in Antigua felt the effects of the drought and we became quite creative when it came to obtaining and storing water. I was awoken each day by an early-morning chorus of squeaking caused by hand-hewn carts dragged through the streets by children as they went searching for water. The carts' wheels competed with the crowing of roosters. The children sought the standpipes with the largest trickles of water. They raced against time to collect sufficient water before going to school, and before the pipes were turned back off again.

The government turned on the water in the morning and in the evening. Every bucket, every bath-pan, every large bowl and large pot was filled with water. I became quite deft at having a shower with one bucket of water and a cup.

One evening Mama Reevah and I sat on the gallery, watching people walking in the street. I was tired, having just filled up our containers with the evening's ration of water. We heard Aunt Sage's feet long before we saw her, for they were pounding their way up the sidewalk in quick running steps.

She burst into the yard and sat on the steps of the gallery, gasping for breath. "They find Seleena," she said. She was crying. "The drought make them decide to clean out the mouth of the gutter at the bottom of

Tanner Street...and they find Seleena skeleton. She wedge-een...she wedge-een...*chak* between two big logs...the same logs that did carry her away...she and the logs wedge-een at the mouth of the gutter and stayed there all this time."

Aunt Sage stopped speaking and sobbed, holding her head in her hands. The sound shook Mama Reevah into action; we were both so shocked that we had sat and stared at Aunt Sage as she spoke. Mama Reevah put her arms around Sage and held her as she cried.

We were all crying now. I felt great sobs pull themselves from my body. I knew that I cried for myself as much as I cried for Seleena and for Aunt Sage, for I held sadness inside me that was waiting to be released.

Finally Aunt Sage wiped her face. "I felt Seleena around me all day. Some days, she is not as present as others; but not today. She was around me for the entire day." She shook her head and I noticed that she looked younger somehow, as if finding Seleena's bones had lifted some of her grief from her. I had thought her quite healed until I saw the effect that finding Seleena was having on her. "There are always layers and layers," I thought.

Seleena's second funeral began in the Anglican cathedral. Everyone in the family dressed in white at Aunt Sage's request. We filled the church with white flowers and strung white ribbon at each pew. Aunt Sage looked regal in a beautiful, softly flowing white dress.

It was not just the lines in her face that had softened since Seleena had been found. Her eyes were clearer and she walked around with a smile on her face, greeting everyone as they came into the church. Her hair was plaited in "Congos" that met at the top of her head, and she had pinned a white *frangipani* over one ear. I told her that she looked like Billie Holiday and she smiled proudly, saying, "Thank you; that is a real compliment." I was quite surprised; I had no idea that Aunt Sage had that kind of style. It showed me that she had really reclaimed her life. More so, I was surprised because I had no idea that Aunt Sage even knew who Billie Holliday was. I had only heard of her because Aunt Helen had several of her records and she had told me about her.

Aunt Juniper Berry wore a soft, white cotton dress that she had made recently to hide the fact that she was in the early months of her second pregnancy. She was not ready to tell everyone; so she had made some outfits that looked stylish, but that were actually designed to camouflage her growing belly.

Uncle Clifford wore a lovely white linen suit, and I giggled unashamedly when he put a foot out of the car and I saw that he wore white loafers and no socks. "You stop that!" Aunt Juniper Berry muttered to me under her breath. "Do you know how hard it was to get him to discard the socks?" Then, as I still giggled, she added: "I like seeing a man without socks; it's sexy."

I laughed as I watched poor Clifford trying to hide his bare instep from the disapproving eye of the dean, who was waiting to greet each family member. As he stepped from the car, his son pointed to his feet and said: "Daddy don't have on any socks!" His sister took up the chant, bringing everyone's attention to poor Clifford's bare ankles.

It was Mrs. Dimitrius who helped Aunt Sage to identify Seleena. She had heard about the discovery of the skeleton and brought Seleena's dental records to Aunt Sage's house. Seleena had never been to the dentist while she lived with Aunt Sage, and so when the police asked for the name of her dentist, Aunt Sage had been unable to supply any information. She had no idea that Seleena had been taken to the dentist by Mrs. Dimitrius.

"We chatted for a while too you know, Reevah-girl," Aunt Sage reported afterwards. "Time is a healer, eh? They are coming to the funeral and that feels quite all right with me. Both Mrs. Dimitrius and Rogain Dimitrius. In fact, I am taking any money that he gives me to help with the expenses.

He offered to pay for the casket and I tell his wife, 'Sure, why not?' And then she say, 'He would really like to pay for all of the expenses of the funeral; would you object?' And I answer her, 'No; I would not object; not at all.'

There was a time that I would not take their money; but I put all of that old hurt behind me; I am past that. I appreciate any help they want to give me."

And so it was that Rogain Dimitrius paid for all of the expenses of Seleena's second funeral and attended with his wife and two daughters. And a proper funeral it was too. The father of one of the children in Aunt Sage's daycare sang a solo. The song was "Oh Perfect Love," and the man had a beautiful voice. People forgot for a moment that they were in church and clapped lustily when he had finished singing.

Next on the programme was a poem written and read by Joyling. It was titled "To Seleena from her sisters." She too received applause. I had been asked to do a reading from the Scriptures; it was Psalm 121. I felt my voice clear and steady: "I will lift mine eyes up unto the hills, from whence cometh my help. My help cometh from the Lord, which made heaven and earth..."

When I was finished, there was a hush in the church, but no one clapped. I was glad of that; it would have been too much really. I noticed that the dean breathed a sigh of relief at the silence.

It was a full programme. The sermon was rousing and meaningful; it addressed the benefits of perseverance. Apparently Aunt Sage had gone to the dean months earlier and asked him to pray with her for her daughter's body to be recovered. He had agreed to do so and had instructed her about how she could strengthen her own prayers.

From the day that Seleena was found, Aunt Sage never stopped praising the power of prayer. Aunt Juniper Berry reminded her that it was the drought that was responsible for Seleena's skeleton being discovered, but Aunt Sage did not answer her. She just smiled a secret little smile. Aunt Juniper Berry still tried to get a rise out of her.

"You going to become a religious fanatic like Mabelay?"

"Of course not! But that does not mean that I cannot acknowledge the power of prayer."

Aunt Juniper Berry pressed on: "Actually, we could go and thank the government for not cleaning the gutter properly for so long. I understand that when the main reservoir dried up, they found dead animals in it."

At that, Mama Reevah shook her head and Aunt Juniper Berry stopped. I think she realized that she had gone a bit too far. I chuckled inside at the irony of it all. Whatever the source of our good fortune, I was just glad that we could give Seleena a proper burial.

We did not make a long service at Seleena's grave. Aunt Sage did not want mourning and weeping. She had planned that after the service, we would go back to her house and play music and dance. She had cooked a big-big pot of Seleena's favourite food, *season-rice*, and had invited several friends to drop by her house. She said that that was how she wanted to say goodbye to Seleena this time. She pointed out that things had fallen into place nicely; she had left Seleena twice and now she was burying her twice. This apparent order of things gave her a deep sense of satisfaction.

After we had thrown the first sod on Seleena's coffin, I felt a great peace come over me. For the first time that I could remember, I did not cry at Seleena's grave. I had a feeling that her spirit would not be visiting me in Toronto any more; she was at peace. She had been found and buried with her shoes. This was much better than being lost forever in a backlog of flotsam and jetsam.

I kissed my fingers and ran them over Seleena's name on the grave-stone that was left intact above the freshly-dug space for her coffin. Then I placed a single white rose on the new mound of her grave. I could almost feel her smile and wave good-bye, the way she used to when we met at school.

While the rest of the congregation sang hymns for Seleena, I slipped away and walked to Papa Emmanuel's grave. I knew that I would sit on his gravestone the way I had wanted to before going to Canada. I would wail out my heart's cares, my fears. I wanted my wail to go out from me and make harmony with other sounds that I released from inside of my body. And I knew that I would ground myself, the way that listening to Coltrane had grounded me...the way I had seen and heard that other family grounding with the earth and their loved one.

My voice grumbled up from my belly, reached my throat, and came off my tongue in a string of sounds. They rattled as they left me, sounding more like sighs as they fell onto the stone of the grave. My sounds shaped themselves into words as I talked to Papa Emmanuel. I told him every-thing; and yet, I had no feeling that I composed my thoughts and spoke them into words. They just tumbled out in a disharmony of sound and turned into order as they flowed and flowed from me, until at last every-thing was said and all had been released.

I sat and allowed a quiet to come. It arrived just as the twilight fell. I listened to my heartbeat. I felt the moment when Coltrane stopped his horn from screaming and smiled at me. When I looked up, Mama Reevah was standing, quiet, watching me. I saw that she heard and that she understood.

We brushed the dirt from our shoes as usual when we reached home. Mama Reevah looked at me as we stepped inside of the house. "You shift-ed something?" The way she said it was a question, but I knew that it required no answer from me and she did not wait for one. She turned away and was busy setting up the cushions so that she could plait my hair while I sat at her feet in front of the rocking-chair.

For the first time since we had begun our ritual of hair-plaiting, I did not do my part in the usual way. I did not want to hear her say the word "Come!" For I was in Antigua. I had already arrived. I had not waited for her to ask me to come home. My head was in her lap before the word was formed on her tongue. She laughed and kissed the top of my head. "I missed you." My answer was made inside. I could not speak.

Mama Reevah had combed my hair, and Aunt Sage and Aunt Juniper Berry had kept a space for me. Papa Emmanuel had pulled me to do my grounding and reasoning at his gravesite. And Seleena had needed me to be a part of her burial. Even Joyling had joined in the energy to bring me home. She saw my arrival as something directly connected to her. "I am so glad you came home to see me" was the first thing she had said when she saw me.

That night, before going to bed, I went out to the backyard of our house on Number One New Street, now renamed Prince Klass Street, and sat under the tree that held the secret of my navel-string. I said a greeting to the tree and to the navel-string buried there. I said that I was sorry for not saying good-bye before I went to Canada. Then I said good-bye, as I knew that I would be leaving very soon. It was time.

Chapter Fifteen

Rashaan's voice talked into the telephone I held at my ear. He was restating his invitation to meet him in Nevis. This time he suggested that I stay, not at his parents' home, but at a hotel for a two-week holiday. He would also stay in the same hotel. "…in separate rooms, Sayshelle," he said seriously. "You did not really get to see Nevis. I had been planning to come and take you and the little girl to see the island. So how about it? I am sure you could use a real holiday after all that you have been through, and especially now that you tell me you had a sudden funeral. You will go back to Toronto refreshed and ready to deal with house and job and everything else."

I *did* feel drained, and I loved Nevis. For one brief moment, I wondered if I was ready to be alone in a hotel with a man, even if we were in separate rooms. And even though it was a man whom I knew well and whom I trusted. I told him that I would sleep on it, and he promised to call again the next day.

Mama Reevah actually made the decision for me. The next day when he called, I was out and she took the call. He told her about his invitation and left a message saying that he would be calling back that evening as he needed to know about booking the tickets. She was delighted with the idea and she reminded me that I would be coming back to Antigua in a very short while. I had agreed to be Aunt Juniper Berry's coach in the delivery room for the birth of her next baby six months hence.

When the twins were born, Clifford had been her coach, but this time, he would need to be at home with the twins and so it would be a help, she said, if I came back and accompanied her. I had a feeling that it was more than the issue of convenience; I think she simply wanted me close and this was one way to make it happen. She was the only person in whom I confided about all that had taken place in my life; and she wanted to help me to get over it. Certainly, returning to Antigua more frequently would help me to heal. The sea alone was a big healer for me. I had soaked in the water at Fort James beach, and had felt my cares melt away in the blue-blue sea.

Three days later, I flew out of Antigua on the first early-morning plane. In Nevis, Rashaan was waiting for me at the airport; he had arrived from Toronto an hour earlier. I realized with surprise that I was really happy to see him. He felt like my link back to the life that I had left, the life that I wanted to embrace in a new way.

The morning was a thing of beauty and joy and peace and calm. As usual, it seemed to me that in Nevis, a fine mist hung over everything. We went to visit Rashaan's parents on the way from the airport and I apologized to them again for the drama that had unfolded in their home. They assured me that they trusted their son's judgement of character and that they knew that everything was all right. His mother said, "It is the father we were worried about. How could anyone be able to find a person so easily? Is he a spy?"

I had never explained anything about Cicero Finley to them, and clearly, neither had Rashaan. I suspected that they were too polite to have asked me. They knew that Rashaan was involved in the Movement and were aware that certain things happened because of that involvement.

At that point, Rashaan took over and smoothed his mother's question away. I saw him catch his parents' eye and they nodded, understanding that this was one of those things that had no explanation.

Their response did not surprise me. They were kind and non-judgemental. Rashaan's father actually brought some humour to the whole thing by saying, "Well, girl, I had thought that he was a prisoner on the run and that you were escaping from him." He play-acted, widening his eyes and dropping his voice to a hushed tone. His wife chided him. "You have been listening to that soap opera on the radio again, nuh? Come and help me with the breakfast, before you have us in a big spy scene."

Rashaan and I avoided each other's eyes. When they left the gallery to go and prepare breakfast for us, we giggled like two guilty school children.

When the attraction was reignited between us, it was not Rashaan who moved to light it. Lunch at the hotel was long and lingering and lazy. Then we went to take after-lunch naps in our adjoining rooms. When we woke up, we swam for a long time, then sat under beach umbrellas and talked for hours.

I was embarrassed to take my insect repellent out of my bag. I thought that Rashaan would laugh at me; but instead, he begged me for some of it. Mosquitoes were taking nips out of him in the same way they had attacked me when I had first arrived in the Caribbean. My blood had begun to lose its appeal to them, but Rashaan's was fresh and appealing. I never got over how sensitive the mosquito was in its capacity to sniff out the fresh blood of a newly arrived visitor.

Rashaan practically bathed himself in insect repellent and then said, "Well, there goes my trying to kiss you; I smell awful now." He laughed and I laughed with him, then without any planning, I kissed him full on the mouth.

I was probably more shocked than Rashaan was. It was not a lingering kiss; we were in a public place, and I was a private kind of person. So I just held his face in my hands and kissed his lips softly. After he got over the shock he looked pleased, but he said nothing and neither did I. My boldness embarrassed me. It was the first time that there had been a kiss between us. When we had first dated, we had never come any closer than holding hands.

That evening after dinner, we stayed for the hotel entertainment. Louise Bennett and The Mighty Sparrow were announced, and we could not believe our good fortune at having such a line up. We laughed until we thought our sides would split as Louise Bennett performed a piece about Black Power. All went well until Sparrow sang "Congo Man" and Rashaan became very offended.

He said that he felt embarrassed that Sparrow had fallen into the trap of declaring white women delicate morsels that the Black man hankered after. He also disliked the presentation of the African as a cannibalistic primitive. "I even dislike the jacket of the 'Congo Man' record," he said. "It shows Sparrow like a primitive, returned to the savage state that white folks insist we came from in the first place. That is the way they justify racism."

He went up a couple of notches in my estimation, because that was exactly the way I felt about "Congo Man." I was a big fan of Sparrow's, however, despite what I considered a lapse in judgement.

After the show, we danced and Rashaan held me as if I were a delicate flower. When we parted outside the door to my room, he took my hand, bent over it with an elaborate flourish, and kissed my fingers. I smiled at the top of his head. "I could get used to this kind of treatment," I thought.

Rashaan was a wonderful travelling companion. He thought of everything. After a while, I stopped asking where we were going and allowed him to do things in the way he designed. On some days, he did not want to tell me what he had planned. We would turn a corner in the pick-up that he had borrowed from his father and I would gasp at the beauty in front of me. Then Rashaan would look pleased and say, "That is where we are going; I wanted you to look down on it first."

The beauty of the island lay for me not in the views, no matter how spectacular or picturesque they were, but in the sense of Spirit that I could feel there. It was a feeling of peace and serenity...just what my soul needed.

At night, we danced wherever we could find music in a nightclub or hotel. It became our habit to dance the night away during the two weeks that we spent in Nevis. Rashaan eventually borrowed some tapes and a ghetto blaster from a relative, and if we could not find a band to dance to, then we danced in his hotel room or in mine. And we talked a lot, sitting on the balcony, or on the beach until the early hours of the morning.

In the mornings, we swam before breakfast, then walked on the beach for as long as we could manage. Some mornings we walked the entire length of the mile-long beach, then returned to our rooms to catch up on the night's sleep that we had missed. We woke late in the mornings, hungry and hot from the strong noonday sun. And we would walk out onto our balcony, almost at the same time each day, and marvel at the timing as we greeted each other.

It felt as if we grew into each other. I knew that this heady, romantic setting was not the best place to make judgements and decisions, but the closeness between us was something that I could not ignore.

I felt now that I knew how to look after myself more carefully than ever before in terms of how I handled relationships. I wanted to visit with Rashaan in the gruelling concrete of Toronto, where things were thick and dense. Then our newfound feelings would be tested.

We agreed to be friends forever and in love, maybe, if the friendship allowed for this shift to take place. We discussed it the night before we left Nevis, as if it was the last time we would ever have to speak so closely, so privately. We agreed to see what was to be. We would not hurry, and we would not tarry if we agreed that it was not to be.

By the time we were packed to return to Toronto, I felt like a new person. I was relaxed, calm, and at peace. I told myself that I was ready for the sale of my house, for purchasing a new home, for finding a new job, and being involved in the Movement.

Chapter Sixteen

It was morning again; night had given way to the inevitable to and fro of light and dark. I looked out of the window of my new house. I was not yet ready to step out into the morning light. The wetness of the rain still hung over everything and there was a damp that my skin was not yet ready to embrace.

I noticed that even though the rain had covered over all of the debris, there were still dribbles of things-past lingering in the new day's dawn. They were no longer assembled on the shelves on which I had neatly folded them. The rain had washed things clean. It had realigned the world: the inside world as well as the outside world.

The fire had burned itself out during the night and wet still clung to everything. I tried to reignite the dying embers in the fireplace. The smell of damp wood was everywhere: my clothes, the furniture, the bed, inside me. It had reached deep inside and touched my heart. Now the dryness of my life grew new skin, brought into being by the dampness.

It looked as if the fingers of light would soon creep up from behind a hillside. When I was little, I had called those big hills "mountains." I had thought of them as high mountains, big and lumpy mountains like Boggy Peak, the "mountain" of my childhood.

"I will lift mine eyes up unto the hills, from whence cometh my help. My help cometh from the Lord, which made heaven and earth."

I thought of those words when I stepped outside that first day in Nevis and looked up at the mountain...which was really a hill. I had thought of those same words when I had looked up at Boggy Peak as a small girl.

"The sun shall not smite thee by day, nor the moon by night. The Lord shall preserve thee from all evil: he shall preserve thy soul. The Lord shall preserve thy going out and thy coming in from this time forth, and even for evermore."

I held the sheet close up under my chin and made a great sigh of comfort that only the night creatures could hear. I never could put an "Amen" to loving the rain. The wind was loud, and the rain fell too heavily to make a space for my voice. I felt drowned in the wetness.

While all else slept, the furies tore at my shelter. It was a strong place, my new house. It was well-secured. Still, the sound and damp of the rain crept into the warm bed. And the fire burned until at last, before dawn, after the eye of the rain made its way to some other place, it gave up the valiant fight. As it died, small spirals of smoke rose up like some grotesque after-birth. The thin grey wisps filled the house and took hold of my eyes. And then I knew that I would flow softly into sleep.

I said the words inside, but I wished that I could stay awake long enough to move my voice to fill the room. Then the silence could be broken.

"He will not suffer thy foot to be moved: he that keepeth thee will not slumber. He that keepeth Israel shall neither slumber nor sleep."

The smile inside me came and enveloped me. I did not begrudge my body the sleep, but I did not want this last slice of time to be robbed by sleep. I sighed and nestled back under the sheets, waiting for my cool body to feel warmth again.

The brush of tree branches against the roof was at first a little whisper. It was not a harsh sound, but it was a new sound in the peace that had come after the rain. The fire had left in good time for the sun to rise brilliantly and fill the void.

The gentle rustle of the tree branches grew louder; then I heard a crash as something banged against the side of the roof. It broke my reverie and brought me quickly out of sleep to discover that the storm had weakened a tree at the root. In its new location, it caressed the side of the house. Its branches peeked into the window, as if it were looking at me, beckoning me to get up and attend to the daily activities of life. For morning-after-rain-freshness had arrived and brought a clearing.

There was a day when the songs in my heart sounded so dim that I wondered if I had ever really heard them. They were so distant now, and their echoes were hardly ever present on the wind. They just seemed to have gone to some place where the air had taken them and made them theirs. Songs of my heart had always been with me. They were sad or plaintive, or strong and lilting and beautiful in their expression of the emotions that ran through me.

Now a new song moved its soft strains through my heart. It held the echoes of a love that I had known and had enjoyed and had hankered after. I longed to touch my fingers to the dying embers of a fire that burned so bright that I would not need to hold myself in check. It would be safe at last to love another person or a place deeply, passionately.

The river ran deep with the fullness of the words of love that filled my mouth, filled my heart and spilled out onto the bank. The grass was damp from the fine spray as the water gushed to the open mouth of the river. It was not really a river, but I thought of it that way, the same way I thought of the little hills as mountains. And I imagined that I spread my clothes on the bank to whiten them in the sun. I could almost see the white-white skirt with matching blouse and white lace edging on the full, puffed sleeves of my girlhood.

It was an idyllic time and an idyllic place. I could make myself believe that time stood still and that the place where I washed my clothes was on the banks of East Pond, also known as Little Pond. And when I laid them out to be whitened in the sun, I could make believe that I was an innocent girl and not a town-woman, urbane and knowing about life.

Then everything could be rendered subtly different from the solid, thick reality that threatened to penetrate the haze that came with the hot sun. And if the flies threatened to mess on my clothes as they lay trying to be white in the sun, in the mud of East Pond, or Little Pond, I would shoo them in the direction of those light-skinned women who avoided the sun, lest it make their skin too dark. Or to those who acted white, spreading suntan lotion and laying themselves out to cook.

My heart's song strums my life. Precious drops of wet still cling to the words as they move out of my mouth. I taste the wet on my tongue, but I do not swallow. I want everything to go out from me. There is no room for them in the bath-pan under my bed. For they have not served me well in storage, not even when I tied them up with a blue ribbon. I want my life to flower in its own season, like the *snow-on-the-mountain* tree, flourishing in its own rhythm.

I could let myself hear my family's song sharply again now, for there is no threat of disharmony between their song and mine. They make harmony with my feelings, and my journeying, and with my heart's desires.

I understand more fully what Aunt Helen meant when she said that the memory of things past kept her whole. "For the present can take you over, remember that." I remember. And I use the memory of things past to imagine that I make flowers on the bank of East Pond and spread them over my whole existence.

It is time to make a list: the dance of rainwater under bare feet, a fine-fine mist that makes smooth-smooth skin under my fingers' tips, a white-white skirt, a matching blouse with white lace edging on the sleeves, a soft baptismal gown...a christening frock, a wedding dress, a funeral shroud, the white-white light, a middle, an ending, a beginning.

I turned the bend and embraced the green of the evening sun as it flashed its ritual meeting with the horizon. And in that moment, the wind rose up and carried me like a bird. I braced my shoulders to leap, on a single thread of faith, into the arms of a new love.

So the nail-head bend; so the story end.